All rights reserved. Printed in the United States of America. No part of this book may be used or reproduced without the author's written consent except in the case of brief quotations embodied in critical reviews.

The Lord Poet is a work of fiction inspired by the true life events of a Lord who lived in London in the early part of the 19th century named Lord George Gordon Byron. The story is fictional and, any and all, names of characters, places, and incidents are a product of the author's imagination and bare no resemblances intentionally upon persons, living or dead, besides the aforementioned Lord George Gordon Byron.

Cover design: Megan M. Franks

Cover photo: Michelle Bentley, Jarvie Bentley, Brittany Bennett

A Drop of Ink Publishing Company.

Logo design: Ryan Fye.

Copyright©2019 by Megan M. Franks

"A drop of ink may make a million think."

—Lord Byron

Acknowledgements

No book is ever the sole creation of a singular person. A lot of other people play an important role in the author's life by offering their support. Whether it is their editing skills, artistic skills, thought or insight, or simply being the first people to read the book, I owe the following people my gratitude:

Thank you!

Kyle Franks and our children– For supporting me and allowing me to follow my dream.

*Holly Byrd–*For providing your years of experience and expertise with editing and grammar.

Ryan Fye – For your amazing artistic talent and support.

Michelle Bentley and Brittany Bennett– For being my "second pair of eyes" and providing your thoughts.

For being my first readers: *Denise Fye, Holly Byrd, Brittany Bennett, Michelle Bentley, Carol Bryant, Janice Galerneau*

For using their creative talents for my cover artwork: *Michelle Bentley, Jarvie Bentley, Brittany Bennett, Amy Willson, Ryan Fye*

The Lord Poet
a novel

Megan M. Franks

Chapter One

    I always knew that I wanted to be an author. When I received my first diary from my father on my seventh birthday—tobacco-colored with an Eiffel tower embossed into the leather—I filled it with a story about a mouse named Ambrose.
    He was a chubby, jovial mouse who would become an unlikely hero, defending his family against a wild gang of tomcats using only his paws. He had the uncanny ability to climb the Eiffel tower and fly from it. I believed, at the time, that he was magical, as no other mouse could fly besides Ambrose.
    I slid my fingertips along the rows of books in Lord Troy's library, searching for something similar —a leather binding or an embossed image. *What relics could I find in such an eminent author's bookcase?* I mouthed the titles—*Idylls of the King, La*

Belle Dam Sans Merci, Don Juan...

The place was unfamiliar in its immensity, and yet if I closed my eyes, I was transported home to my father's study—the pungent scent of cigars, leather and paper unfurling like a flower. I could spend hours curled up here, absorbed in the infinite amount of words written within these pages. But my cousin Agatha had other plans.

"We're here to socialize—besides—I haven't seen Lord Troy come in. I've been looking around everywhere," she murmured excitedly, bobbing and weaving in an attempt to catch a glimpse of him.

She had to speak louder now, the crowd was growing by the minute. A piano played in the background, ordinarily a mellifluous sound; it was drowned out by the cacophony of voices.

"Maybe he's waiting to make a *grand* entrance," I said, before scanning the crowd.

"I should certainly hope so, we've been waiting long enough—speaking of—where is Ezra?"

She made a low note of discouragement in her throat and twirled a lock of her hair around her finger. She plucked a champagne flute from a butler passing by and handed one to me. I took a hesitant sip.

"This is quite good...Like the ebullient cousin of wine!" I said, watching as the golden bubbles fizzled to the top.

"Lord Troy always serves champagne...from what I've heard," Agatha advised with a satisfied grin.

I left home a week earlier to spend the summer with my aunt, uncle, and cousins in London. An invitation solicited by my mother to experience "the Season". It was the expectation that this would be the perfect circumstance to find suitable, potential husbands and introduce Agatha and me into society.

I grew up in a fishing village—far from the society of London's elite— and it was the first I'd ever been in the home of a Lord. Agatha, who only met him briefly, described him as "*Robustly handsome— Roman god-like.*"

If nothing else, he had a remarkable library; all of the walls were lined with ornate mahogany bookshelves, filled to the brim with novels, poetry and the like. Thick, purple drapes hung across a span of floor-to-wall windows running the entire length of the room. A garish, oversized fireplace sat at one end, surrounded by plush couches, and a grand piano graced itself in the corner.

My cousin Ezra made his way to us, standing like a tall, blonde pillar against the men behind him. Two big, blue eyes peeped from behind his round eyeglasses.

"Heaven and Earth! Where have you been?" Agatha asked, looking her brother up and down. One of his pale brows rose before he spoke.

"I've been making acquaintances—one of whom I'd like to introduce to you." He motioned to a woman who stood beside him. She was in a gown the same exquisite olive green as her eyes.

"This is Imelda Hawthorne," Ezra declared, motioning to her with a flick of the wrist.

I'd heard of the great actress before, but seeing her in person, it became apparent to me, that there was no exaggeration of her beauty. To see her beside Agatha was something of a study in contrasts. Agatha, in a sky blue gown, had the same fair qualities as her brother. Her hair, the color of citrine, gave her an angelic quality. Imelda was dark and mysterious. Her olive complexion and red lips gave her an alluring appeal. Her hair—the darkest shade of black— had an incandescent glow about it, as if it reflected light. Both women had an intrinsic beauty about them, Agatha's classic, and Imelda's exotic. I couldn't help but stare at them —*yin and yang*—and wonder if I fit somewhere in between.

"It's a pleasure to make your acquaintance, Agatha Greenman." Agatha bowed before waving to me, "my cousin, Catrina Bennett."

"A *pleasure*—indeed," Imelda replied, giving us a reserved smile before looking out at the crowd.

It was sweltering. The combination of bodies and muggy summer heat covered the room like a blanket, and I could feel the sweat bead and roll down my chest. The effects of the champagne, combined with the stifling heat, made the edges of the room fuzzy.

"I am sure we can expect Lord Troy at any minute."

It was a statement, but Ezra directed it to Imelda.

"He likes to make an entrance to events like this—a good deal of people come just for the spectacle of it," she said, looking around for any signs of a commotion. But the crowd was immersed in conversation, blissfully unaware of Lord Troy's absence.

"Spectacle?"

Agatha cocked her head. But before Imelda could reply, a loud crash and the sound of glass breaking rang out through the room. A chorus of gasps, and then a hush fell over the crowd as everyone looked around for the cause of the sound.

Near the piano, a man swayed in his spot, wobbling like a skittles pin as he attempted to pick up a glass. He was swiftly shooed away by a butler, who was on his hands and knees, sweeping up shards of glass.

"I a-a-apologize."

He held the remaining piece up to his face taking in the light from all angles, examining the intricacy of the design. His mouth hung open with awe.

"Such a fool! Getting himself buffy in no time at all," Imelda groaned as she set her empty glass down with a loud clank.

"Who is that?" Agatha asked, standing on her tip toes to get a better look.

"Sam," Imelda groaned, "Lord Troy's longtime chum."

"I s'pose that isn't *quite* the spectacle Lord Troy had in mind?" Ezra suggested. He began to chuckle, but cleared his throat upon seeing Imelda's face. She gave him a surly glare before disappearing into the crowd, weaving her way to Sam.

The sound of cutlery on glass made everyone turn their head again, this time to a man in a black suit near the doorway, clanking a knife on the side of a champagne flute.

The gentleman smiled, revealing a remarkable set of straight, white teeth. His sleek hair bobbed as he spoke, exposing a tuft of dark waves.

"That's him! That's Lord Troy," Agatha squealed, nudging me excitedly.

I studied him from a distance, acknowledging how the light favored his features—his aquiline nose, deep-set eyes, and the perfection of his lips. I had to admit—Agatha did not embellish in her musings—as he had quite the pleasant countenance.

Lord Troy held his champagne flute up

and with a tip of the head, began to speak.

"I'd like to introduce everyone to my closest confidant—and most valuable friend— Sam, a fine fellow indeed."

The roar of laughter rolled over the crowd like a wave. Everyone's eyes drew to the corner of the room where Sam swayed. A ruckus of cheers, whoops, and hollers rang out.

Sam held his empty glass up to Lord Troy and gave him a sloppy grin. Sitting on the edge of the piano bench, he rubbed his chin where a patch of facial hair sprouted and took root. His eyes were glossy and dark, like two black orbs.

"My introduction to our next guest won't be as outstanding as the one I've given Sam, but the show must go on," Lord Troy boomed. A chorus of laughter erupted from the crowd again.

He waved a hand to the doorway, where two gentlemen emerged, wheeling in a massive, covered box. They rolled it to the center of the room before Lord Troy gave them a nod, where they withdrew the blankets to reveal a large beast.

"I'd like to introduce you all to Socrates," Lord Troy announced, as he sauntered over to the cage.

A low susurrus swept through the room. Inside the cage, a giant black bear shuffled and grunted, picking up a massive paw and pressing it against the bars before setting it down again.

I took a deep sip of my champagne, lamenting that I'd almost reached the bottom, as beads of sweat rolled down my chest and back.

"Well, isn't *he* the cock of the walk?" Ezra remarked, and turned his attention back to his champagne.

I leaned over and whispered into Agatha's ear, her eyes—as large as teacup saucers— were transfixed on the spectacle.

"Is he...*mad*?"

She shook her head.

"I can't say he isn't, but—how *magnificent!*"

Ezra and I shot each other a look of bewilderment before turning our attention back to the scene.

"I give you my sacred honor that he is a tame bear," Lord Troy remarked, looking over the animal with a satisfied grin before unlocking the cage.

Several people near the front instinctively leaned back. Some receded into the crowd, bumping into one another, spilling their drinks and eliciting more than a few gasps, sighs and grumbles. Some of the more curious, than fearful, filled their place, shifting into the empty spaces at the front— eyes wide with fascination.

"Come now, Socrates." Lord Troy stood beside the cage, summoning him with a click of his tongue. The bear, alert to his master's presence, grunted as he lumbered out of his cage, the light sparkling on his dark fur as his big, black body shifted. His nose—a being of its own—quivered over the landscape, coming uncomfortably close to the front row.

A brave, or drunk, woman stuck her hand out for the bear to sniff. She giggled uncontrollably as the nose tickled her palm—the people beside her watched, eyes wide with tentative intrigue.

"By Jove, would you look at that?" a man beside them exclaimed. The woman's husband attempted to get his wife to put her hand down, but she seemed enthralled with the idea, the bear's nose exploring her fingers like a separate being.

"I believe you've made a friend, Mrs. McAllister," Lord Troy beamed, giving Socrates a tender tap on the shoulder. The woman—now known as Mrs. McAllister—giggled again, throwing a sloppy hand to her flushed face. Once the bear moved on, parting the room like Moses in the red sea, the relief visibly washed over her husband's face, as she gave the beast a dainty wave goodbye.

"Do you s'pose he has other wild animals?" Ezra whispered, as he leaned closer to me.

"Perhaps," I said, envisioning a menagerie somewhere in the courtyard.

"I'd really like to see a lion," he added.

Agatha shot him a look.

"Do you think he sees colors—the bear?" he probed, careful to avoid his sister's disapproving glare.

I shrugged.

"I can't be sure. But, if he did, he'd be perusing about for something tasty—say—a tart or pudding of sorts," I surmised, stifling a grin.

Agatha overheard and gave an audible huff, hoping her brother would take the hint and behave himself. I couldn't resist, however, as I nodded at a robust woman in a violet dress.

"Plum pudding," I whispered.

Ezra chuckled.

"Very good then," he said, as he searched the crowd. His eyes landed on a woman with a maroon-colored dress, her hair adorned with a head full of white feathers.

"Rack of lamb."

"That's uncannily accurate!" I sniggered. Ezra gave a bow, before we dissolved into a fit of giggles. Agatha glowered at us.

I pressed my hands to my face. A red, hot heat was radiating from my cheeks. *Was it the alcohol?* Although I was certain that my feet were planted firmly on the ground, I felt myself sway.

Lord Troy made a full circle before calling out to the gentlemen near the door, assuring they were prepared to take the giant beast away. One of the gentlemen took the bear by the leash and guided him into the cage, shutting and locking the door behind him. Then both gentlemen carefully pushed the cage out of the room to loud applause. Lord Troy took his hands and lowered them.

"Thank you, Thank you. Please. Socrates does not like applause. It frightens him. Thank you." Lord Troy took a bow.

The applause died away, fizzling out into the quiet drone of conversation, and Lord Troy disappeared into the crowd— who engulfed him with admiration.

Feeling dizzy, I took the opportunity to escape to the hallway.

~

I steadied my elbows on the ledge of a window looking out at the lawn as it pulsated in and out of focus. I relished the feel of the wind on my face, as it blew in, billowing the drapes with each inhale and exhale, like a giant set of lungs. The lanterns on the hallway walls flickered inconsistently, the halo of their bright light growing at one moment and ceasing to exist in another. It was a welcome break from the heat and noise of the library.

"You aren't m-m-much like your s-s-sister."

Startled, I turned to see the man Lord Troy had introduced as Sam, leaning up against another window. His hair was a mop of tousled, dirty blond locks, so unruly, it looked as if he'd never seen a comb. I wondered if it always had that type of character, or if it were merely the results of his sloppy drunkenness.

"She's *not* my sister," I said, looking back at her in the corner of the library, immersed in her storytelling. She had a love for an audience and was soaking up the attention.

"She's my cousin, my maternal cousin, my mother's sister's daughter." I swallowed, forcing myself to stop the words from coming back up.

"I s-s-see..."he stuttered again, clearing his throat and attempting to hide a grin.

"Per aspera...ad astra-a-a." He gazed out the window with his head tilted far back—eyes to the sky.

"I beg your pardon, sir?"

"Latin. It means, through the hard-sh-ship to the s-s-stars." He pointed a finger to the sky.

"Come with me?" he asked, turning to me and motioning with his hand. "There we can s-s-see the s-s-stars forever under the blue blanket."

He pointed down to the lawn, an open spread of grass that ran as far as the eye could see.

"Come where? Down *there*?" I exclaimed, gazing down at the yard below.

He set his glass down on the window sill, and a bit of gold liquid splashed out the side. He grumbled to himself as he tried, unsuccessfully, to mop it up with his hands.

"Are you *mad*?" I cocked my head.

Ignoring me, he stumbled towards the door, almost tumbling head first down the stairs before catching himself. I followed reluctantly behind him, hoping he had the sense to catch himself should he fall.

In the darkness, the lawn was the pale gray color of a shadow. A walkway—stark and white in the reflection of the moon—framed a fountain and gardens that were lined by hedgerows. In the distance, where the estate lawn ended, a tree line—as black as onyx— rose like a jagged, miniature mountain range.

I breathed in the scent of dew-covered grass and the intoxicatingly sweet aroma of viburnum, together, they created a musky, but honeyed, perfume.

I followed him to a bench where he plopped down unceremoniously.

"I had to follow you for your safety, and now that I see that you are safe, I must return," I said.

But before I could leave, he reached out and grabbed my hand. It was an audacious move. I removed his fingers, one by one, shaking my head with annoyance at the effects of alcohol.

"Have you ever s-s-seen a s-s-sky so clear?" he blurted.

He was right. I was admiring it from the open window, but from here, in the open, it was a sight to behold. There was nothing quite as beautiful as the dark sky with the scattering of a million stars, each like the small glow of a candle flickering against the black.

"Bright s-s-star...would I were s-s-steadfast as thou art— Not in lone s-s-splendor hung aloft the night," Sam began and then looked over at me, one of his bushy eyebrows raised.

He sang more than spoke. His arms spread up towards the sky like a sermon in the middle of a psalm — no doubt the confidence a gift from the copious amount of alcohol he'd consumed.

I smiled at him, the memory of my father beside me reading through a book of poetry came into mind. He read my favorite and then his own, asking me to recite along with him— the warm blaze of fire alight on his face as he spoke.

"And watching, with eternal lids apart, like nature's patient, s-s-sleepless…" He stopped to glance over at me again this time, a quizzical look across his brow.

"Eremite?" I suggested, feeling pride swell within me.

"Er-r-r-emite." An accomplished grin spread across his face when he said it. I chuckled under my breath.

"The moving waters at their priestlike task of pure ablu-blu-tion 'round earth's human sh-sh-shores."

He paused for a long moment, searching the inner recesses of his mind.

"You sh-shknow Keats?"

"I do…" I said, biting my lip.

The soft glow of the moon—full and bright—spread across his features. Whenever a smile broke out on his face, deep-dimpled lines grew in his cheeks.

I looked up again and was surprised to see a whirl of black and bright spots of light. The alcohol was still bubbling in my blood, pulsing just below the surface and lending me an air of social freedom. A faint whimper faded in and out.

"Do you hear that?" I leaned toward the sound coming from the garden. But Sam shook his head.

"It's...it sounds like someone...sobbing?"

A sniffling sound emphasized my comment.

"Eh, let it be," Sam huffed, stripping the needles from a shrub and concentrating on rubbing them in between his fingers.

"I can't seem to get a good look."

The garden was lined by hedgerows making a dense privacy fence.

"Let it b-be...Miss..."

"Catrina Bennett," I answered before turning back.

"Catrina...C-a-a-a-trina...that's a fun name to say...C-a-a-a-trina," he said again, with a big ridiculous grin on his face.

"It's rather *queer*—is it not?" I added.

He ignored me, plucking at another bit of shrubbery. I doubted very much that Lord Troy would appreciate his landscaping being molested, but bit my tongue. I sighed and walked toward the archway.

"Where are you off to?" he whispered loudly, "let me b-bear your company."

A small grin spread across my face at the thought.

"I should think it would be *just fine* of you to stay where you are."

He smirked, and continued plucking the needles off one by one.

The moonlight reflected off the smooth, white stones that lined the walkway casting an ethereal glow to the garden. I stepped lightly, hoping not to cause anyone alarm. Seeming to notice my arrival however, the sobbing ceased.

"Is someone there?" I called out. Hearing my voice waver, I cleared my throat and called out again.

"Do you need help? Is there someone there?"

Sam, hearing me from behind the hedge, responded.

"C-a-a-a-a-a-trina."

I spun around, annoyed.

"That's *not* very helpful," I whispered loudly back at him.

I looked around again, but saw nothing but the rows of manicured English roses, black and glossy, under the night sky, and a few uninhabited benches waiting for patrons.

Returning to Sam, I found him slumped to the ground.

"I have a s-s-seat for you, but I can't get up to offer it," he said, looking up at me. I suppressed a grin.

"The poor creature...I can't imagine why anyone would be out here sobbing," I replied, ignoring Sam's offer.

"Oh, any number of reasons...I'll be b-bound that it's-s-s one of Edmund's many admirers."

"Edmund?"

"Eh...it's not a m-m-matter of much consequence," he said, picking up a small stone and chucking it onto the walkway where it made a "ping" sound before bouncing into the lawn.

"Do you d-d-do this often?" he asked, one of his eyebrows rose in my direction.

"Do *what* often?"

"Obsess-s-s-s?"

"I do beg your pardon." I felt my jaw drop.

"Forgive me...must be the sh-sh-drink speaking."

"I certainly *hope* so...is the grass wet?" I asked derisively. He ran a hand over it and then looked up at me and nodded.

"My bum'll leave a print in the grass-s-s-s," he stuttered, looking grudgingly behind him.

"You really ought to have stayed on the bench."

"Now *that's-s-s* a capital idea!" he agreed, leaning his head back to look up at the stars.

"Sam! Is that you? I've been looking all over for you!"

A woman called to him from the shadows, her figure obscured by distance and darkness.

"Don't you sh-shworry about me," Sam slurred.

"Oh, I think I *must*." The woman made her way across the walkway, grumbling to herself about the lawn.

"Lordy me! I'm covered in wet grass," she cursed.

When she came closer, I could make out Imelda's slender hourglass figure.

"Catrina." Imelda bowed to me curtly.

"Imelda," I replied.

"Come along now, Sam. Perhaps we should get you to bed." She turned back to look at me, narrowing her eyes into two dark slits while Sam got to his feet. I shrunk into myself, avoiding her gaze. Sam stumbled, then got up and held onto her.

Lord Troy's home stood like a large lantern— its windows casting long, rectangular patches of light onto the lawn— guiding them back. I watched as they walked off—*filly and foal*. And when they'd finally disappeared into the shadows, I called out again.

"Is there anyone there?"

But there was no reply. I heard nothing but the nocturnal symphony of summer insects and the distant sound of a train whistle.

Chapter Two

Lord Troy—Edmund as he was known to his friends—rolled over from his back to his belly. Next to him, a woman slept. She was still deep in the throes of slumber despite the early morning sun that peaked through the window, her breathing was rhythmic and steady.

She was sprawled across the bed with her arms above her head, her fiery hair encircling the pillow like a wind storm came through. Her arse was nice, firm and round, in fact, it very well may be the nicest arse he'd ever seen. She sputtered in her sleep, and he caught a glimpse of her open mouth and the drool rolling from it, puddling under her chin onto the pillow. He shuddered. He was so perturbed by her noisy breathing and the saliva running down her face that he couldn't stand it anymore and got up.

He flung the sheets off of his legs and sat there a moment examining them. His right leg was graceful—the muscles weaving in and out like artwork—defining and smoothing his skin. His left leg, conversely, was marred by a silver line that ran from his hip to his knee. What should have been a mirror image was distorted and ugly. He forced himself to look again, imagining what his leg looked like *before* the accident, before the scar. He stared for a moment before sneering at it, perplexed with himself and his strange inability to look away, wondering why he forced himself to study it. But he *had*. *Every day* he had.

    He went to his wardrobe where ready and waiting, a man—like a silent shadow—had his clothes neatly pressed. He helped Edmund in every aspect of his dressing before hurrying off to attend to other matters of the estate, leaving Edmund to examine himself in the mirror on his washstand.

    Edmund's eyes stared back at him—the infinite spiral of his soul unfolding before him through his blue irises. He used Bandoline to tame his hair, but his wave—unwilling to relinquish its full strength—bounced subtly back. He squared his shoulders, proud of what he saw in the reflection. He was blessed with the captivating charm of his father's side and the Romanesque good looks of his mother's side—an advantageous marriage.

    He made his way to the door, taking no time to look back, where his cat Whitman greeted him. He seemed delighted to see Edmund, rubbing his long and lean, striped body up against his leg, eliciting a friendly rub on the head and chin. His purr vibrated, enthusiastically, as his master stroked him. Just as soon as he appeared, however, he disappeared, walking away in the opposite direction with his tail posed in a 'question mark'.

A maid scurried down the hall.

"Florence?"

She stopped in her tracks. She was a thin waif-like woman with a tuft of strawberry blonde hair that seemed infinitely frizzy.

"Yes, My Lord."

"Please see to it, that the missus is given a full breakfast."

He couldn't very well leave the poor girl *nothing* for her efforts.

"Most *certainly*, My Lord."

She bowed and turned to leave, overeager to perform her duties.

"Florence?"

She turned again—as if drawn by a string.

"Yes, My Lord?"

"By the by, please see to it that I am served a glass of water as well...before the day starts."

She nodded, looking up at him and displaying a surprisingly, pretty pair of blue eyes, before scuttling off in the opposite direction.

Byron, released from his confines for the night, came running in full speed from the front door when Raymond, the butler, opened it for him. Raymond stumbled back a moment, his eyes wide with surprise. He looked like a startled old tree, with his limb-like arms swaying about.

"Come along now, boy!" Edmund bent down and rubbed behind the dog's ears. The dog playfully nudged into him, almost knocking him over with attempts to lick his nose.

"Did you have a grand time in the stable?" Edmund cooed.

The dog followed behind him with his big brown eyes. He was attempting to translate his human's words to no avail but loving the sound of them, nonetheless.

Edmund had an affinity for animals and attributed it to his mother's fondness of them during his childhood. His childhood was filled with a virtual menagerie of animals of all sorts— dogs, cats, birds, snakes, bears, goats, and–for a short period of his childhood–a trained jaguar.

His mother named her animals after Roman gods and goddesses, but Edmund much preferred to name his pets after famous poets or philosophers, having possessed on his own accord— his dog Byron, his cat Whitman, his bear Socrates, and up until recently, a parrot named Dickens, and a goat named Shelley.

The sun spilled into the foyer as he opened the door. A sprawling blue sky cascaded over the estate, holding the sun like an orange in a bowl as it rose steadily. He took in a deep, invigorating breath, grateful that the humidity broke overnight. A flustered kitchen maid scurried up behind him, tentative as a mouse near a cat.

"My Lord."

Chubby, with a permanent patch of red on her cheeks, she dodged and weaved behind him, doing her best to avoid being in Edmund's way, as he and Byron played together on the floor.

"Yes?" he answered, without meeting her eyes.

"Do ye wish for yer breakfast, My Lord?" She scuttled around him, careful not to fluster him.

"An orange will do."

She gave him a tight-lipped grin before speaking up again.

"My Lord, we've made plenty of Abernethy's. We have pork, cheese, eggs, treacle, tea, coffee..."

He shooed her away with a hand.

She opened her mouth fleetingly, and then decided against it, before shuffling back into the kitchen, her substantial bottom swaying to an imaginary rhythm.

She emerged from the kitchen a minute later with an orange and reluctantly handed it to him. He tossed it into the air, catching it as he stepped out the door with Byron on his heels.

~

The auburn-haired woman opened her eyes. She rubbed them for a moment and then attempted to focus on her surroundings. Her vision first adjusted to the gilded frames, the prominent wardrobe, the ornate mahogany bed with the scrollwork, and the garish canopy—a vibrant blood red material that flowed to the floor. It took her a moment to realize that she wasn't in her own bedroom and when she came to, she immediately searched around the room for her fleeting companion. *Where was he?* She wondered, feeling a pit in her stomach develop.

She lay there for a few moments, her head on the pillow looking up and her mind lost in thought. She was grateful to hear the click of the door and see the maid pop in, her strawberry blond hair, a frizzy mess, as it poked from the sides of her cap. The maid scurried about, placing a silver tray beside the bed table and lifting the lid, before picking up some fresh linens she left on a chair. The scent of bacon and butter filled the room, making the auburn-haired woman salivate.

"Miss...Miss," she called out timidly.

"Yes, Misses. Is there somethin' that I can do for ya?" The maid peeked over the linens in her hands, the stack so high they almost reached her eyes.

"Uh, yes...it's umm...I haven't a way home. Is there somewhere I can catch an omnibus?"

"Oh no, no, no, no mah dahling."

She shook her head, her puff of light hair staying remarkably stiff under her cap.

"We've a carriage—can arrange for to take ya home."

She turned away and headed to the door, shutting it behind her, and leaving the woman by herself once again.

~

Edmund strolled through his lawn enjoying the warmth of the sun on his face. By the time he planned to return home, he knew that the woman he'd spent the evening with, would be gone. He grinned at the thought, as he bent down to pick up a stick and throw it to Byron.

He sauntered through his garden, enjoying the sweet floral scent that hung in the air, and the soothing sound of the fountain that trickled behind him. He planned his day as he walked along— first, he would spend the early afternoon roaming down to Roehampton for a game of cricket, after the game, he would stop by the Green Man for a bite to eat, and finally, he would meander his way through Putney Heath, taking in the wildlife, before heading home.

He was surprised to come across Sam in the garden, sitting on a bench in the sunlight. He had his diary on his lap, writing zealously. He was lost to the world. He empathized with this type of deliberation and focus, the writer's consumption with their own realm beneath their fingertips.

"What's this?" Edmund nodded with his chin to the diary, while he peeled the layers of his orange. The scent of fresh citrus was now pungently drifting between them.

Sam looked up. It was just enough time to leave an unsightly blob of black on the sheet.

"Dash it all! Look what you made me do! You're a ridiculous distraction." He gave Edmund a derisive look. "If you must know, it's a new bit of prose I've been working on…"

"Hmm," Edmund replied indifferently, as he bit into a slice of orange—the juice bursting in his mouth. "May I?" He held his hand out to receive the diary, and Sam grudgingly handed it over.

"*Night beguiles the subtle wiles that hang aloft in mind, betwixt the beating of the heart, indelicate and divine*," Edmund spoke aloud, letting the words roll skillfully off his tongue.

"Rather fine indeed—*however*," he said, handing it back to Sam and setting the half-eaten orange on his lap. He picked the stick up and tossed it to Byron again, watching as Byron wagged his tail and spun around, trying to find the best way to pick it up.

"What is it?" Sam asked.

"I am sure that you are well aware that Romanticism is dying— nearly dead, in fact," Edmund remarked.

Sam tapped his pen to his chin.

"I am *unfortunately* well aware..."

"It is a struggle for us, as I fear that we are both of the same kind of...*heart*." Edmund looked out at the vast expanse of his estate, his eyes deep in thought.

The truth was that he hadn't written anything of substance in a while. He picked up a pen a few days past, but drew only the letters of the alphabet, dazing off as he did so. The words never came as fluidly as they used too, the ink drying up from his pen before he had a chance to write. Most of the time, he sat idly, passing the time in his office smoking a cigar or rolling an old ink blotter around.

"It's a capital day ...Queen's weather," Sam said, seeming to notice the worry on Edmund's face. "Where have you been, friend?"

The frown that settled on Edmund's face, a moment before, had been replaced with a smirk, but he didn't meet Sam's eyes. Edmund pretended to be invested in throwing a stick to Byron. His big padded paws hitting the ground with heavy thuds as he raced across the lawn.

"Another one? Good god, sir. Can you *not* control yourself? I'll be bound that you can't even recall the name of the woman!" Sam jeered, jabbing his pen in Edmund's direction with a wry smile on his face.

It never surprised Edmund when Sam knew he was being evasive. They lived together long enough to learn each other's tells, nevertheless, he attempted to remain coy.

"If I recall correctly, her name was Eliza," Edmund countered.

"Very well then, what of Eliza? Is she still enjoying her breakfast?"

Edmund raised his shoulders in response. Sam pressed his pen to the paper but sat idly.

"I've lost my concentration..."

"Perhaps your writing wouldn't suffer as much if you'd enjoy yourself a bit more," Edmund chided, the visions of his conquest still fresh in his mind.

"One could argue that those moments of enjoyment also bring about moments of distress."

"I've yet to have any myself...moments of distress, I mean... of course," Edmund said contemptuously, as he bit into the last slice of his orange, a challenge evident in his tone.

"I could argue that," Sam said with a wry twist on his lips as he began to write.

"Indeed?"

"*Indeed!* Last night, we heard a guest giving way in the garden. I took it upon myself to find out who it was that was sobbing and why, however, I never did see a face. But it sounded very much like Olivia Frederickson."

"Olivia Frederickson?" Edmund huffed, "She's absolutely mad, you know that— *everyone* knows that!"

"I'm just glad she didn't have the inkling to come into the party and make a spectacle of herself," Sam remarked.

The sun was directly above them now, its rays causing both of them to squint. The sounds of ducks quacking came from the distance. Byron had found a few and began taunting them, and they taunted him back, turning it into a game of cat and mouse.

"She was always quite..." Sam drifted off.

"Queer?"

"Something of the sorts, yes," Sam agreed.

"She's off her head. Obsessed," Edmund added, looking out at his dog, who was now on his belly with his ears back, on the shoreline of the pond. Byron was watching warily as the ducks went about their business, fluffing their tails and waddling about, baiting him for another game.

Olivia Frederickson was a lady of upper-class breeding. When they first met, she fascinated Edmund. She was, not only incredibly beautiful, with a head full of thick golden hair and bright blue eyes, but also captivatingly mysterious.

He'd never met a woman who shared his intense fascination for travel or literature, and she seemed to be a rather notable creature in her expertise in *both* areas. They had a torrid love affair that ended shortly after it began, leaving Olivia distraught. She proclaimed— after Edmund had no interest in dealing with her dramatic flights of fancy—that she would end her life at one of Edmund's public functions. Thankfully, she had been discouraged by fellow sympathetic females, who pulled her away from the knives.

He didn't regret last night's social event, however. Without it, he'd never have had the chance to meet Agatha.

"Do you recall Agatha?" Edmund asked; as he bent down to rub Byron's head. Byron grew tired of being mocked by the ducks and meandered back to him, his black fur shining in the sunlight, gleaming like obsidian. Sam shook his head.

"She came with another lady—her sister, I believe. Her name was Catherine or something of the likes, but I didn't have a chance to speak with her," he added.

Sam's brows pressed together. His forehead scrunched into a few smooth lines as he thought.

"I don't recall either a Catherine or an Agatha."

"I don't doubt that you can't recall them. You were *gone* most of the time..." Edmund chuckled, giving Sam a knowing look.

"I have to say, I was quite *taken* with Agatha. She rebuffed me in a way I found *intriguing* more than irksome." Edmund said, looking off into the distance.

It was her voice that caught his notice first, high pitched but soft on the ears. The way she floated into the room demanded attention, a certain unspoken appeal radiated from her—like the aura that glows around anything in the moonlight.

"I see that you like a challenge?" Sam remarked, looking up from his diary. Edmund shot him a glance.

"A rare belle à croquer?" Sam jested, but Edmund ignored him.

An image flashed into Edmund's mind, of he and Agatha intertwined in a tangle of flesh and legs, her breasts on his chest and their heartbeats racing together. It was these visions that kept him content for a moment in the knowledge that, *one day*, he'd succeed; he'd have a chance to seduce Agatha. She was a prize waiting to be won, and who would be worthier than *him* to win it?

"Ah, I know who you are speaking of! They're not sisters they're cousins, Agatha and Catrina, I believe," Sam interrupted.

"Ah, Yes! That is it! Would you be good enough to deliver this message to her—to Agatha? Raymond, the old fool, I can't trust him to get his trousers on in the morning. The man cannot remember a thing. Certainly can't trust him with a letter. He's just not up to dick anymore, I'm afraid." Edmund handed the letter to Sam who nodded and tucked it carefully in his pocket.

"I'll deliver it tomorrow...How old do you suppose Raymond is anyways? I'd be willing to bet he lived through the Seven Years War," Sam added, and they both laughed.

"What would that make him now?" Edmund rubbed his neck with a hand, deep in thought, "Over a century?"

"I just hope to recall my name when I'm his age," Sam said.

"I shan't care if I do—only that the ladies do," Edmund quipped.

Both men laughed. Once their laughter died down, Sam turned to Edmund in earnestness.

"You know, one of these days, a lady you are bedding is going to surprise you and pull out a knife and slit your throat." Sam took his pen and pretended to slash it across his throat for emphasis. "I'd hate for that to happen to you..."

Edmund stroked his dog's large head paying no regard to Sam's response. From the corner of his eye, he could see Imelda as she made her way across the yard. Her baby blue dress swayed across the lawn with a grace all of its own. He hadn't noticed her until she popped into their conversation. She had an unsettling way of doing that, appearing out of nowhere like a ghost. It unnerved Edmund, but he didn't let on that it had.

"Imelda," they both said, tipping their heads to her.

She fumbled with her gloved hands, rubbing an embroidered handkerchief as she stood.

　　"I hope you are doing well?" Edmund asked cordially, but his tone lacked feeling. Imelda wasn't discouraged, she stepped a bit closer to him.

　　"Very fine." she twisted the handkerchief in her hands, "Would you do me the honor of coming with me into town? I plan to walk about the park, perhaps play some croquet. I don't have to practice my lines, as I don't have a show this evening. I won't need to be rushing off." She stared at him, her olive green eyes wide and entrancing.

　　"It would be an honor—but I regret that I have plans," he said, as he got up from the bench and called for Byron.

Chapter Three

  I finished the morning's lessons with Agatha and Aunt Beatrice on the formalities of dinner parties earlier than expected, and I was grateful to escape. I was looking for a place to write and Ezra, being quite familiar with the territory, guided me to a meadow. I meandered my way there and huddled up comfortably under the base of a large plane tree. I unbuttoned my shoes and dug my toes into the cold, gritty dirt. *No one here to judge*, I thought.

  It was a perfect, incandescent afternoon, and the meadow came alive with the sights and sounds of summer. Flowers weaved their way, like an intricate embroidery pattern, among the sedge. The tart yellow, deep amber, and pale violet buds, spread among a veil of tiny white petals, popped up through a thicket of green. It was mid-afternoon now, and the heat was growing more intense. A welcome breeze blew through the field making the leaves on the tree above, twirl like ballerina dancers by the ends of their stems. A determined damselfly attempted to land on the sedge, its iridescent wings flitting as the wind interrupted its persistent efforts.

  "You're very much like me," I whispered, as it attempted in vain to perch itself. "Somewhere *foreign*...attempting your best to fit in."

On a blank page, I wrote: *Blue bodied damselfly, holding onto the sedge*

I glanced down at my diary and bit my lip. Despite the beauty of the location, I'd been uninspired.

I read through my notes:
—*Big, black eyes of a horse*
—*The orange and black dotted wing of a butterfly*
—*The night sky, pitch black but filled with stars*
—*Sam gazing at the stars*

Anything that I found fascinating, I would jot down in my diary. Whenever I felt uninspired—as I had now—I would turn to the notes I'd written and read through them, hoping for inspiration to strike.

Frustrated with the lack of motivation I felt, I leaned back and closed my eyes. The sun's rays grazed my cheeks, and the wind rustled my skirts. A flock of birds fluttered overhead. They flew from the plane tree, and to the forest and back, chattering with one another. The faint scent of summer hung in the air— dirt, sunshine, and wildflowers.

I hadn't thought much about home since I left, but now that I was alone, my mind began to wander. I was drawn, almost immediately, back to the sea. It was the *sound* I'd missed most. The sound the waves made as they hit the shoreline, only to be slurped back across the sand into the depths moments later. I paused for a minute to listen, wondering if I could still hear the swell of the waves as they lapped the sand. Much to my dismay, the only sound I heard was the wind. The heather gave a resounding answer to my thoughts.

~

I woke to someone tapping my foot, and pushed myself up as fast as I could, landing clumsily on my forearms. The face of a man stared down at me. My vision, fuzzy and distorted at first, became clear, the features slowly coming into focus.

"Sam?"

He appeared to be enjoying the novelty of finding me by the grin on his face.

"Please do let me help you up!" He held his hand out to me.

I glanced out at the field, and a patch of violet tufted grass waved back in response. Judging from the distance of the sun, it was around five o'clock.

"Sir, I must ask you to please turn around for a moment."

He gave me a queer look but obliged. *What did I look like? God only knows what my hair looks like, or what I smell like, or if I drooled...please say I didn't drool!*

I bent down and attempted to button my shoes up, brushing the dirt away from the soles of my feet before putting them back on.

Sam turned away, but was doing an

insufficient job, as he peeked repeatedly over his shoulder—a smirk on his lips at the sight of my fumbling. I finished buttoning one shoe, grinning satisfactorily at my progress.

"Would you please?" I asked, motioning to him to turn around.

"Pardon me," he mocked with a bow, his smirk still evident as he turned. I finished buttoning and stood up.

"You're *quite* cheeky. Even when you're not..." I bit my lip.

"Drunk?" he asked boldly.

"Well...that's not exactly how I'd put it—*but.*"

"*Am I?*" he interrupted, amusement evident in his tone.

"Are you...Oh, cheeky...yes, I dare say you are."

He turned around, so we faced one another again, uncertain what to do next. We stood there a moment in silence, examining one another, the light of day offering a new dimension.

He had a distinct crook to his nose, it jaunted slightly to the left. It didn't detract from his overall appearance, however. By contrast, it only served to compliment him. *Had he broken it while fighting in battle? Or while wrestling a bear? Perhaps, he broke it when he jumped into a river to save a child?* I lost myself briefly in thought before he spoke again.

"I have a message to deliver to your

cousin Agatha...but it appears that I may be lost." He surveyed the field. "And *you*?"

"Reading...mostly." I clutched the diary to my chest.

"What sorts of things do ladies—such as yourself—read?" he asked, eyeing the diary.

"All sorts of things, but mainly magazines about fashion, etiquette, cooking...*those* sorts of things."

He paced around me and then stopped, meeting my eyes. The glow of the sunlight exposed the deep chestnut color of his irises.

"But...*not* you?"

"I beg your pardon?"

"Well, I suppose you don't often quote Keats in public." He picked up a stick and, absentmindedly, started to whack at the grass, the sound making a soft 'thwack.'

"I suppose I don't..."I said, silently cursing myself. I *need* to learn to hold my tongue under the influence of alcohol.

"You have a bit of something..." he trailed off, "in your hair." My hands frantically raked through my scalp, plucking out grass and twigs and other debris while Sam looked on, his lips pressed together.

"What? What is it...do you find this...*humorous*?"

He shook his head.

"Not at all."

"You are..." I huffed, wondering if I

were amused or upset.

"Charming?"

"Charming? I should think *not*!" I teased.

He gave me a sideways grin before focusing on getting his bearings. Squinting, he looked off into the distance, his eyes tracing the line of the forest.

"Care to join me?"

"I thought you didn't know the way?" I asked, feeling my brows purse.

"Unfortunately, I don't. That's what I need *you* for," he said, as he smirked again, exposing one deep dimple, "After you..."

~

My floral skirt swooshed against the forest floor creating a song, a melodious path by which I envisioned myself as the pied piper leading his mice. It was cool under the vast underbelly of the trees, a welcome relief from the stifling, unbearable heat of the sun. Enormous oaks and yews stood like protectors of the copse, their leaves intercepting the light and reflecting it like an emerald watercolor painting below. A faint miasma of decay clung to the air, intermingled with dirt and vegetation. I paused to wipe a bead of sweat from my forehead before leading the way.

Sam came up beside me. His jacket, a rich brown pinstripe, harmoniously coordinated with the trunks of the trees around us. He fiddled with his cravat, a bright red material that clashed terribly with his ensemble. I couldn't help but grin at the sight of him fiddling, wondering if he were preening for my benefit. I glanced down at my gown, its eau de nil cotton blending in with the other shades of the forest.

"If you were an animal where would you live?" He strolled up beside me, derailing my train of thought.

"I beg your pardon?"

He looked over at me, and our eyes met for a flash before parting, sending a jolt of unexpected vigor through me.

"We have some time. I don't suppose it will hurt to talk about something *interesting*. Where would you live, if you were an animal?" he asked again, eyes wide with enthusiasm.

My thoughts immediately drifted to the ocean. I'd spent the majority of my life bathing in the essence of it, whether it was the bosom or the foe. It was the only thing that I knew so wholly that I felt as if I'd been born to the sea and would one day return to it.

"The ocean."

He raised a bushy brow in my direction.

"*Infinite* possibility!" I said, as I stepped over a sycamore log with his hand for guidance.

"Outside of all the ravenous sea creatures who want to *eat* you, you mean?"

"Indeed."

We both laughed.

"How about *you*—where would you live?"

He thought for a moment and responded. "Here, in the forest. Not too many large animals capable of eating me."

"I suppose not," I said, examining our surroundings. Emerald moss ran like wildfire across the fallen logs of the forest floor. Underneath the ferns and other underbrush, a squirrel would skitter about, running from tree to tree. Overhead, the rustle of leaves and branches, promised that the wind had returned.

"Where would Lord Troy live?" I asked.

Sam rubbed his chin as he thought, the dirty blond hair springing away in a phobic manner.

"The ocean, of course—where else can a sea serpent live?"

"Well, I certainly hope that 'said' sea serpent is congenial toward house cats."

"Why ever *house cats*?" Sam frowned.

"I'm fairly certain that Agatha would be a house cat," I said, turning to watch his reaction. He broke out into laughter again, light-hearted and buoyant.

"Such an interesting perspective...and why is it that you suppose Edmund...Lord Troy is interested in 'said' house cat?" He leaned closer, our shoulders almost brushing as we walked.

"Well...for starters, she's caught the

eye of quite a few suitors when she came out a few weeks prior...She's very much desired."

"Ah, perhaps *that's* it..." Sam exclaimed, as he lifted his hand to me while we stepped over a fallen log.

"What is?"

"Edmund loves a challenge."

It was no surprise to me that anyone of Lord Troy's position of wealth and esteem would find Agatha attractive. She was beautiful, a prime article, and would be a fine catch for any male socialite...despite her rather dismal lack of talents.

"She's a fine lady...*but*, does she quote Keats?" Sam asked, reading my thoughts.

I shook my head.

"She'd no sooner know how to quote Keats than she'd know how to make bricks."

He sniggered.

"I'd be bound that she can quote Mrs. Beeton's?" he said with a chuckle.

"I'd be bound that she could also."

We looked at one another in a brief moment of connection and grinned, his dimples forming deep rifts in his cheeks.

"Besides Keats...what other famous poets can you quote?"

"Plenty, I suppose—much to my mother's chagrin." I looked down, watching my feet as they padded along the forest floor. The feel of the solid earth beneath me felt reassuring.

"I suppose it isn't in a mother's favor for her daughter to be open–minded and well–spoken—one must be meager and meek—of the most timid sort." He cocked his head to me as he spoke.

"Yes, I suppose it is my greatest regret that *I* was not born a male," I replied, concealing a smirk. I was leading, and he fell behind, so I paused for a moment, allowing him time to catch up. There was a moment of poignant silence between us that I broke by grinning and then we both started to giggle.

"I'm *not* serious...why ever do you ask?"

"Curiosity—mainly, I haven't known a great many women to *know* of Keats let alone be able to quote him—at least not openly—I'm surrounded by...*fluffery*." He emphasized the word as he waved his hands out in front of him.

"Fluffery?"

"Yes—*fluffery*—you know the type—encouraged from birth to remain stoic and weak, to not have a single care in the world—'least not one that can be shown...*fluffery*."

I nodded, Agatha instantly popping into mind.

"To be honest, it was a moment of weakness brought about by the copious amounts of champagne," I admitted.

"Ah, but *is* it a weakness?" he asked, bending his chin down and looking up at me. I ignored him, turning the question around.

"And what others do *you* know?"

"Longfellow, Tennyson, Shakespeare, Whitman..." he rattled.

"Who's your favorite?"

"Difficult to say...Whitman, perhaps. Whitman loved Shakespeare and many of the other greats. He read quite a few books in his time too. Although, I do suppose I also enjoy the work of Emerson. Both men held nature in great esteem."

"I agree," I said, taking in the surroundings. "I'd much rather be in nature than anywhere else."

The sun dodged and weaved through the canopy, creating a mottled appearance to his face, at one moment casting it with shadows and in another casting it with light or a varied combination of the two.

"Do you hear that?"

We both stopped and looked at one another.

"It's a creek!" he said, as he peered around me, attempting to locate the source of the sound. "Once we find it, I'd like to take a dip."

My eyes grew wide.

"Feet only, of course!" he assured.

~

I directed him to a shallow creek that wound its way through the forest floor like a snake. The water was as clear as a looking glass. In spots where it wasn't agitated, you could see the silt-covered bottom, two or three feet below. Littered around the banks, moss-covered boulders sat like guardians of the river. The scent of moist earth permeated the air, wafting up and rolling across the ground.

"Do you want to take a dip?"

I shook my head, as he took his shoes off and placed them neatly on top of a boulder. He rolled the cuffs of his trousers up to his shin and stepped in. The water—like liquid glass—rolled and whirled around his calves. He tipped his head back, exposing his neck and closing his eyes as he embraced the feel of the water on his legs. The sound was just as soothing, swishing and sloshing as it made its way down its path, ebbing and whirling into eddies. After a moment, he opened his eyes and put a hand out to me.

"Come, now. If you can take your shoes off in a field, you can take your shoes off to feel this water!"

A gush of warmth spread within me at the revelation, and I shook my head. *I can't very well be exposing myself again...*

"Trust me, I've seen *plenty* of ankles with the company that Edmund keeps," he avowed, with the slight shadow of a smirk before it dissolved. My eyes went wide, but he turned to avoid my gaze.

"You mean, women run about shoeless there?"

"*More* than shoeless..."

My jaw dropped, and my eyes popped wide— as if the two were interconnected like the strings on a puppet.

He nonchalantly picked up a stone and tossed it in, watching as the water consumed it with a 'plonk' before sinking to its new resting place on the bottom. The tide rolled around his calves, lapping anything it came in contact with. A dace or chub—like a glint of silver lightning—shot through the water nearby.

I leaned up against one of the large gray stones, the coolness seeping through the cotton of my skirts, as I set my diary down beside me.

"The ancient Greeks hardly ever wore shoes. Some have been known to live their entire lives without wearing shoes..."

"Goodness me! That's rather...interesting," I observed, clearing my throat.

"Perhaps, Plato didn't wear shoes..." Sam thought aloud, and we both laughed.

"Perhaps, not," I said, shrugging.

"In that case—let me be like Plato. I do hate to wear shoes." He looked down at his feet—seemingly mesmerized by the way they looked distorted through the rippling water.

"I suppose it's not all that bad of an idea...I do rather enjoy the feel of the dirt on my feet," I said, looking down at my toes constricted in their leather confines, the buttons laced to the top of my ankle. I could feel them pulsate as the blood pooled in my heels.

"See now! That is the thought." He meandered slowly along the stream, the water rising and falling against his calves as he moved. Inspired, I picked up my diary and added:

—*Sam wading in the creek. The look of joy on his face. The coolness of the water is a relief.*

He looked up from his feet that were sloshing about the bank.

"Now, since I am Plato—who shall you be? Hmm. Well, not Hydna...she swam, and you don't take your shoes off," he joked.

I crossed my arms across my chest.

"Certainly not Phryne." He rubbed his chin, and I thought I could see the faint glow of pink touch his cheeks.

"You do write...or, I *presume* you do, judging by that diary you have beside you." He pointed to my diary, and I felt a jolt of panic run through me.

"Not anything of consequence," I exclaimed.

"Nonsense...every great writer feels this way! Ask Edmund and the piles of uninspired paper and the hours of torment deep into the night, and the pints and pints of ink he must go through...and pints and pints of liquor, I might add. I can attest to the torment, as well..."

"You write?" I asked, tilting my head.
"Feverishly."

An image of him popped into my mind as he wrote—an old fashioned feather pen in hand as he whipped through page after page.

"Poetry?"

"Novels, poetry, articles...I've written a few for Punch," he said, looking down, as the water swirled around his feet.

"You haven't!" I gasped, and a sheepish grin spread across his face. "That's nothing but satire!"

"*Is it?*" he asked with a jerk, pressing a hand to his chest. "One must start somewhere I suppose..."

"I suppose..." I replied, unconvinced. The shadow of the trees moved across his face, at once exposing and then concealing, a glint of something in his eye.

"Have a look," he said, nodding to his diary which sat on a boulder next to his shoes. He gave his chin a jerk in that direction, "if you'd like."

I picked his diary up and rubbed my fingertips across the smooth, black leather binding, turning it over in my hands. Despite the heat of the day, the leather remained cool. I flipped open the pages landing on one in the middle of the book. The first title "*Fauna*" had been scribbled out and replaced with "*Spring Song.*" I read the title aloud and cleared my throat, looking up at him to ensure he was still comfortable with the idea. He gave a small nod in return.

"*Delicate the breeze that blows through your meadows, stirring one's soul from the burdens of winter. Steadfast the sun's rays that defy all the shadows, and a promise of the ice it shall splinter. Bewitching the soil with her dainty reach, entrancing the buds and their petals to seek, on the newborn night's eve, doth the flowers beseech, that night shall be short and the day shall it keep, of the springtime that lasts and the blooms how they hope, of such dreams of the gentleman and the lady: elope.*"

"It's...*remarkable*," I gushed, closing the book slowly. He gave me a tight-lipped smile before making his way to the bank, where he sat on one of the boulders rubbing his feet to remove the dirt that stuck to his wet heels. He bent over and put his shoes back on, eyes drifting off to someplace inside his mind.

"I am well aware of the changing tide...Romanticism is a dying art. Perhaps, this is why I am troubled," he said suddenly, as he bent over to pick up a stone, rubbing it in his fingers before tossing it with a 'plop' into the water. "I have a project that I'm working on...I suppose it's different than other projects I've done. But I'm not ready yet to unveil it to the world."

"And what is that?"

"When the time comes, I shall divulge it to you…perhaps, I shall ask for your opinion on my work."

He looked as if he were mulling something over in his head, his hand rubbing methodically across his chin.

"Perhaps, we can both be of assistance to one another!"

I cocked my head.

"How?"

"Lord Byron…what did Lord Byron and his colleagues do?" He held his hands out, eyes wide with excitement. I shook my head and shrugged.

"He had help! He had friends…friends who were also poets and authors. They worked together; they critiqued and encouraged one another."

"But…we *hardly* know one another," I said, hunching inward, holding my diary taut to my chest.

"Perhaps…that's better." He was pacing now, his hands on his hips. He turned to me whenever he spoke, his arms animated with his thoughts.

"Whatever do you mean?"

"Well, if we can critique one another's work…without bias." He met my eyes, waiting for my response.

"Critique each other's work? I critique yours?" I asked, feeling the sentence drop off.

"Yes! And I, yours."

"No, no, no…Absolutely not!" I shook

my head, as I held steadfast to my diary and turned to walk away. He raced to catch up with me, putting his hand out.

"This can be our writing spot...is it not the finest place to write?" he implored me to look, as he waved a hand at the surroundings.

Admittedly, it was intrinsically peaceful, the sound of the stream as it slowly trickled along, the sporadic sound of woodland animals scurrying about, and the sunlight as it filtered through the leaves, creating a sage-colored ambiance to the world below.

"Is there such a thing? A writing spot?" I asked.

"I suppose there could be..." he laughed, his eyes crinkling.

"What is it that you plan to do while we are here?"

"Write—of course—and share our thoughts on the other's progress..."

I pursed my lips.

"And if you shall not feel like sharing, you will not be obligated to do so, but as fellow writers, we should support one another..." he added, noticing the look of hesitation on my face...

I nodded slowly—mulling it over.

"Well then, we shall meet here every...Monday at 3:00?"

I shook my head.

"I have lessons with my Aunt Beatrice and Agatha..."

"How about Tuesday then? If I walk to this spot from Edmund's estate, I can reach the river, this river," he pointed to the stream, "in about twenty-five minutes...shall we meet at 3:00 in the afternoon?"

"Tuesday at 3:00...yes, I suppose that will work. It can't hurt if no one finds out about it," I sighed.

A smirk developed on his face, exposing one deep dimple.

"Capital! We shall meet here every Tuesday at 3:00 sharp in the afternoon."

~

We made our way through the forest and reached the edge of a field. We were getting closer to my aunt and uncle's estate, and by the pang in my stomach, I imagined we were far past lunch and now into dinner. Almost as if he'd read my reaction, Sam squinted and looked up at the sky. The discomfort of the raw daylight made us feel like moles, and we each grimaced at the brightness.

"I could really have a go at a squab pie."

"Squab pie?" I shot him a look, and he shrugged.

"Not much different than pigeon pie, although I suppose some make it with mutton and apple—anyways—I've lost my thought..." he chuckled.

"I'd much rather have a nice plate of

chicken. Chicken medallions perhaps or pork…a few potatoes, asparagus, beets…" I drifted off into thought. My mind filled with the ecstasy and aroma of dinner wafting as it piled up from a plate, hot and steaming. My mouth was watering, and I licked my lips, absentmindedly, ignoring the rolling and gurgling of my empty stomach.

"And of course a pie or some sort of pudding," I added, not wanting to forget dessert.

"Cherry tart!" Sam blurted out. We nodded at one another in agreement.

"Now that we have dinner settled…"

We both snickered.

I was grateful for the breeze that blew across the field, stirring the tall grasses. The furry tips of them tickled the tops of our calves as we moved. The wind stirred a few warblers in the trees, squabbling amongst one another as they flew off to a more peaceful resting spot. A blaze of orange wildflowers spread across the field, the tops of their bright, spiky heads popping out of the grass ignominiously. Despite the sun's descent, the heat was still substantial, and I could feel the beads of sweat forming along my temples. Tiny wisps of my dark hair sprang up, disobediently, near my ears.

"We will meet here on Tuesday?" He looked over at me—the sun casting its long sideways glow on his features— the rays exposing blond and ginger tones in his darker facial hair.

"Perhaps...or perhaps not," I said coyly. My heart suddenly made itself known within my chest, as it beat faster and harder in response.

Chapter Four

There was a soft glow cast on the wall by candlelight — the flicker growing longer, and then shorter, as it moved across the wall like a dancing ghost. Uncle Harold liked the ambiance and novelty of candlelight chandeliers. He was wealthy enough to afford gas lights, but either from sentiment or frugality, he chose to have dinner by candlelight every night, much to my aunt's dismay.

"Where's all the food?" Uncle Harold sat down at his seat, folded his napkin on his lap and regarded the table with a furrowed gray brow.

"It is a very *fashionable* thing to serve dishes sequentially. All the ladies at Martha Ogleby's are talking about it! It's certainly a change that we can *all* benefit from," Aunt Beatrice stated.

"I find it to be *less* than satisfactory!" he barked, as a frown appeared under his salt and pepper mustache. I bit my lip to stifle a giggle.

"It's de rigueur for dinner to be served á la russe, Papa," Agatha added proudly, as she dipped a spoon into her seafood bisque.

"I see that you are practicing your French, Agatha... that should be for a worthy cause." He grunted before looking down at his meager plate. Ignoring her husband's grumbling, Aunt Beatrice spoke up.

"It helps with digestion, dear."

"As much so as eating in the dark, I suppose!" Uncle Harold shot back as he patted his paunch. Uncle Harold, a stout, older man with a tuft of thick black and gray hair, had a substantial belly that protruded like an uninvited dinner guest at the dining room table.

"Where is Ezra?" He gazed around the room, finding his son's seat empty. Aunt Beatrice, quite the opposite of her corpulent husband, waved a frail hand in his direction, focusing her attention on buttering a roll.

"*That boy*...when is he going to learn that he's an adult now?"

"Please, Harold. Can we discuss this in private?" She eyed their guest and gave her husband a thin-lipped smile.

"Always out and about, *gallivanting*...fishing or hunting or doing God knows what..." he moaned. "His work ethic is a *disgrace!*"

Aunt Beatrice, undaunted by Uncle Harold's ranting, grinned at him amicably.

"Well, there is *some* hopeful news about his future. I've spoken with Madeline Foster, and she says that Lillian would be an exceptional option for Ezra. She's an excellent pianist, studies the arts and also has a fine hand at painting..."

Uncle Harold threw his hand up and grunted.

"Won't be much good if he can't keep a job! He needs to start taking his future career more seriously...boy's going to end up being a costermonger *for God's sake*...I didn't work this hard for nothing...the boy's an ungrateful sow!"

"Harold, *please!*" Aunt Beatrice bent her head down, glaring at him from across the table. In an effort to avoid further conflict, she promptly addressed Sam.

"I've heard that you've come to deliver a *letter*?" she inquired, as she buttered a piece of bread and took a delicate nibble of it, setting it down on the edge of her plate. Agatha was bubbling over like a pot of stew from expectation. If not for the faux pas of outright asking, I could see her leaping across the table and strangling him until he gave up the letter. She tapped her fork subtly, but impatiently, on the table to calm her nerves.

Sam, suddenly aware that he was addressed, swallowed and blotted his face with a napkin before responding. "Yes, Mrs. Greenman." He patted his pocket before he took a sip of water from his glass.

"Mmmhmm," Aunt Beatrice gave a noise of vague interest, assuming that Sam would liberally continue, but he hadn't, and she was much too formal to ask outright.

The kitchen maids scurried in and replaced the empty soup bowls and bread plates with the second course of meat and vegetables. The scent of hot beef, butter and asparagus filled the room.

"I assume the letter is about the fabric I ordered from Gambitt's?" Aunt Beatrice piped up. Agatha's mouth dropped slightly, as our eyes met. "I ordered purple silk from Italy a few weeks ago. It's called mauve, I believe... and it's *absolutely* stunning!"

"And how much is this new fabric going to cost me?" Uncle Harold didn't look up, just continued to eat his food. He set his knife and fork down onto his plate where a pea accidentally rolled off and onto the table. Without waiting for an answer, he picked his knife up again, jabbing it in his wife's direction like a finger.

"I don't see why you couldn't choose *English* silk...or even French silk...not an import tax on the stuff anymore."

"It *far* surpasses either English or French silk...once you see it, you will be certain to agree," she said, taking another delicate bite of her asparagus.

Sam opened his mouth to interject, as he reached hesitantly into his pocket for the letter, but abruptly shut it. Uncle Harold looked up and gave a low grunt in his throat and then went back to cutting his meat with a little more vigor than necessary.

"*Foolish*...paying to import something we have loads of," he continued, the knife having successfully cut through his beef and hitting the plate with a low screech.

"It isn't for me, Harold. *Heaven*

forbid!" she said with a bit more bite, and all of us dropped our heads to our plates, feeling the emotion of the room drift into uneasiness.

"How shall I expect our daughter to marry a fine gentleman if she is not dressed her finest? You believe that we shall live like you're a measly clerk, is that it, Harold?" Aunt Beatrice met Uncle Harold's eyes across the table and held them for a moment before going back to eating. She had the same blue eyes as Agatha, however, hers wore the lines of experience and wisdom.

If she were to marry her daughter to a wealthy business owner or someone with a title, she would need Agatha to be dressed her finest, and they had the money to do so. Uncle Harold was one of the most laudable Civil Engineers in London. He'd shown promise after his contribution to the Crystal Palace Exhibition in '51, and his work won him many accolades and future commissions putting him and Aunt Beatrice in a position of wealth as much as status.

But old habits die hard. Uncle Harold grew up as an apprentice's son. It was only by luck that he managed to wedge himself into his career, becoming an apprentice on behalf of his family and showing considerable talent.

Ezra waltzed in and sat down casually across from his mother. He huffed on the lenses of his glasses and used a handkerchief to wipe them clean before putting them back on to reveal two large owl eyes.

"How pleasant of you to join us," Uncle Harold scoffed.

"I do apologize for my tardiness...*but*...I have news. The Barrymores' have offered to allow me to fox hunt on their land with them. We don't have a hound, but I'm sure they'll be plenty along with us for—"

"Well isn't that *grand*?" his father interrupted, lowering his eyes at him. Taking this as a queue to refrain, Ezra looked down at his dinner and spooned out some soup. He shrunk his shoulders in, which did little to conceal him, as he was so tall. It would be difficult for Ezra to disappear in a crowd, let alone a room of six. Aunt Beatrice gave her son a look of understanding before sighing and turning her attention back to Agatha.

"It is our *duty* to find her the most suitable gentleman," she continued, eliciting a huff from someone at the table. Sam cleared his throat ready to intervene, but was largely ignored.

"Ahh, *indeed*... and who better, than the finest gentleman, to marry my sweet Agatha– a prince, *perhaps*?" Uncle Harold shot back scornfully, glancing at both Agatha and Aunt Beatrice as he took a sip of his port. Agatha glared at him, as he brushed a crumb from his robust belly. Ezra stifled his laughter, pressing his lips together and blotting them with a napkin.

"A sweet lady she is...our Agatha," he said with an air of sarcasm that caused his mother to look up and Agatha to glare at him, her jaw clenched for fear of lashing out.

"How *are* the prospects?" Uncle Harold lifted his spoon, filled with peas, but stopped just short of putting it into his mouth when he realized his blunder. All the women's eyes were glued on him as if watching an animal in the zoo. His topic was utterly *taboo* while having outside guests at the table.

"Bahhh...I've never been good at this stuff," he scowled, before he shoveled the spoon in. "I hope that you are correct in your assumptions, my darling...for if not, we shall be..." He looked over at Agatha, then Beatrice, and thought hard about completing the sentence. "We shall be spending a good deal of time finding her the *appropriate* suitor." He dabbed his mustache, the gray hairs shining from the port.

Sam took the opportunity of distraction to hand Agatha the letter. He dug it out of his jacket pocket and bent over to her, thankful that he didn't have to reach over anyone to do so.

"I beg your pardon, I know this is not ideal...*however*, I feel like this may help the matter at hand."

They all looked at him with looks of confusion and mixed amusement before he cleared his throat and sat down. All eyes then drew to Agatha as she carefully opened the envelope. She read it to herself, conscious of everyone watching, and then handed it over to her mother.

"It's a letter...*from the Lord*!"

Aunt Beatrice read with an indistinct expression, but her foot tapped impatiently beneath the table, exposing her genuine thoughts on the matter.

"*Bless my soul*, we have *found* a prospect!" she gushed, as she folded the letter and handed it to her husband.

~

"Do you s'pose we'll get married—Lord Troy and me?" Agatha giggled as she sat up on her elbows. She undid her hair for the night, and her long blond locks hung lax against her shoulders, except for a small strand that she coiled with a finger. We retired to her room, bidding Sam farewell shortly after dinner.

"I should have known! I threw an apple seed in the fire, and it *popped*!" she exclaimed.

She was referring, of course, to the ritual of throwing an apple seed into a fire to see if it would burst loudly...*or* if it would burn quietly. If the apple seed popped, loud enough to hear, it was a sign of good fortune, and a sure sign that the person you loved *also* desired you. I found it hard to believe that she had heard anything *at all* from something as tiny as an apple seed; moreover that she put so much hope into a simple act of nature.

"But—you hardly know the man," I said, as I brushed my hair, dislodging any of the dirt or leaves from the days' adventures. It was thick and difficult to untangle, and I cursed silently as the brush became ensnared in it.

"It hardly matters!" she asserted as she sat up, wide-eyed. "I trust it...don't you?"

I nodded unconvincingly.

A fine smattering of freckles spread across the bridge of her nose and cascaded down her cheeks. I'd never seen them before, realizing then that I'd never consciously seen *any* flaws in Agatha at all—at least not physically. She'd scrubbed her face clean revealing the telltale marks, and I wondered what other marks she possibly concealed.

"Oh, I almost forgot..." she said as she got up, the bright light of the oil lamp casting her shadow against the wall as she moved. My eyes followed her over to the table where she picked up the envelope. I hadn't wanted to prod, but I *was* insatiably curious. It took no probing on my part for her to hand it over, and I sat with it happily in my hands, eagerly waiting to open it. She shuffled onto the bed and took the letter from the envelope and read it aloud.

> *Dearest Agatha,*
> *I hope that this letter finds you well.*

There was a blank space and a small blotch of black ink where he paused for too long.

> *I have asked that Sam deliver it to you in hopes that I can see you again soon. I have so enjoyed your visit the last we met. It seems as though fate has brought us together and I shall not be a foe to fate.*

Agatha stopped and let out a squeak of excitement after reading the last sentence.

> *Please join me at 3 o'clock on June 13th at my estate for afternoon tea with your dearest cousin, Catrina.*
> *With great affection,*
> *Lord Edmund Troy*

She twirled her hair around her finger, and a grin spread across her face, reaching her eyes.

"He wants me to be there?" I asked, feeling queer about the idea. Agatha gave me a quizzical look and then sat up.

"Of course—I *must* have a chaperone! Don't you know these things?" she asked with a giggle.

Would it be awkward to be someone's chaperone? What did an escort do?

Without giving it a second thought, she stood up. "I've never read any of his poetry before," she said, as she rifled through a bookshelf near the bed and pulled out a green book with a small, gold ivy border. "I'll start... the first poem is called *Dolcezza...*"

~

 I stared up at the ceiling for a long time in an attempt to sleep. It was night now; the lavender darkness crept in from the window and made it impossible to see anything but your own shadowed figure. The noises here were strange. Instead of the rush of waves, I heard the sound of Agatha softly snoring. She had been asleep for a good hour or more, the book held to her chest, reminding me of a child with a favorite toy. A grandfather clock chimed on the hour, breaking the silence and the soft rhythm of Agatha's sleep.
 But it wasn't just the sound of home I missed. It was the scent too, the salty, briny scent that wafted in from the depths and became the permanent cologne of my older brother's hands. The vision of my father helping my brothers cast nets out into the open water, and mama descaling fish for supper, flashed vividly into my mind, and I found myself giving way. The warm tears ran silently down my cheeks. I frowned, feeling my chin quiver. In my stomach, a hole began to form, whittling away around the edges like paper that caught fire.
 What does a fish become when out of the sea? I wondered. *What would become*

of me if I, too, were to find a suitable prospect for marriage? Would I have to sacrifice my love of writing and literature for the love of husband and child? Even worse...what if I didn't have the means to write and publish a book under my own name? I reached to the nightstand for my diary and started to write—"*The sea is a looking glass...*"

Chapter Five

The cucumber sandwiches and tea settled happily in their stomachs as they walked around the estate lawn. Lord Troy studied the way Agatha moved. Reservations, like bobbing corks, popped up inside of him before Agatha and Catrina arrived. *Had his drink betrayed him the night of their first meeting? Was the dark too cunning?*

But he found himself feeling relieved at the sight of her, as she sauntered ahead of him with a slight bounce to her step. She stepped so lightly, that for a brief moment, it appeared as if she could float above the ground. The even lines of her dress framed her silhouette, a feminine hourglass of perfect proportions.

When she moved, she swayed her hips from side to side, taunting him. He struggled to maintain his composure, forcing himself to think of arbitrary things to take his mind away from her— or from the things he'd like to *do with her.* He spouted off in his mind random stream of conscious thoughts: *Cricket, Tea, Tobacco, Ferns, Fox Hunting, Horse Racing, Gambling.* He'd thought of anything to corral his unsavory thoughts at the moment. But the visions were merciless and popped up frequently, *despite* his efforts. Grateful for a distraction, he welcomed his dog when he came barreling toward them.

"This is Byron," Lord Troy announced, as he bent down to scratch the dog's large black head. The dog looked up obediently, his mouth agape. Drool coagulated on the side of his jaw, forming a slime-like substance that dribbled to the ground.

"I've never had the...*pleasure* of owning a pet," Agatha uttered, as she gave a tight-lipped smile and folded her hands neatly in front of her.

Catrina, who stood stoically near Agatha until now, bent down and patted the dog briskly on the head.

"Hello there little guy! Well, I suppose you are a *big* guy. Come over, Agatha, he's friendly!" She motioned to her cousin, who was leaning back. Her face was contorted with distress.

Lord Troy gave her a polite nod to acknowledge her, but turned his attention back to Agatha. Agatha gave a wary glance at Byron, but started to soften and lean in on her cousin's guidance.

"Have you had the pleasure of meeting Socrates at the gathering?" Edmund asked, patting Byron again on the head. The dog nudged him impatiently to continue when he stopped.

"The bear?" Agatha asked—her eyes lost in thought. She was attempting to puzzle together what he might be implying. "He was marvelous! I could not believe that someone would be capable of owning such a magnificent creature and have him in captivity...but it truly is incredible that you own such a...such a beast," she stuttered. She bent her head down, twirling a long lock of her hair.

"Byron looks much smaller now when you look at him, doesn't he?" Lord Troy inquired. Catrina laughed—a genuine chuckle that caught Lord Troy off guard—and made him grin in response.

He hadn't paid much notice to Catrina. When compared to her cousin, Agatha had the kind of beauty that was noticeable to anyone regardless of age or sex. But it wasn't just a physical manifestation either, she moved with the grace of a lady and even her voice and mannerisms oozed with femininity. But Catrina's laugh, a sweet and innocent sound, filled the air for a moment with something *so* —uniquely intriguing— that it caused him to take notice of her.

She was taller and lither than her curvaceous and petite cousin. Her hair was dark where Agatha's was light, as if *she* were the night and Agatha the day. She had a fine face. Her eyes were large, on anyone else they would seem oversized, but they fit her perfectly. She had a petite, but flawlessly shaped nose. There was nothing outwardly remarkable about her like her cousin, but she wasn't hard to look at either.

He was drawn back to Agatha when he

noticed her making a tentative move towards Byron, eyeing him like he was a tiger about to attack. Catrina bit her lip suppressing a grin. Without warning, the big dog put two massive paws up on Agatha's skirts. Her eyes flung wide and she shot back so fast she fell straight on her bum, letting out a shriek on her way down. She shook her head and put her wrists down to the ground, catching herself before falling all the way back. She startled Byron, who started spinning around before shooting off in the other direction. Her brows scrunched together for a moment and then bounced back, her eyes wide and as large as marbles as she watched Byron flee. He and Catrina raced to help her up.

"Are you well? Shall I fetch a doctor?"

Edmund's face was relatively calm—the effect of consistent expectation. His Adam's apple, however, bobbed up and down giving his true feelings away. She shook her head as they bent down to help her to her feet.

"I'm terribly sorry; there is no excuse for this! May I fetch another dress for you before our outing?" He put his hand out to her to offer his assistance, but she shooed it away.

"I'm quite fine, *thank you*," she hissed, her tone wavering on short, as she continued to brush off her skirts.

"Well, I suppose the good news is that he didn't lick you," Catrina piped up, breaking the tension. Agatha eyed her and gave her a reticent smile, her brows still furrowed. Lord Troy stifled his laughter, cleared his throat, and followed Agatha and Catrina back to his home.

~

While I was never interested in architecture, I found Westminster Abbey to be an undeniably, sophisticated feat of beauty. One could hardly stand in its presence without their jaw-dropping at the immense artistic display it was, and yet, Agatha spent more time looking down at her nails, than the centuries-old manifestation of Gothic architecture and history.

The scent of polish, dust, and age lay thick in the air. Immense pointed arches stretched skyward from their shafts and pillars, spreading as they reached the top like branches. The entirety of which gave a vein-like appearance, as if the ceiling were a beating heart, and the arches pumped in the blood. Light filtered in through the windows, exposing the dust which floated and swirled like tiny snowflakes through the haze.

I treaded lightly at first. But Agatha—being Agatha—had no qualms. She strolled about as if she were buying new hats in the Burlington Arcade.

"Attending a service here on Sunday would be quite the sight..." she said impartially, as she glanced to the ceiling, before looking back at her nails.

"Did you know that Westminster Abbey was, at one time, a Benedictine Monastery?" Lord Troy strolled up next to her. Agatha smiled charmingly at him before sighing and rolling her head back and forth when he looked away.

We walked for some time until he stopped in front of a large open hall. He motioned with a hand behind him, sending a few thousand particles of dust in all directions.

"But this—*this* is why I brought you here—the Poet's Corner."

"Poet's Corner?" Agatha eyed the hall, as she twirled a piece of her hair with a finger.

"The Poet's Corner is where the most brilliant poets are buried," he effused, a sense of reverence radiated from his expression.

Statues and plaques of varying size and structure ran the length of the walls. I was tempted to run my finger along the smooth marble, but swiftly withdrew it. I stepped toward one of them and mouthed the inscription to myself—William Shakespeare. The statue rested his head thoughtfully on his fist, his elbow pressed onto a stack of books. His other hand held a scroll with his written word. His eyes, round and barren, looked outward onto an invisible scene, deep in thought.

I made my way to a bust of a man with a stern face bedecked with grape leaves in his hair. His epitaph was written in Latin, so I continued, as Lord Troy sauntered up beside me.

"It reads," he took a hard look at it before translating, "sacred to the memory of Samuel Butler." He cocked his head to the side, deep in concentration. "Who was born in Strensham...in Worcestershire 1612 and died in London 1680, a man of extraordinary...learning, wit, and integrity. Peculiarly, happy in his writings...not so in the encouragement of them."

I felt my eyebrow rise at the sentiment.

"The curious inventor of a kind of satire among us."

My mind immediately drifted to Sam.

"The rest carries on about his integrity and such."

"Interesting," I said, gazing at the empty eyes. "This place...I've never been to such a place. It's really quite...*extraordinary*!"

"It is," he agreed, as his eyes drifted upward. "I've been all around the world, or at least this *part* of the world, and I can say— with certainty— that the English know what to value."

"The arts?"

"The arts, literature, astronomy—all great things flourish here—whether they are born here, or are brought here," he said with an air of flourish, before starting off down the hall. I followed dutifully behind.

Agatha, more or less, seemed uninteresting in the whole event. She was only satisfied, based on her smile and sparkle in her eye, whenever Lord Troy looked her way. She was quick to turn on her charm and even quicker to let it fall by the wayside whenever she wasn't being noticed...or thought she wasn't being noticed. When Lord Troy turned to examine the Chaucer monument, she pulled me aside.

"I've lost one of my hairpins!" she whispered loudly. "Can you distract him?"

"I'm sure he won't mind if we try to find it," I said.

Her eyes grew wide.

"This isn't my *cup of tea*...to be honest," she mumbled, looking down at her nails again. The obvious having no need to be stated, but I nodded in agreement.

It wasn't an unexpected response from Agatha. She never cared for poetry or literature arts in any means. She did read, but far more from her father's pressure to do so, than for the actual enjoyment of it. The only thing she read for pleasure were ladies' journals, and she read these mostly to find fashion plates and see what was going on with the elite culture of the London wealthy.

She held a steady finger on the pulse of the bourgeois zeitgeist of the Piccadilly neighborhood and had fashioned herself among one of them. While she *was* among the upper crust, the exclusivity of Piccadilly came from residing in the area as opposed to pretending too, and thus, leaving her less favorable among the friends she made by happenstance in the area.

She was off, methodically tracing her footsteps while holding a few wayward strands of her hair balled up in her hand. I shook my head as I watched her hunched down, shuffling across the floor like a crab. Finding no use in attempting to lure her back, I entertained myself by reading all of the inscriptions following behind Lord Troy.

He paused next to the statue of the poet Joseph Addison and took in the sight of his marble features. He was draped in material, holding a scroll to his side, a mission of knowledge and art both present in his devoid marble eyes. He nodded before turning back to me.

"Can you paint, Miss Catrina?"

I slowly shook my head.

"I regret to say that I cannot...at least not *well*."

"I don't regret it at all. I find it a most *useless* talent. Unless, of course, you paint like DaVinci or Michaelangelo."

We both snickered.

"A few of my chums come to paint the gardens at my estate." He strolled casually beside me. "I have been told they are the finest in England."

"They are fine gardens indeed, My Lord." I nodded.

"To be honest, I can't really tell the difference between a rose bush and a rhododendron," he chuckled. "I regret that one of my only talents is my ability to write…"

He paused, looking up at a bust, staring past its empty eyes.

"It is a most *dreadful* living, really…I find it heartbreaking, while at the same time unavoidable, as if I shall wither and die if I do not do it…" His hands slowly formed into fists at his sides and then released. "I both love it—*and* loathe it. How can such a thing be?" He was circling the bust; his eyes were roving over it, but not seeing it. "It has some sort of *power* over me that I cannot comprehend!"

I nodded, feeling something take flight within me. It is a writer's *duty* to write—a burden and a challenge—but a duty nonetheless, I thought.

"Perhaps it would all be worth it, to be buried here…" He drifted off as he walked around the statue, taking it in from each side. "I'd like to imagine that this would be my final resting place one day—be an artist at rest, among my fellow companions in the poet's corner—Alas, we all have our demons…and the scariest monsters are the ones that lurk within our souls, are they not?"

I felt my lips press together at the

reference.

"Edgar Allan Poe?" I asked. A look of surprise crossed his face before he commented.

"I can thank him for the wit of the sentiment—but the *truth* is eternal."

I nodded, unsure of my feelings on the topic.

"Although, I *suppose* that if a man can claim to live to one hundred and fifty-two and secure his spot among such notables, I shall likely have a chance..."

I giggled.

"One hundred and fifty-two? That would be...preposterous. No one has lived to one hundred and fifty-two!"

"Your frankness is quite refreshing," he replied with a grin.

"You must tell Thomas Parr that! Old Tom Parr claimed to live to one hundred and fifty-two years old and King Charles, having taken pity on the old fool, laid him to rest here when he died, which, by the by, was from an incident largely caused by his inability to cut meat...He choked at the dinner table."

"While dining with the king?"

"Or so the story goes..." he said, looking off into the distance.

"Surely, among anyone, you would have the greatest opportunity," I spoke up. "I've read your works, My Lord."

"Hmm," he said thoughtfully, as he ran a hand behind his neck. "Do you often read,

Miss Catrina?"

"I'm a huge fan of poetry…and novels…"

"I presume then that you can quote some?" He leaned in with one brow piqued.

"I shouldn't like to be so forward, My Lord."

"Mmm…but you *can*?"

I nodded politely, as he peeked around my shoulder.

"Where has Agatha gone?" he asked, looking down one corridor and then the next.

Chapter Six

We were all famished by the time we arrived back for dinner. We stopped only once at a street cart, somewhere between the manor and Westminster Abbey, for a nibble of spice cake and tea. It did little to satiate our appetites, but the zing of spice and the warm tea were a welcome mid-day treat.

"My cook makes the finest lamb," Lord Troy remarked, watching as his kitchen maid hurried off, offering the slice to Agatha who reluctantly accepted it. I knew she preferred nearly anything to lamb, but of course wouldn't say as much, as I imagine she was quite hungry.

"There's mint jelly for it, as well, if you'd like." He nodded with his chin, to the green gelatinous blob sitting in a cup on the table. The entire room smelled of roast lamb with the faint hint of mint. Agatha took a gingerly nibble of her slice and swallowed. The shadow of a grimace was still on her face as she went in for another bite, but thankfully, Lord Troy was much too busy garnishing his own lamb to notice.

Something bizarre sat in the middle of the table, and I couldn't take my eyes off of it. It looked as though it was some sort of...*fruit or vegetable*, but it was unlike anything I'd ever seen before. It was oblong and brown with ...are those *spikes*? *Yes, I suppose those are spikes...or spines*? I caught Agatha's glance from across the table, her big blue eyes were as round as marbles.

"Whatever is *that*?" She pointed at it, one eyebrow raised, her curiosity getting the better of her.

"It's called a pineapple," Lord Troy said casually, as he cut his lamb and took a small bite without looking up.

"It's a fruit that comes from an island called Bermuda... near America." He watched as the cryptic expression on Agatha's face softened.

"Very rare here...and all the more reason for me to display it," he added.

"Have you...*tasted* it?" She tilted her head, taking in the spiky top with a look of piqued inquisitiveness.

"Is it bitter?" I asked, as I studied the spiny skin.

"I've heard...that they have a sweet taste, but I haven't tasted one myself," he added. "I have plenty of unique plants. It's sort of a hobby of mine."

I looked around the room before Lord Troy spoke again.

"I collect rare ferns. I have a few of them in my parlor...from my travels abroad. Fern hunting is, in fact, quite a sport. I've heard some outrageous stories from my chums about their adventures fern hunting..."

Agatha caught my eye from across the

table, as Lord Troy took a sip of port and set it down carefully beside his plate.

"Some people have gone to such extremes to find rare ferns that they've accidentally died in the process! Fallen off cliffs, fallen down holes, been attacked by wild animals... it is a rather *dangerous* sport," he sniggered peculiarly. Agatha joined in, and I felt the awkward desire to participate, hearing her polite, but nervous giggle.

"Perhaps we shall go one day..."

He stopped eating and met both of our eyes, his bottom lip held between his teeth, holding back the slight mischievous curl to his lip.

"Of course we shall be of the utmost safety!" he said, allowing the grin to spread from his lips.

"You will have to excuse me. I am feeling...*unwell*." Agatha interrupted. She had a faint hint of green to her face, resembling the hue of the mint jelly. She blotted her lips with a napkin; her skin was dewy with perspiration.

"Shall I call for someone?" Lord Troy's Adam's apple bobbed nervously in his throat as he analyzed her. Without responding, she stood up and made haste to the door, holding her hand to her mouth and crouching as she ran.

"Perhaps I should check on her myself?" he questioned himself aloud, rubbing the back of his neck. He sat up and then sat back, conflicted.

"Or perhaps I should give her time to settle...yes, I believe I'll do that."

It was quiet for a few minutes. The only sound was the clanking of flatware against our plates, before he spoke again. The room, with its cream-colored wallpaper and gilded picture frames and mirrors, appeared friendly and warm when I'd arrived, but now felt enormous and foreboding. The table, a long span of glossy mahogany, fit to feed twelve or more hungry patrons, seemed infinitely vast. I tapped my foot nervously beneath me, and bit my lip with my teeth, holding it there.

"Do you...*reside* with Agatha?" Lord Troy asked, breaking the silence as he bit into a roasted potato.

He had, unfortunately, caught me while I was chewing.

"Only for the summer, My Lord," I replied.

"Mmmm, I see. From where *do* you hail then, if not from London?" he asked, without looking up as he cut a substantial chunk of lamb, oozing with the sticky mint jelly.

"I'm from Weymouth, My Lord."

"Weymouth...and do you have a family?" He looked up at me, his tone belying his lack of genuine interest in the topic at hand, I thought. He caught my eye, and I felt my skin prickle. His gaze was unforgiving, roaming over my face and fixating somewhere on my lips. Finally coming too, he cleared his throat and looked down, feigning interest in the rest of his dinner.

"Please...carry on." He flicked his wrist at me, before forking another potato.

"I have a mother, a father, and three brothers. All of whom live in Weymouth, My Lord," I continued.

My eyes were drawn to the glass filled with port, its deep crimson color catching to the sides as he swirled it around with his hand. I bit my lip again.

"And...what is it that your family does...for a living, I mean?" He set his fork down with a clang and tilted his head, looking up at me through his eyelashes.

"I come from a fishing family, My Lord...Three generations of fisherman."

"Say than...how *is it* that you have such profound knowledge of the arts and literature?" he challenged.

"I was fortunate enough to befriend a wise, little old lady...Mrs. Cullwick."

He nodded for me to continue.

"Mrs. Cullwick's husband was a professor of literature. A lover of the arts and the written word, he had tons of books—more than I'd ever seen, actually—and he died, leaving the books, of course, with Mrs. Cullwick. Whenever I'd come to see her for the day, I'd borrow a book, read it and return it the next day." I grinned at the recollection, a bittersweet memory.

"Mmmm...And how is it—beg my pardon—but how is it, that you learned to read without the resources of a...say...governess?" he asked suspiciously.

I sat straight up before meeting his eyes.

"Forgive me, My Lord. But there *are* other ways to learn to read."

He pressed his lips together in a thin line before nodding and looking back at his plate.

"Indeed," he replied feebly.

"My older brothers taught me. They all took turns teaching me...and if I did not know a word I came across in a book, I would simply find someone who did."

"Your brothers?" He motioned to me and drew a hand to his chin, deep in thought. "They knew how to read?"

My shoulders tensed.

We are not all ignorant despite our lack of wealth, My Lord, I thought before swallowing my pride and answering.

"Yes...they learned at school."

His eyes grew wide. The light was dim but bright enough for me to see that they resembled the color of the sea.

"School? They have such a thing in fishing villages?"

"No...But they did at a nearby village...and my father was adamant about sending them to be educated."

"And you?" He pointed a butter knife in my direction. "What do they think of *you*...knowing to read?"

"Well, my mother is certain it will do me no good—my *only* lot in life being to secure a husband and mother children." I tilted my head to the side and waited for him to laugh, but he didn't...

"No, my papa, he loved the idea...he's the one who bought me my first diary." I continued, feeling a swell of pride at the thought.

"I imagine a costly thing for a fisherman?"

"I imagine so," I said, biting the corner of my lip. "And you? Do you have a family?"

A strange look crossed his face that I couldn't read.

"I have a half-sister," he said quietly, as he took another sip of his port.

~

The jostling and jolting of the carriage made my stomach ill. I looked over at Agatha with sympathy, as she bent her head down between her knees.

"Are you well? Shall I ask the coachman to stop?" Lord Troy studied her. She looked ghastly pale in the moonlight. I reached a hand down to comfort her, and she took it, keeping a handkerchief clutched in the other.

The gust of wind that came from the open curtain offered a small bit of solace, but it was still sultry, much like the night we first met Lord Troy.

"Perhaps you should have stayed with me and rested," he said, bending his head so she could hear. She shook her head slowly side to side and muttered something indiscernible to him.

Longing for fresh air myself, I laid my head close to the window and watched as the landscape rolled along. It was always interesting to me how things looked at night. A stretch of familiar land would become almost unrecognizable with the moon's bleaching features. As if the vibrant color of mid-afternoon leached into the ground leaving only the pale spirit of the earth. It was either a somber way, or a menacing way, to look at it, but there was no denying the power night had to transform its surroundings.

"Damn lamb," I heard Agatha whisper to herself. I looked up to see if Lord Troy noticed, but he hadn't appeared too, or he was merely being polite and hadn't said anything. I imagine the latter, despite the clatter of the wagon's wheels.

Although she couldn't display it, I knew that Agatha must have been overjoyed when the coachman stopped. With the assistance of Lord Troy and me, she gingerly made her way down the steps and into the garden. I took a long, deep breath in. The heat and cramped confines of the wagon made my legs and neck tense. It was a relief to get some fresh air, even if it was thick with humidity.

"Can I call for someone?" Lord Troy asked as he examined Agatha. She was crouched down, her head facing the ground. But there was no time, Aunt Beatrice caught a glimpse of her from a window and hurried out to the lawn.

"Agatha?" she called out, as she rapidly made her way across the lawn. Uncle Harold resumed his normal pace until he caught up with Aunt Beatrice at the end of the walkway. She eyed me, Lord Troy, and then looked back at her daughter, bent over the grass, before coming over to Lord Troy, a look of mixed emotions on her face

"Your servant, My Lady." He took her thin hand in his and gave her a gentle kiss on her knuckles. Aunt Beatrice stood like a statue, as an odd grin grew on her lips.

"You honor me so," she blushed. I knew from the glint in her eye that she was already planning a spring wedding before he could speak again. A grunt from Agatha drew her eyes away. Her face was as pale as newly fallen snow.

"Aunt Beatrice, meet Lord Edmund Troy." I put a hand out to him, and he gave a regal bow.

"Indeed it is. My Lord is there anything...*anything* at all that I can get for you?" She was eyeing him like a Christmas ham. Agatha shot her a glance, but she was too bewitched to notice. His brows pressed inward before he cleared his throat and shook his head.

"I am very well. Thank you...Agatha, however."

Aunt Beatrice looked down at her forgotten daughter and with a sheepish grin, bent to check on her.

"Please forgive our manners, My Lord," Harold said. His gruff voice broke the entrancement, momentarily.

"Please, call me Edmund," he said with the flutter of a hand.

"Mr. Harold Greenman, but you may call me Harold."

Lord Troy huffed amusingly, but it was so quiet, it was almost unnoticeable as Uncle Harold motioned with a hand to Aunt Beatrice, "and my lovely wife, Beatrice."

"A pleasure," he said, with a slight hint of haughtiness.

Aunt Beatrice motioned to me, and we both helped Agatha to her feet, her head dangling like a heavy globe between her shoulders.

"Please do come in...I can settle Agatha and—" Aunt Beatrice began, but Uncle Harold interjected.

"We can take a rest from all of this *drama*...have a smoke?" A chuckle erupted from Harold, his pudgy belly vibrating with good humor. Aunt Beatrice stared at him in disbelief, jaw agape. But Edmund gave a warm smile in return.

"I regret that I must be heading home. I have a very early morning appointment tomorrow."

Aunt Beatrice waited for him to continue, perhaps hoping he'd change his mind, but he didn't elaborate, and there were a few moments of awkward silence. Harold cleared his throat obtrusively.

"Well, I suppose another time..."

Beatrice's eyes glanced at her husband, a look of desperation evident in them that was largely ignored.

"Good night, My...err Edmund." Harold bowed and turned to walk away, much to the dread of his wife who stood frozen in spot, paralyzed by mortification. Lord Troy hadn't noticed and walked a few paces to Agatha, who abandoned standing up and bent over the side of the walkway.

"I hope that tomorrow finds you feeling well again," he said. She tried her best to smile, but her lips were tight and pale.

"Catrina." He stopped in front of me, and picked up my hand, leaving a light kiss on the knuckles. I bit my lip, looking down at the spot, the moonlight glowing softly on the place where his mouth met my hand. I bowed to him belatedly, as he entered his coach. Resigning to his departure, Aunt Beatrice bowed once again as well, before stealing her eyes back to Agatha.

Just as the coach churned its way down the dirt road spitting up chunks of rock and dust, Agatha bent over and heaved.

"Bloody lamb," she cursed, as she pressed her palms into the dirt. Aunt Beatrice drew her hair back and sighed, strands of it were already wet with vomit.

"Bless my soul, Agatha!" she scolded. "You *must* see him again!" There was a long moment of silence. "Absolutely *no* Lamb though!"

Chapter Seven

It was a day like any other, except for the undercurrent of excitement. She couldn't explain it, but the moment she woke up and heard the birds chirping in the garden and saw the bright, open blue sky, she had an unmistakable feeling of *hope*.

She ate her breakfast, brushed her skirts and washed her face with a smile. Happiness bubbled inside, filling her with a warmth that spread through her entire body. Despite her unsightly vomiting episode the night before, she was filled with an uncanny sense of hopefulness about her future with the handsome and eligible bachelor, Lord Troy.

Agatha lost herself in a daydream, a vision of her laying scandalously in his lap as he read prose after prose to her while on a bench, listening to the steady rush of a waterfall. She couldn't quite determine where the waterfall would be as she hadn't seen any on the property, but that was irrelevant. She dreamed of them laughing, as they fed each other picnic food under the shade of a large oak, specifically a string of red grapes, as she'd seen the Roman god's do. Or she envisioned them taking a moonlight ride on horseback, where the night ended with a romantic, utterly immoral kiss.

All of the signs were pointing towards

him, and she couldn't deny the signs. The fortune teller she consulted told her that she'd meet and wed a handsome and wealthy suitor in the near future. It had only been three short months since her cards were read. Even the woman who'd consulted the crystal ball agreed; she could see the face of an attractive gentleman that would soon offer her his hand in marriage.

When the post was delivered, she finally realized what the spontaneous feelings of hope were about. Among some correspondence of her father's, she found a neatly decorated white envelope. Curiosity, getting the best of her, she ripped it open and pulled out an invitation with little decorum.

Lord Edmund Troy, The 4th Baron Troy, Requests the honor of your company:
Sir Harold Greenman and the ladies of the house, to the Annual Summer Ball Friday, June 24 at the Bellmont Manor
Dancing 9
Carriages 1

Agatha let out an ecstatic screech, wiggling in her spot like a fish out of water. She handed it to her mother to read as she watched her reaction. She read through it quickly, her eyes lighting up.

"Harold! The day has finally come," she cried out from the hall, putting a hand to her chest. She gave Agatha a warm, but stern smile, before adding—"I certainly hope, for your sake, that he doesn't serve Lamb there."

Chapter Eight

Edmund sat at his desk listening to the rain pound on the roof. The scent of moist earth rolled in from the open window. Dark gray, looming clouds and constant drizzle always left him discontent, as if he were a caged beast. He longed to be free, to run wild. But even then, he thought, were I to be free, *where* shall I run?

He looked down at the stack of papers littering his desk; every last one of them was a late notice. He sneered, shoving them further away from him, as he took a sip of brandy and savored it. He closed his eyes off from the world before swallowing it, the amber gold bitterness a salve for his soul.

He knew it would come to this...Romanticism was a dying art, and he'd ridden the coattails out, mopping up with him every last bit of success he could squeeze from it. His previous book was a flop and largely ignored by his followers. They praised him on his earlier works. But even *he* knew they would eventually turn their heads

He attempted to harness the transformation, motivating himself to carry on and prosper, and yet, his opportunities were dismal. They dried up before him like a trickle in a drought. He tapped the pen to his chin. The humidity caused his hair to curl, much to his dismay, and he kept brushing it off his forehead with an irritated flick of the wrist. He *desperately* needed inspiration.

He paused for a moment to look out the window, the bottom two inches exposed to the rain as it pelted the frame. He didn't have much faith in the idea that the window should be open, regardless of weather conditions. He knew it was a commonly held belief and one that Agatha was adamant about, but couldn't ignore the scent of wet soil much longer. He wondered where she'd even heard the information, but thought better of it to ask. Wistfully wondering what it would be like to carry on a conversation with a woman in the way he had with his chums.

He rubbed the back of his neck, as he watched the rain pelting the trees and ground below, blurring them into soft blobs of green. He leaned back with his arms behind his head and sighed. It was quiet except for the ominous sound of a grandfather clock near the door—its "tick-tock" driving him to near insanity before he got up to pace around aimlessly.

He expected words to flow through him with the ease of water, having found himself consumed with the idea of Agatha, but much to his vexation, it appeared to be quite the opposite. His mind kept drifting, and he found himself coming back more and more to her cousin Catrina. He replayed her laughter over and over in his head. The vision of her gleaming white teeth as she threw her head back. She was so pure, so natural. There was something intrinsically desirable about her, but he couldn't put his finger on it.

He sat down and put his head in his hands, feeling the full weight of it. The ink pen sat on the page with nothing but the lines... *"Dearest Agatha."* There was a rap at the door, and he sat upright, a little dazed.

"Who is it?"

"It's me...Imelda."

He sighed, but motioned to the door. "Come in."

She pushed the door open, gliding over to him, hesitantly making her way to his side. The silky, forest green gown flowed along the ground beneath her, like a shadow. He imagined the smooth texture of it on his skin, envisioning her undressing and draping it across his thighs, but quickly shook his head to release the thought.

"Are you *well*?"

She took a seat next to him, rubbing her hands nervously together. She was so close now that he could smell the sweet balm of her perfume. *Was it gardenia?*

It was dark in the room, outside of a small oil lamp lit on the table. She motioned to a maid to assist in illuminating the rest of the room, but Edmund shook his head.

"I much prefer the room to match my mood," he said, looking at the paper under his hand.

"Could you have the goodness to help me with my lines? I have much to study, and I've been having terrible difficulty focusing lately..." She leaned closer to him. Her long dark lashes fluttered as she looked up.

Minx, he thought.

He struggled to avert his eyes, as he leaned back in his chair. He ran the length of his pen across his bottom lip, feeling something come alive in his groin.

"I am afraid we've both come a cropper. I haven't had any luck lately myself."

"May I draw you a bath?" she asked, leaning in as she traced a fingertip along his jawline. He shivered slightly at her touch.

"I'm very well, thank you." He shook his head and kept a closer eye on her hand, wondering where it would travel next.

She pressed her finger across the top of his desk and bent forward displaying the whole of her chest like a ripe fruit basket. Edmund felt his Adam's apple bob up and down relentlessly in his throat. His eyes, like magnets, drew back to her chest, the narrow divide that formed as she pressed her breasts inward, exposing the supple and smooth mounds.

He sat back and took in the view for a moment too long, biting the tip of his pen as he grazed it subconsciously across his lip. One false move and she would burst her stay lace. He struggled to look away, instantly regretting that he'd fallen prey.

"You *know* this cannot work." He forced himself to look up at her. "*You and I...*"

He watched her lips form into a frown; they were the color and texture of a ripe peach.

He grabbed hold of her by the shoulders, holding her gaze. She had such pleasant eyes—alluring. He shook his head to rid himself of his primal thoughts, before he continued.

"We *must* carry on proper..."

She shook her head and Edmund could feel a small quiver run through her, like the tremors after an earthquake.

He forced himself to turn, focusing instead on his pen, as he pressed it forcefully into the paper. They sat in silence a few moments before she spoke up.

"What is this?" She glanced at the invitation on his desk and motioned to it.

"The invitation to the annual summer ball."

"Hmm," she uttered, nodding her head and licking her lips. There were a few moments where the sound of rain, pinging softly on the roof, filled the room until Imelda spoke again.

"I suppose this will be like any *other* ball?"

"Mmmhmm," he mumbled, pretending to focus on his work.

She returned to making circles with her finger on his desk. He regretted her ability to do so, watching as she left her mark in a film of dust.

"Am I to assume that the Greenmans' will be guests?"

This caught his attention, and he stopped writing enough to look up at her, one eyebrow askew.

"Yes, is there something about this that you find...disagreeable?"

She looked away, feeling the intensity of his gaze as it followed her.

"No, it's *only*..."

He knew that she saw the flicker of anticipation within him. She could see in them now, the intensity by which he wished her to carry on, but his unwillingness to ask her of it.

"Sam *has* been spending a good deal of time over there."

"And what does this suggest? I have sent him on an errand for me...to deliver a letter to Agatha. "

He leaned back, rubbing his neck.

"Mmmmm...Yes, that *is* true...I suppose he could be there to see Agatha...*or* Catrina," she added, shaking her head in agreement, a silky black corkscrew of hair fell from her shoulder and moved with her. His stomach clenched at her name.

"Do you know more?" he demanded, sitting straight up in his chair. He thought the rain came down harder on the roof, but he couldn't be sure if it was only his imagination.

"I know nothing...except that he's never here anymore," she surmised, looking behind her and back at Edmund. Her eyes were expressing what Edmund thought was false sincerity.

"I see..." he said, as he sat back and pressed his fingertips together before waving a hand at her. "You may leave now."

"But...Edmund," she interrupted.

"I said...you may leave now." He used a hand to motion to the door, and she begrudgingly got up, her dress rustling behind her as she moved. She took long, deliberate strides, stopping midway before turning to face him again.

"Do you ever wonder…who it was that was in your garden the night of your party?" A frown played on her lips as she turned back around. She closed the door behind her with a soft click, as Edmund sat, listening to the rain pour steadily overhead for a long time.

Chapter Nine

I cocked my head and looked over at him. He was dangling a foot over the river from the boulder he sat on, and I wondered how much longer he would maintain his balance before falling in. It was the second Tuesday that Sam and I met at the river.

It rained the day past and through the night, leaving a dank smell of wet soil and new growth. My shoes were caked with mud and Sam—being the gentleman that he was— offered to wash them for me.

"Why do you always try to persuade me to run around shoeless? Don't you realize the implications?"

He shrugged and looked back toward the river, calculating the distance from the top of the boulder to the surface of the stream, as he ran a hand through his hair. His hair didn't spring back at his touch, like Lord Troys'. Its texture was different. It was thicker and straighter and the color of raw honey.

I sat down on top of one of the rocks and opened up my diary to a new page. Seeing the light come through the trees, and spreading over Sam's hair, I was inspired and began jotting down everything that came to mind:

—*The way the light hits Sam's hair. A million colors—amber, gold, champagne, honey.*

— His reflection in the stream below.
But I was quickly interrupted.

"I regret that I wasn't able to attend your outing the other day."

I cocked my head at him.

"Outing?"

"With Agatha and Edmund..." he replied as he jumped down. He stared at his feet as he spoke. It was unusual for him to avoid meeting my eyes.

"Oh, Yes! *That* outing...well, it was quite...interesting."

"Interesting...Hmm?"

He fumbled around in his pocket, to produce an apple, which he rubbed clean on his waistcoat, revealing its shiny, red skin. He needn't draw attention to this article of clothing of his, it was anything but humble with its bold turquoise and silver embroidered peacock feathers. He noticed me studying it, so he stood erect.

"What is it that you find so intriguing about my suit, Miss Catrina?" he inquired, with good humor.

"I find your style to be..." I swallowed, attempting to polish my thoughts before I blurted them out, *"fascinating."*

He took a bite of the apple, exposing the crisp white inside, before giving me a sideways grin.

"Fascinating? Is that your terminology for...*handsome?*"

He leaned back against one of the boulders, crossing his legs at the ankles and pressing his back into the stone so his chest was straight. I bit my lip, feeling my mouth twinge. I was struggling to contain my laughter.

"You have no lack of confidence, I give you that," I jested playfully, pretending to write. I looked down at my diary and pressed the pen to the page, but wrote nothing, leaving a rather unsightly blob of black instead.

Sam looked down at himself and pretended to preen. He dusted away imaginary dirt and looked back again.

"Tell me of this...interesting event," he continued, seemingly satisfied with my response as he saw me rip the page from my diary with a sheepish grin.

"Lord Troy took Agatha and me to see the Poet's Corner in Westminster Abbey."

"Did he, now?"

I nodded.

"Did you enjoy it?"

"How could I not?" I swooned.

He showed the apple to me as an offering, and I shook my head. The scent was enticing, but I was too invested in my thoughts to stop speaking.

"There were statues, and monuments, everywhere! There was even one there that reminded me of you."

"Eh?" he muttered, as he took another bite.

"Samuel Butler," I said, attempting to garner his attention. It worked, and his eyes met mine, a twinge of humor evident in their creased corners. Suddenly, he started laughing.

"What? What is it?" I was beginning to feel my cheeks in their early stages of embarrassment, as the blood rushed into them.

"Who read the epitaph?"

"Lord Troy, of course. I can't read Latin," I replied. My stomach was beginning to tense into a knot, and I wondered if I should have mentioned it or not.

"Latin? Ahh...no, no—the *comment* on the epitaph by Samuel Wesley."

I shrugged and shook my head.

"I'm not aware of any comment," I said, attempting to envision the plaque in my memory.

Sam started laughing again, this time holding his belly. He sat the apple down beside him where it rolled into a crevice on the boulder.

"What is it?"

"If I recall correctly, it goes something along these lines..." He cleared his throat and held one hand in front of him and another behind as if he were preparing to address royalty. He stuck his chin out and looked down his nose. He looked so ridiculous I started to giggle.

"Quiet, quiet please...this is serious," he said, narrowing his eyes at me humorously.

I cleared my throat and bit my lip, holding back my laughter.

"Ok...where were we? Oh, yes... Samuel Butler..." He looked around again as if a crowd of bystanders were waiting for his speech.

"Butler, the needy wretch, no patron would a dinner give when starved to death and turned to dust, givin' with this monumental bust. The poet's fate is shown...he'd asked for bread, but was given stone."

We both started giggling which turned into outright belly laughter.

"That's...marvelous," I said, clapping my hands.

He took a formal bow.

"Of all the authors there, Samuel Butler is the one who reminded you of me?" He looked up at me through his lashes.

"For the satire, of course," I said shamelessly.

Satire for a satirist. Is there anything more fitting? I thought.

"Have you considered writing epitaphs now? You could have a prosperous career in them if any more satirists tragically die. I assume you are an expert...having written articles that were published in Punch." I pressed my teeth into my lip and smirked gingerly at him.

"Very funny!" he retorted.

A broad lop-sided grin filled his face, however, and a faint tint of pink touched his cheeks, cheeks punctuated with deeply grooved dimples.

Whenever they appeared, I felt a satisfying ripple roll through me. I was tempted to tease them out more, to feel the rush they elicited within me. I may have been inconspicuous about my motivations, but I wasn't very good at hiding my glances, as he caught my eye more times than I'd like to admit.

"And what of *your* career...have you written anything worthy enough for Punch?"

He raised a bushy brow at me, a dubious look on his face as he leaned back against one of the boulders and reached for his apple. A faint echo of a dimple appeared in one cheek.

We both laughed, but I felt a pang at the thought.

Had I? The thought tumbled around in my head, leaving a trail of doubt.

"I don't write satire!" I shot back.

If I had...would it be good enough to publish?

I peered off into the trees, thankful for the sun as it peaked in through the leaves overhead. Gradually, the surrounding area was drying. The drops on the leaves seemed to be disappearing before my eyes. Sam took a generous bite of his apple, the juice sprayed in all directions. The welcome scent of it filled the air, and I felt my stomach rumble. *Perhaps I should have accepted his offer.*

"What is it that's holding you back?" he asked, interrupting my thoughts.

I am a woman —for one thing—I have no money, no wealth, no property and no opportunities...

"Besides...*everything*?" I asked with a laugh.

"Everything?" he gasped disbelievingly.

I nodded.

"Everything..."

"I see no one here to take your pen. Besides...I'll be bound that your work is extraordinary!"

"Extraordinary? Do you mean...extraordinary for a woman...or *truly* extraordinary?"

He cocked his head.

"Is that it? Is *that* the problem?"

"One of them," I said before I closed the diary with a soft thud.

"What is it that you plan to write? Do you plan to write *fluffery*?"

"What is it with you and that word?" I exclaimed, feeling my pulse hasten.

"It's a perfect word to explain something—vapid," he said, as he stared off into the surrounding wilderness.

There was a moment of silent contemplation between us, where I soaked in the sounds of the river— the calm, resonant sound of it babbling along through the forest bed, broken only by the sound of him chewing obnoxiously on his apple.

"Well, no. I don't plan to write only— *fluffery*," I replied, feeling a sense of calm come over me at my decision.

"Have you considered publishing your work with an alias?"

"I have..."

"And?"

"I cannot." I swallowed, wondering if he could sense my apprehension.

"I'm not certain that I understand."

"The world has changed—and for the better, I might add—but *when* will the work of women be honored as the work of men is honored?" I looked up to catch his glance. My temples were throbbing with the blood that was now racing through me.

"The answer to *that?* I really don't know...but to deny myself the ability to be...to *encourage* other women to write as themselves...then what value has come from my work if I cannot speak my own mind with my own name? Yes, they will enjoy the written words—but the *message*—They will *miss* the message!" I preached.

He paused for a moment, lost in thought.

"I see..." he said, as he rubbed his chin thoughtfully. It was something I enjoyed watching, as his wild hair sprung away from his touch.

There were a few moments of silence before I started writing again, only to be interrupted when he appeared beside me. He was so close that I could hear him breathing.

"Must you?" I asked as I looked over my shoulder.

He leaned back, with a smirk.

"Pardon me, but I'm having a difficult time reading your diary...did I see my name?"

"Have you no *decency?*" I shouted, clamping the diary shut and promptly pressing it to my chest, tightening my grip on it.

"If you cannot share with me...how can you share with the world?"

"You—sir—are *not* the world." I bit my lip and narrowed my eyes at him. "Besides, when shall I view your project?—the one that is clandestine, I see."

"That's different."

"Different?" I tilted my head down, eyes looking up at him through thick lashes, "That is no different than what I'm writing here!"

I scrunched my lips to the side.

"Is it a romance novel? I've heard that's the only thing women are capable of writing!" he said, changing the subject abruptly.

I gasped and put a hand to my chest.

"That's...*abominable*!" I felt my pulse race, the sound of it thrummed in my ears. A fire slowly burned in my gut and threatened to spread to my limbs.

He sneered, exposing one deep dimple that carved into his cheek.

"You are also *no* gentleman..." My jaw clenched, as I slid down the boulder. I attempted to turn away from him, but he reached his hand out to my shoulder. I turned, reluctantly, but kept my head low.

"I know...what it is that is stopping you," he said, drawing my chin up with his hand so that our eyes met.

"Fear," he whispered, as he boldly cupped his hand around my cheek. It was the closest that I'd ever been to a man. The fire, which started from animosity, had shifted course and blazed hot from his touch. I felt a tear spill from my eye and poignantly roll down my cheek onto his fingers.

I felt my shoulders soften. Reluctantly, I moved forward, so we were closer. One more step and our noses would touch. The idea of being this close to him was bewildering, but also, intoxicating.

"Let us make a promise—here and now—that we shall be the only ones to review one another's work," he asserted, breaking the silence and leaving me longing for more. He looked up at me, before continuing, and I gave him a small nod.

"And we shall choose to be constructive with the works of one another—for the sake of improvement."

He scrunched his lips to the side as he turned around and ran to the boulder, grabbing a pen and his diary, before rushing back to me.

"Here," he said, opening his diary up to a fresh sheet and pointing to a line, "sign it."

I cocked my head at him.

"We agree to honor each other's work."

I stared down at the blank page and back up at him. I bit my lip and wrote my signature.

Catrina Mae Bennett

Chapter Ten

There was a rush of excitement filling the air as we rode to Lord Troy's manor. We followed in a caravan, with Aunt Beatrice and Uncle Harold in front of us, the coach clipping along at a steady and rhythmic pace. Agatha, overly eager, had her head pressed against the window, gazing.

It was dark now. The last of the summer's day sun slid down the horizon, leaving behind it a trail of royal purple, before succumbing to the earth. In its absence, a pitch black sky with a sliver of moon emerged. It was so dark, you could scarcely make out the rough border of the forest as it spanned for miles behind the shadowed heath.

The last several hours Agatha, Ezra and I perfected our knowledge of ballroom etiquette, but I couldn't suppress the uneasiness in my chest. My breathing was so shallow that I wondered if I would faint. I presumed it could be nerves, although Aunt Beatrice suggested that perhaps it were the corsets. Agatha, all but fainted, putting hers on. She'd begged me to lace it as tight as possible. I looked over at her as she attempted to breathe, wondering where, and if, any air got in.

I sat up straight, grateful for the sense of relief from the irritating boning in the corset. The gown I'd borrowed from Agatha wasn't the most comfortable garment I'd ever worn; it was cream-colored silk with lace appliques that rubbed annoyingly against my arms. I was a good two inches taller than Agatha, requiring the dress to undergo an ad hoc hasty tailoring where Aunt Beatrice had a few inches of cheap lace sewn to the bottom.

"Who do you suppose is on the guests' list?" Agatha leaned her shoulder into me with a distant look in her eye. Her hair fell down her back in enviable gold curls, and she had just a touch of pale pink rouge, enough to look as though someone had pinched her cheeks. The heavy scent of her perfume—a concoction of orange, lemon verbena and neroli—wafted into my nose. She smelled as though she bathed in it. I leaned away to catch a draft of fresh air.

"Charles Dickins, George Eliot, Queen Victoria," Ezra quipped as he ran a hand through his hair, which appeared to be, uncharacteristically, well tamed. Adorned in his finest, a pitch black three-piece suit, he looked dapper. The metal rims of his glasses even shined. He scrubbed his face revealing a fresh, almost boy-like appearance, despite his mustache, and even that was trimmed and neat.

Agatha glared at him.

"It's a possibility," he said, taking a more keen interest in the countryside as it bounced by his window. Ignoring her brother's comment, she carried on.

"It's an *awful* shame..." She drew out the sentence, leaving the end dangling like a worm on a hook. I looked over at Ezra wondering who of us would sacrifice ourselves to ask "What is?" I was grateful that she continued. I met Ezra's glance, and we leaned back with looks of relief, neither of us had to give her the satisfaction of playing fancy to her dramatic whims.

"It's really quite a shame that I will have to dance with other gentlemen. I really have *no* interest in anyone—other than, *the Lord*, of course." She leaned her head back looking down her narrow nose, twirling a ringlet of her gold hair around her finger mindlessly.

"I believe it'd be quite a shame for him to host such a ball, and *only* dance with one lady," Ezra retorted. He had the glimmer of a smile on his face. I had to turn away to avoid giggling as she folded her arms across her chest.

"Well...whomever he decides to dance with, I will—assuredly—be his *most* memorable," She scowled, as she straightened up the lace berthe that lay at her collarbone, her dress fluffed out in front of her like the feathers of a large, irate bird.

"I'll be bound that there are plenty of doctors, lawyers, and other prosperous gentlemen here—many of whom would make excellent suitors—do you agree, Catrina?" Ezra asked, catching me off guard. I was currently preoccupied with finding a flow of fresh air.

"I suppose you're right..." I said mindlessly as I looked out the window, watching the rows of gray fields ebb and flow into one another.

The conversation dwindled off, leaving us each to contemplate the expectations of the night. I was grateful for the moment of solitude as I stared out the window, my eyes were going in and out of focus as I lost myself in a daydream.

A vision of Sam appeared. He was wearing a suit similar to Ezra's, a coal black three-piece ensemble. His body was the only clear image, amid an array of blurred faces and colors. His hair— as wild as ever— lay tousled across his brow as he sauntered toward me. I could hear nothing, outside the sound of his voice, but the words he said...*What had he said?* Whatever they were, I seemed delighted by them. His eyes came alive under the glow of the chandelier, exposing the deep russet I had known them to be when the sun hit them. He leaned in, as he had when we met by the river, and placed his hand on my cheek, cupping it gently with his fingers. *Oh, how I longed to feel his fingers on my cheek again.* I shook my head, feeling the sudden exodus back into reality.

"Eeee!" Agatha squealed, disturbing my thoughts. "Heaven and earth! Would you look at that?"

Despite attending a dinner party at Lord Troy's manor a few weeks past, it was a breathtaking sight to see it come alive with light. Rows of manicured lawn surrounded the house, which sat like a tremendous white island in a sea of green. Tier upon tier windows lined the exterior—each filled with a bright, yellow glow that spilled out into the darkness. The light cascaded down its white walls, which boasted pillars and pointed arches reminiscent of Westminster Abbey. A lush garden surrounded the circular roadway that led to a massive gothic-style arch, which appeared to stand sentry, near the entrance.

I was in awe at the sight of people funneling in, like a colony of bees returning to the hive. Bright golden light spilled from the entry like someone had tipped a pot of honey, and it slowly trickled out.

"Can you *believe* it?" Agatha gushed.

"I cannot." I shook my head.

~

Lord Troy was standing near the door, the glow of light favoring his winsome features. I could now see his resemblance to the Roman Gods, the dark curls, the angular profile, and the prominent, but well-defined, nose. His jawline was firm and taut when at rest, and defined when he smiled; exposing a row of straight, white teeth. I could see how he made women swoon. Agatha—a vision of physical perfection herself—seemed a most advantageous match with the handsome Lord Troy.

He was standing in the entryway, the golden glow of the light surrounding him with a resolute aura. Like all the style conscious men, he was in the standard black three-piece suit. But, unlike the others, he wore a white silk waistcoat beneath with a thin black cravat and garnet stick pin. The garnet stood out like a glimmering spot of blood against the white of his waistcoat. He gave us a broad smile and bow before motioning for us to continue.

Lord Troy bent down, giving Aunt Beatrice a delicate kiss on the hand. She giggled coyly in return. Uncle Harold cleared his throat and urged her on with a gentle, but firm, hand on the shoulder and they disappeared into the crowd, just the top of her blond curls visible from a distance.

"I expected the help to welcome us in," Ezra whispered, but Agatha gave him a firm nudge, before turning around to give Lord Troy an overconfident smile.

"Ah, Ezra, Agatha, Catrina—it is a pleasure to see you again. I am pleased you were able to make it. Please, do come in," he said, ushering us toward the main hall.

We were lead to the ballroom, where before us, a sea of colors emerged—women in gowns of amethyst and topaz, emerald and pearl with their hair—adorned with feathers, flowers, and ribbons—bobbed and weaved across the floor besides Men in their nicest suits—their hair sleek and neat—as they mingled in a conglomerate of polite society. An intense aroma of lemon, rose, bergamot, lavender, and bay rum filled the room from the skirting board to the ceiling.

Above, massive gold chandeliers filled the room with light, reflecting like glowing white orbs on the polished floor. A fresco, in an ostentatious gilded frame, of Baroque angels in pink and sky blue clouds, looked down from the ceiling, a consistent reminder of the piety expected of those beneath. It was a resplendent fantasy!

Agatha nodded in the direction of a woman who was causing quite a stir, her sapphire gown, swaying gracefully from her hips as she walked, following some form of self-made melody. Her face was obscured from view by the mass of people she stopped to speak with, but three black feathers sprouted from her dark hair like beacons. Agatha stood on her tiptoes to get a better view.

"She must be some sort of...nobility," Agatha reasoned, still craning her neck, before glancing down at her own gown. The mauve silk Aunt Beatrice ordered came in last week and was promptly transformed into her ball gown. The color drew a roving eye from a few of the ladies, who gossiped and pointed, as they ogled her dress. Aunt Beatrice was accurate in her insistence that Agatha wear it tonight, for if not, the woman in the sapphire gown would have drawn away *all* the attention.

Agatha hadn't seemed to mind being the envy of the ballroom. She'd truly relished it. *How did it feel to be the source of so much adoration?* I looked down at my gown, with its flimsy lace trim, and sighed. *Would Sam even bother to give me a second glance?*

I felt a glimmer of hope, however, when I looked into the mirror after Agatha did my hair. She'd pinned my curls, cocoa-colored and bountiful, atop my head, and I couldn't resist the feel of them as they coiled and sprang when I walked. She put a dab of rouge on my cheeks, proclaiming that the cream brought out the rosy tones in my skin. I stared at myself and felt a sense of pride at, whoever it was, looking back, with the big tawny eyes and the rose-colored lips.

I studied the room, searching the moving heads as a slick film of sweat formed on my palms. Whenever I saw the shadow of a man with honey-colored hair, I felt my heart start to race. *Where are you, Sam?*

Agatha yawned, before nudging into me.

"Who is he, dear cousin?"

I bit my lip, feigning interest in the surroundings, my eyes drifted to the walls, roaming them for something worthy of my attention.

"Whatever do you mean?" I asked, feigning indifference.

"Oh, come now! Don't be silly," she frowned, turning her attention to the room. Her eyes roved the crowd for anyone of interest. She started bouncing up and down in her quest, drawing even more attention to her—and unfortunately—to me. I sank into myself.

"Is he here?" She scrunched her shoulders up, a huge grin on her face. She looked like a dog with a bone.

"Shall we go for some refreshments? With all the people in here, it's getting rather hot." I attempted to turn around, but Agatha was relentless. She tugged on my arm.

"*I*...have an idea of who it might be..." she said with a wide smirk on her face, a curl of her hair rolled around one of her fingers.

"Will you, *please...let it be*?" I tried to remain calm, but the thought of him caused my stomach to flip. I could feel the heat rise through my face threatening to expose me.

"*Follow me...*" she said, grabbing hold of me by the wrist and whisking me off.

~

As we weaved our way through the ballroom, we found Ezra absorbed in conversation with a group of gentleman. He saw us approach and waved to catch our attention. I heard Agatha huff under her breath, irritated that she'd been interrupted in her mission.

"May I have the pleasure of introducing you to a good friend of mine?" he asked, looking at Agatha and me, as he pushed his glasses up with a finger. "Mr. Thomas Atwell."

Agatha—ever the eager lady—gave a poised bow, making an adequate effort at appeasing her brother.

Thomas had a prominent nose and a weak chin, but his eyes were friendly. The color was oddly entrancing too, the same blue-green of algae, an amalgam of earth and sea.

"It is a great pleasure to make your acquaintance," he said as he gave us a cordial bow. He swept his husk-colored hair to the side, giving Agatha a shy, polite grin. "Are you ladies enjoying yourselves? Can I escort you to the refreshments? I hear they have some excellent oysters."

Ezra shot Agatha a look, when he assumed no one else was watching. He was doing his best to provide his sister with other opportunities, despite her resistance. It was to Agatha's chagrin, however as she had no inkling to dance with anyone other than Lord Troy. *But* society dictated otherwise, and I could see the resignation in her eyes as she turned to me.

"Care to join us?"

I shook my head.

"Thank you for the offer, but I must decline."

Agatha gave me a cold stare before responding.

"Very well then..."

They turned and left, as I made my way to the outside edges of the ballroom. Pleased to find myself a flute of champagne from a passing butler, I took some dainty sips under the watchful eye of a few couples before I saw Lord Troy making his way through the crowd.

"If you are looking for Agatha, I—"

He shook his head as the butler handed him a champagne flute. He put it to his mouth, taking a small swig. I noticed as he drank, that his lips formed a bow, the upper lip making a full "M" shape.

"Is the night everything that you've expected it to be?" He turned to face me. I was up near the wall, rather enjoying the novelty of not being bothered until now.

I took another sip of champagne, relishing the bubbly dose of courage as I swallowed. I needed all the courage I could get, feeling lightheaded and at a loss for words when he was near.

"It is an honor, My Lord. To be invited to such an occasion." I bowed my head looking up at him through my eyelashes, hoping he'd see it as coy and not foolish.

"Mmm," he mumbled, disinterestedly, as he tipped his head up at the crowd. "And your dance card? I presume you've found *gentlemen* with whom to dance?" He leaned against the wall, his eyes contemplating the mass of people on the floor, a fusion of different hues in a frenzy of laughter and joy. The swell of a band in the background, violin, cello, and pianoforte caught our attention fleetingly.

"I have," I lied, giving him a shy grin. I took a lingering sip of my champagne. *Please, give me courage.* I swallowed, feeling the impending quiver inside my spine. There was a moment of quiet between us, Lord Troy staring off into the abyss before turning toward me.

"Will you share a dance with me?" he asked. He meant it earnestly. His eyes met mine, revealing the depth of blue in them. How deep *were they*? I wondered, feeling the strange tug of the ocean within them.

I looked down, at the card within my hands, wondering if it were possible to deny his request. *Goodness me! How would Agatha react? What would Sam think?* I took a look around the crowd, looking for the familiarity of his disheveled blond hair. *Where are you, Sam?*

"It would be an honor, My Lord," I said, handing him my dance card as I held my arm steady, feeling my pulse begin to throb against my wrist. I felt myself hunch inward.

"I see that I am the first." He looked up at me, both brows arched. I opened my mouth to explain, but he just grinned and put a finger out to stop me. When I looked up again, I saw Imelda wandering through the crowd toward us, her stare fixated on Lord Troy as he handed me the card.

Her dress was the deepest hue of sapphire I'd ever seen, complementing the silky raven wave of her hair. Atop her head, were the three tell-tale black feathers, of the mystery woman. She had a glass of red wine in her hand, from which she occasionally took delicate sips, before peering up at me through thick, black lashes.

I rubbed the card between my hands. In the space labeled *Quadrille*, Lord Troy wrote his name in the most beautiful, eloquent print I'd ever seen. Before he bowed and turned to leave, I blurted out.

"Will Sam be joining us...at the ball...*here*?" I felt immediately foolish.

His brows puckered and then the realization dawned on him.

"Ah, yes...*Sam*..." He looked around the crowd before meeting my gaze. "I hate to be the bearer of unfortunate news. But I feel that I must inform you...Sam is presently away...in Bath. He never has cared for balls, at any rate..."

I bit my lip, feeling my shoulders slump.

"That is *queer*..." I thought aloud. But, Imelda just made a noise in the back of her throat and looked away, as Lord Troy gave an involuntary shrug of his shoulders.

"It is my pleasure...*and honor*, Miss Catrina to have a dance with you. I sincerely look forward to our time together." He bowed, taking my hand in his, as he gave it a gentle kiss before he disappeared into the crowd. He weaved in and out, stopping temporarily to speak with his guests before I lost sight of him altogether.

It was surreal, as if I were part of a watercolor painting. All of the colors swirled and blended with the sounds, as my mind attempted to make sense of the past few minutes. I have to find Agatha, and tell her the news, *before* she finds out from anyone else, I thought. But when I turned to leave, I bumped straight into Imelda.

"*Enjoying the ball?*" she asked, taking a sip of her wine and leaning in, meeting my gaze with her cat-shaped, green eyes. "Lord Troy has requested a dance with you, I see?" She raised a wiry, dark eyebrow at me.

I avoided her gaze, studying the room, attempting to find a way back to Agatha through the maze. *Where was she?*

Imelda pressed a fingertip to her lips, tapping it methodically, before addressing me again.

"It is one thing, to have a dance with the Lord...it is quite another, to deny your...*intentions.*" She gave me a steely glare, before leaning in to whisper, "You don't fool me."

"I *do* beg your pardon," I said, standing up straight. I felt my fingers stiffen around the stem of my flute, as my pulse began to throb faster and faster. She gave a low disapproving grunt as she circled me like prey, a sapphire snake about to lash out.

"*Edmund,*" her eyes found him within the crowd, tracing his body greedily, "can possess *any* lady he *wants* in this room. What makes *you* think you are worthy of his possession?"

I felt my stomach turn, wondering if Lord Troy had any inkling of Imelda's unsavory infatuation with him.

"One can never be entirely sure what types of things ladies would do *just* to have a chance to be with him," she carried on, keeping her eyes on me as she paced back and forth. "So desired is Lord Troy that ladies have gone to extremes to be with him—disguising oneself as a man, following him around the world, even feigning their own deaths...*can you imagine?*" she gave an ominous chuckle. Her eyes drew back to him, and then to me.

"Agatha—" I began, but Imelda interrupted.

"*Others* though," she added, as she rubbed her hands together. "They prefer to do things a little *differently*...they prefer to *ensure* that he remains in their hands..."

I shirked back into myself, feeling the room become smaller and smaller.

"I promise you, that I have *no* intent for Lord Troy, except my cordiality in accepting to share a dance with him. You are mistaken in your accusations," I hissed, folding my arms defensively against my chest.

"Hmm," she cleared her throat, taking a long, purposeful sip of her wine before glowering at me. "Let us hope that you are truthful, hmm?" she glowered. "Because I know, that he —*only*—asked you to dance because he *pities* you..."

I felt as if someone kicked me in the stomach. A wave of nausea came over me as the words rolled around in my head. *Pities...he pities me?*

"I have only honored his request to share a dance. Now, if you will please excuse me..."A lump of fire lodged itself in my throat. I swallowed hard, trying to shove it down before my eyes swelled as I attempted to move past her. Suddenly, I felt a gush of cold liquid dribbling down my neck and the strong scent of wine.

"Oops...I'm *so* clumsy."

I looked up to see Imelda's hand, the wine glass dangling from its stem in between her fingers—empty. My eyes darted to my dress, where a shadow of red wine blossomed across my chest, like a raw gash against the cream-colored silk. I stood with my hands out beside me, my jaw dropped.

"You...*You*...I cannot...believe..." I felt my jaw clench, and my hands form into fists.

She put her hand to her mouth, one thin brow rose, as she stared at me with mock sincerity. For a moment, a look of satisfaction flashed over her features.

I stood there in shock, feeling the sticky residue roll down my chest in tiny streams, before I turned abruptly and ran for the doors—feeling the eyes of everyone in the room on my back.

~

My first thought was to dash outside, but a group of men smoking cigars, formed an impromptu blockade near the doors. I quickly abandoned the idea, choosing to find refuge somewhere else, as I rushed down the hall and found myself in front of a familiar set of French doors—bright red with gold handles. I pushed the door discreetly, thankful to find that it swung open.

I felt a sense of relief at the sight of the bookshelves that lined the walls. *At least this was somewhere I was familiar with*, I thought.

Finally alone, I looked down at my dress and began to sob. While I didn't love the lace berthe or the lace around the arms and bottom, it was, undoubtedly, the most elegant dress I'd ever worn. *Damn beast! Confound you, Imelda!*

I wanted to scream at the top of my lungs! I felt my body urging me too, but reluctantly, the tears rolled down my face silently, as I sobbed. I found a chaise lounge to lay down on and curled into a ball.

This is all your fault, Sam! If you were here right now, none of this would have happened.

It felt like an eternity passed before I felt whole enough to sit up, but when I did, I found myself staring silently out the window. The sky was now a deep onyx. I could count the stars as they glimmered in the darkness, each a soft, white glow against the black. The window was cracked, letting in the crisp night air. The row upon row of books— a multitude of greens, reds, and browns in daylight—appeared dull and colorless in the dark. The fireplace was empty and desolate, the only light was coming in from the hall and the crack from beneath the door. Somewhere down the hall, and coming closer, I heard the padding of soft footsteps. I braced myself.

"I see that you've found a place you feel more comfortable."

The voice was deep and masculine— and Lord Troy's. I breathed a sharp breath of relief, not bothering to turn around as I heard him walk, slowly and confidently, in my direction. I prayed my eyes didn't look as raw and puffy as they felt.

He came and sat at a chair beside the window, adjacent to me. We both sat in silence for a few moments. He didn't look over at me, and I was thankful for that. I feared I looked as bad as I thought I had. My hair fell loose while I ran down the hall; a few lopsided curls sprang free from their pins.

"Have you had a chance to explore the library?"

Despite the darkness, there was a sliver of light that cascaded like a long, narrow triangle into the room, allowing me to make out the shadowed features of his face as he spoke.

"Pardon, My Lord...*explore?*"

He waved a hand at the bevy of bookshelves behind him.

"You said to me, that you are a reader...*most assuredly* there are books in these shelves you have not read..."

"Oh yes...I presume this is true. I agree, My Lord...but I haven't...I don't like to—"

"Come, follow me!" he exclaimed as he escorted me to the bookshelves.

"Surely...you will be *missed*. Won't anyone come to look for you?" I asked as our eyes met, only the faint glow of his irises shined white.

"Let them wait...Bloody dark in here, *isn't it*? Pardon my expression," he said, as he lit the gas lanterns. The rows of books came alive with color again, burgundy, emerald, amber, and bisque bindings lined the shelves.

"*Come,*" he motioned to me with a finger, "You may pick any book you'd like..."

"I mustn't...that's very kind of you...but...*I couldn't!*"

"Please...*I insist*...it's the very least I can do for your trouble." He looked down at the dark smudge on my dress, and I felt the faint twinge of pink begin to fill my cheeks. I folded my arms and shook my head, but timidly made my way over.

The new light flooded the room with a warm glow. Lord Troy's face, once shrouded in shadow, had emerged like a butterfly from a cocoon—an impossible, natural exquisiteness about it that defied the ability to look away.

I tried to study him, inconspicuously but found myself to be inadequate at it. He knew I was examining the way his lips formed a perfect bow or the way his jaw seemed sculpted from clay. When I looked up and met his gaze, he gave me a subtle— but definite —smirk, before turning back to the shelves where he ran his fingers seductively along the length of bindings.

"*Don Quixote?*"

I shook my head and he continued.

"*Les Liaisons Dangereuses?*"

One of my eye brows rose.

"*Candide?*"

I shook my head again.

"What is that you have *not* read and care to read?"

"I have not read *any* that you've mentioned, as I cannot read Spanish...or French very well," I said looking down at my hands, as I nervously rubbed my fingers. Our eyes meet in a moment of understanding before he nodded and turned back to the bookshelves, one hand rubbing the back of his neck beneath a few defiant dark curls.

"*Frankenstein?*"

"I *have* read *Frankenstein*," I said enthusiastically.

"And?"

"Intriguing...however, wildly unrealistic..."

He nodded and moved on.

"*Jane Eyre?*"

"I shall never work as a governess..." I said, with the hint of a smile.

He chuckled, as he continued to run his finger along the line of books, stopping abruptly when he touched a brown, marbled binding.

"*I've got it!*"

He pulled the book out and whipped around, handing it to me.

"*The Count of Monte Cristo*," I read aloud, before looking up at him.

"Have you read it?"

I shook my head as I studied the cover.

"It is the English version. I have it in French, as well. This is a first edition," he said with a satisfied smile.

I studied the cover, running my fingers over the words before pressing it firmly to my chest.

"I will take great care of it."

He gave me a warm grin, before motioning to the door.

"*Come*...let us find you another dress. We have a dance to do..." He gave a nod to the hall, and I followed him out.

Chapter Eleven

The party was in full swing when we returned. There was a sense of exhilaration in the air, brought on by the roaring crowd, the loud trill of the band, and undoubtedly fueled by the copious amount of drinks that were consumed.

I glanced down at my gown, feeling a sense of panic (*what would Imelda do?*) but, undoubtedly, a sense of unbridled *excitement*. When I first slipped it on, I had to admit, that the gown was far superior in quality to the gown I'd borrowed from Agatha. It was made of silk— light pink silk, with a fitted bodice adorned with lace appliques. The skirt was bountiful, filled with layer upon layer of shiny ruffles that felt satisfyingly abundant. Whoever wore this gown before me was similarly taller and thinner than my femininely silhouetted cousin.

"These will complete the ensemble," Lord Troy said, giving me a nod of approval, before handing me a pair of elbow-length gloves.

I stared out at the crowd—looking for Agatha— desperate to explain the situation to her. A million questions flew into my mind. The sooner I could find her, the easier it would be to divulge the truth of the matter.

"I believe this is our dance," Lord Troy placed his hand out, waiting for me to accept. I leaned back diffidently, before coming to my senses, and graciously accepting him, I did not want to be viewed as an ungrateful guest, despite the worry that was swirling within me now. I swallowed, feeling my throat tense and my mouth dry up.

I followed behind him, as the crowd surrounded us. We took our place on the floor amidst a mass cacophony of sounds— laughter, chatter, the clank of glass, the shuffle of feet. Everything about this moment was surreal.

I glanced overhead, regretting that I'd done so, as I caught sight of the painted angels and their inquisitive eyes. *Would they divulge this secret to Agatha...Imelda.* Surely, this was common, expected actually, the Lord indisputably spent a good deal of time dancing with other ladies—but to be whisked away and return with him... I shoved the thought away, and looked down the row of ladies beside me.

No Agatha, and for that matter, no Imelda either, thankfully. I sighed, a moment of reprieve from the impending storm. *If I could just finish this dance...maybe I could find a place to run off too.*

I peeked shyly at Lord Troy, who was standing across from me. It was hard not to compare him to the others in the line beside him. He was *so* fascinating and well-read. A voice in my head quickly added—"He is also *dashingly* handsome." I swallowed, feeling my pulse accelerate at the thought. "But, Sam? He, too, is handsome." My conscious argued, and I nodded to myself.

But I couldn't deny that, *some part of me*, found Lord Troy attractive. In fact, he very well may be the most attractive man I'd ever laid eyes on. And nothing solidified that testament quite as much as standing him in a row next to other men.

Thankfully, my thoughts were diverted when I heard the swell of music. I hastily got into position, meeting Lord Troy's eyes from across the room. The corner of his mouth quirked up—I couldn't help but do the same, gazing bashfully at the floor.

The swell of music announced the beginning and I found myself floating tranquilly toward him. I focused on my feet, at first, worried that I'd somehow fumble, but the more we moved, the more confident I became.

There was an ethereal quality about being on the dance floor– and I found myself enchanted with it. The wind, generated from our quick movements, billowed my dress, the chandeliers spilled out a warm glow that casted on aura on the dancers—making them appear as if they were gilded in gold, and the quartet played a grand mix of music.

Finding Lord Troy again, I leaned in.

"Humor me—your favorite book, My Lord?"

He spun around, leaving me briefly before making his return. My breath still caught in my throat with anticipation.

"*The Count of Monte Cristo,*" he whispered into my ear. His warm breath sent a shiver through my body.

He disappeared again, returning gracefully as he had before. His movements were just as poised and graceful as I expected them to be.

"Is this true?" I looked up at him through my lashes. I turned again, feeling the gush of breeze swell my skirts.

"Do you believe it is true?" A smile tugged at his lips.

"I see I shall have to guess then..." I shot back quickly, before we both twirled away from one another.

We met again, drawn by our eyes, as if an invisible string had pulled us together.

"*Call me Ishmael,*" he said, before turning abruptly.

I tapped a finger to my chin.

"*Moby Dick?*"

He gave a solid nod as we passed one another, our hands gripping together firmer than necessary.

"Is that not a book, entirely about one's obsession that ultimately led to his failure?" I asked precociously.

His back was turned, but when he faced me again, I could see that he was thinking of a response.

"That is one perception of the theme..."

"And, My Lord...*what is the other?*" I goaded.

His eyes met mine, the iris dissolved into the pupil in the inconsistent light.

"One may die in their pursuits of their obsessions, but does one not pursue for the joy of pursuit, itself?"

Just then, the music came to stop and we bowed to one another. He took my hand in his and gave it a kiss. He came up slowly, his eyes transfixed on mine, drawing me inward.

"It was an *absolute* pleasure, My Lady."

I heard a gasp and turned to find Imelda, hand to her chest, with her jaw agape.

"*Is that*...is that *my dress?*"

She made a noise that was part shriek and part squeal, her eyes darting from me and then to Lord Troy and back again in succession.

As if by some act of misfortune, Agatha came up beside her, Thomas by her side. Her fair brows where furrowed as she attempted to make sense of the situation. She, too, stared from me to Lord Troy, repeatedly.

"I can't *believe* this! *You!*" Imelda pointed a finger at Lord Troy. "This was *your* doing...wasn't it?"

I stood between them, feeling increasingly uncomfortable. My hands began to sweat as I bit down hard on my lip. *Had I become invisible? Perhaps, if I wished it so, I could melt into the floor and run away.*

She was yelling and drawing a crowd. People began to turn from their conversations, eyes drawn to her with looks of shock. She had no qualms about shouting in public, it seemed.

"This is a simple matter of confusion," he said as he reached calmly for a flute of champagne when a butler flitted past. He narrowed his eyes at her, but looked away quickly, evading the notice of his guests.

"We shall meet in the parlor to discuss this...when the time comes," he stated, pragmatically, leaving Imelda in near tantrum. She snorted audibly, but he ignored it, as he turned to leave.

Agatha's expression turned from one of confusion to dismay. She interjected, seemingly unfazed by Imelda's outburst.

"Edmund?" She addressed him, pushing herself up in front of Imelda, who scoffed and crossed her arms.

Edmund turned around to face us again, his demeanor swiftly changing back into his gentlemanly affability as he walked over to greet her. He brushed past me as if I were a ghost. I swallowed hard.

"Agatha, My Lady." He bowed.

She narrowed her eyes at him and cocked her head, before she gave him a tardy bow in return.

He bent down and kissed her knuckles. "I bid you adieu while I attend to these matters. May I offer my butlers' assistance with anything that you shall require while I am away? Are you enjoying yourself?"

Thomas' head popped up from behind Imelda, his eyes drawn to the exchange between Agatha and Lord Troy. I saw a faint hint of envy touch his eyes, before he sunk back down into the crowd. Imelda's gaze seared into the back of Agatha's head.

Agatha moved to cross her arms, but reconsidered it, and instead gave another bow before responding.

"I am very well, My Lord."

"I wished it so," he said, his attention focused solely on her, as if she were the only person in the room.

"Very well, then. Please, continue to enjoy yourself and I will be back momentarily."

He looked up from her now and addressed the crowd that had turned to watch the spectacle.

"I implore you all to take advantage of the festivities and the refreshments. They are only good for the remainder of the night. I would hate to have to drain my undrunk champagne into the Thames!" he said jovially. The crowd laughed, some of them holding their flutes up in the air to him as a riotous cheer rang out among them.

He turned away and gave me a fleeting glance, before walking off into the crowd toward the doors.

Imelda snorted as she passed me, her arms crossed and her brows knitted across her forehead. Agatha just stood there, staring at me with a look of bewilderment.

Chapter Twelve

Edmund jolted awake. He sat up and held his hand to his heart, feeling it pound beneath his palm.

He was alive. A sense of relief washed over him as he took a deep breath and laid back down, looking blindly up at the ceiling. It was pitch black, and he could barely make out his hand in front of his face.

He remembered the dream briefly—the face of two beautiful women appeared to him. It took him a moment to realize that the women were Imelda and Agatha.

Agatha called to him, her fingers curled in a "come hither" movement that summoned him. Her alluring hourglass shape and narrow waist, seduced him. She had her hair down—the results of their copious lovemaking—with a look of evident satisfaction on her face.

Imelda had a fan and was flapping it alluringly. Her legs were crossed, exposing her ankles and bare feet. Her hair—the wild rebellious waves of a sea siren—flowed down her back. She licked her lips, the vivid red was a surprise to him, and he found himself quaking with excitement.

Without notice, Imelda began to laugh, pointing her finger at him, taunting him. Agatha looked over, her eyebrows arched with curiosity. She discovered the source of Imelda's entertainment—his mangled leg—and she *too* began to laugh.

Panicked, he lifted the sheets off and ran his hands down his legs searching and feeling in the darkness. His fingers finally brushed the raised skin where it rolled into a smooth, long silver line.

He felt an odd sense of relief and anguish at finding it there. He had hoped so many times as a child that it was only a dream, that he hadn't suffered the disfiguring mark. He'd spent nights wishing it away. But now his fingers defied him, as they traced the blemish.

He was glad his mind had failed him at the memory of its cause. Memories of his mother's anguish were enough of a reminder. He had been told that she left him on his own and he had wandered off. From the account of neighbors, he was discovered with a large gash that ulcerated his thigh from a branch. They surmised that he climbed a tree and fell onto the branch, at such an angle, that it did him considerable damage.

It was only luck that saved his life, as he lay unconscious. A trapper, and friend of the family, came across his lifeless body shortly after the incident. He was fevered, but by some miracle, he managed to survive.

His mother— who suffered from bouts of hysteria—lost all sense of reality after the incident, spending days upon days weeping and wailing in the confines of her room while his nurse brought him back to health.

Catrina came to him in his visions now. Her brows were puckered with worry. Her hair fell down her back, thick and coffee-colored, almost the same deep color of her eyes. She took his hand in hers, and rubbed her fingers across his palm. Her skin was alabaster—so white it glowed in the darkness.

He reached out to touch her, wondering if he was losing his mind. The dark permeated through his fingers though, and her vision dissolved around him. He closed his hand into a fist, his stomach tightening, at the realization that she was *only* a figment of his imagination.

He closed his eyes beckoning her back. To his surprise, she came willingly. Her snowy white skin was covered only by a sheer gown that flowed with her as she moved.

She pressed her lips against his, and he tasted the sweet tang of wild strawberry. She sank into him then—dissolving, and at once, becoming one with him—in a frenzy of warmth, skin and sensation that rolled over him like a wave.

He soaked in her scent, a mix of lavender and woman, before he felt himself shudder and let loose, his limbs becoming heavy and fatigued. His body floated somewhere above him, in a euphoric mix of tranquility and resolution before he succumbed to sleep.

Chapter Thirteen

I flipped open *The Count of Monte Cristo* and put the pages to my nose, the scent of paper unfurling as I closed my eyes. It was an intoxicating aroma, the pure scent of knowledge and imagination. Someone's sweat, blood, tears, and angst went into these pages, Alexandre Dumas' to be exact.

With the lessons of the day complete, and leisure now available to me, I sank into a cozy chair by the window, grateful for the peace and relative quiet that followed. The only sounds were the mid-afternoon birdsongs and the occasional rattling of a carriage passing by. The harsh light at this time of day was perfect for reading, if you sat far enough from the window.

I ran my hand over the first page, losing myself in daydream. *What was it about this book that captivated Lord Troy? I wonder if Sam has read The Count of Monte Cristo? Why had Sam simply disappeared on holiday, without as much as a farewell?*

The thoughts rolled around my head as I licked my lips. Without realizing it, I'd been clenching my hands together, my knuckles had turned white.

I swallowed and flexed my fingers. Perhaps it's better not to think of such things right now. I laid my hand on the cover of the book, running my fingers along the embossed title, as I mouthed the words of the first page:

"Marseilles—The Arrival. On the 24th of February, 1810, the look-out at Notre-Dame de la Garde signaled the three-master, the Pharaon from Smyrna, Trieste, and Naples."

And read until my eyelids could no longer stay open.

Chapter Fourteen

Edmund walked outside to the sound of chirping birds. He made the rounds this morning, feeding and watering Socrates, petting Whitman and throwing Byron a stick. Whitman allowed him to rub his belly, but only for a few moments before he tired of the game. Edmund watched as he darted off down the hallway.

After his morning work was finished, he made his way outside with Byron dutifully following behind. They sat quietly next to one another, enjoying the warmth of the sun as the sound of the fountain burbled somewhere in the background. A bird, or two, flew into the garden searching for bees or other insects, their wings fluttering softly.

He rubbed the top of Byron's dark, shiny head as his tongue drooped happily from his mouth; Byron was overjoyed to be with his master. When Byron went off to chase a squirrel, Edmund pulled a letter from his pocket and unfolded it. He'd read the letter before, once last night and one time previously when it was first received, but he opened it up and read it again.

Edmund,
It is I, Sam.

I have been called away to Bath, by my sister, for an urgent family emergency. I am, regretfully, unable to attend the annual summer ball. Please send my apologies to Catrina, as I am aware that my presence is to be expected by her.

Please also, if you may, let her know that I will presently be unable to meet with her this upcoming Tuesday and possibly the next. We meet at the river bank in the forest at 3 o'clock (about 2 miles west of your estate at the boulders). For matters of privacy, at her request, I cannot divulge the topics of discussion for which we meet.

Affectionately, your friend,
Sam

He refolded the letter and tucked it into his jacket pocket, patting it with his hand firmly to ensure it was safe.

What could Sam possibly want with Catrina? he thought.

He felt a sudden strange, and unpredictable, jolt run through him. He rubbed his neck—his fingers brushing against the curls—as he sat there for a long time, lost in thought.

Chapter Fifteen

It was two o'clock in the afternoon on Tuesday. I felt a pang of guilt at stepping into the forest. Aunt Beatrice was under the impression that I was off to Mrs. McGillivrey's to work on my embroidery. It had been a few weeks of this elaborate lie, and still, I wasn't found out. I was hopeful that I could use Mrs. McGillivrey's feeble mind to my benefit if need be. But thankfully—as of yet—I did not need to prove myself.

I felt this way whenever I went off to meet with Sam—a mix of apprehension and excitement. It was a welcome break from the stuffy formalities I endured in my daily lessons with Aunt Beatrice and Agatha.

It offered me the chance to discuss *my* interests with someone. Days upon days of etiquette training and reading ladies' journals filled with nothing but *fluffery,* was torture. Fluffery seemed an apt description for it—I'll have to remind myself to remark as such, to Sam, when I see him.

I felt an uneasy tightening in the pit of my stomach as I weaved my way through the thicket. I hadn't seen Sam in weeks. I knew I was irrational about my expectations, but I had to admit to myself that I felt strangely *lost* without him. He didn't owe me an explanation. The sad matter of fact was that he owed me nothing, *and yet...*

I felt my throat become raw as I strained to swallow, the thought forming a lump at the base of my neck.

Without the disturbance of my unwelcome thoughts, it was peaceful here. I paused to take a deep breath in and calm my senses. The air was crisp and clean, with the slight undercurrent of greenery and churned up dirt. The sun poked through the canopy—spreading rays down in big lines to the earth—like holes in an enormous green umbrella.

The forest was quiet, outside of the spirited activities of the woodland animals going about their business for the day, the pattering sound of a squirrel, or rabbit, running around the undergrowth, stopping only to listen to my footsteps as I interrupted their course.

If you listened carefully, you could hear the stream bubbling along its way. I wandered, stopping every now and again, to hear the sound of it babbling, ensuring I was heading in the right direction.

A crack rang out breaking the silence, and I turned abruptly.

Nothing.

I scanned the area, the thick, tall trunks, the shroud of brush, the stillness of everything in the area. I could feel the pulse in my neck start to thrum wildly.

"Sam?" I called out.

It was strange to hear my own voice, as it interrupted the solitude and spirit of the forest. A few feet away a plump, brown rabbit sat with grass in his mouth.

"Was it *you*?" I asked, bending down to take a look at him. He sat next to a hollow log in the thicket; his big black eyes were studying me. He hopped further away, and when he reached a distance he found comfortable, he sat down again to keep watch on me. He went on chewing mindlessly, presuming that I was harmless after he studied me for a while. I stood up and started to walk again, bidding my rabbit friend farewell.

Finally reaching the stream, I found my favorite boulder and perched myself on top. It wasn't an easy task in a dress, and I found myself balancing precariously as I attempted to sit down. When I finished adjusting, I searched the banks for another rabbit friend— feeling strangely alone, but no other animals were around.

I took my diary out and set it beside me, drawing a pencil from my pocket and tapping it lightly on my knee before jotting down my thoughts.

—Rows and rows of books, purple drapes, blood wine stain, perfect bow-shaped lips, statuesque. Apollo?

Sam came into mind and I added: *Deep brown eyes— the color of coffee, strong tea, the fertile earth. Lost.*

Where are you, Sam? It must be three o'clock already. I rolled the pencil mindlessly over the cover of my diary.

"'Why...'Ellllloooo."

I turned suddenly, almost toppling from the rock, to see a man standing beside me. I clutched my heart instinctively.

"Hello," I said guardedly. I hoped he couldn't see the pulse beat chaotically in my neck.

"What brings ye about these parts...milady?"

My eyebrow shot up, and then down again, in a series of surprise and concealment.

Sam...where are you? I need you, Sam!

"Taking a walk on such a lovely day, looking for some wildflowers..." I replied.

He raised a doubtful, wild eyebrow at me.

"My husband is out with me...he'll be along soon," I added, looking around frantically for Sam. I prayed he would pop up from behind a rock.

The man eyed me skeptically and grunted. He was two times my size, with a mane of bushy, dark black facial hair. Dirt and grim mottled his face, and yet despite the filth, I could see a prominent port wine stain above his left eye. I should have been aware of his presence plainly by his stench. He reeked of rotten food, beer, and soiled clothing.

"Aye, I see..." he took a breath and looked around, "and where might the lad be abouts now, *mo leannan?*"

I swallowed. My throat felt as parched and dry as paper.

"He's...*about*...he shall be coming shortly. He wasn't much behind."

I looked around aimlessly, my fingers clenching to my skirts, as I made a conscious effort to release them.

Please Sam, Please, Come quick! I screamed in my head, begging the forces of my mind to transmit the message. I could feel my palms begin to sweat. I looked up to see him examining my hand.

"It seems ye don't have a wedding ring, *lass*..."

He stared at me. His eyes black and shiny like the rabbit's. He rocked back and forth on his heels with his hands in the pockets of his ratty trousers.

I felt my breath catch in my throat and instinctively slid down the rock before brushing the dirt from my skirt, readying myself to run. I watched as his eyes followed me.

"I *lost* it..." I said, looking down at my barren ring finger. One of his brows rose again, looking very much like a caterpillar poised to walk.

Feeling the weight of my feet on the earth below relieved me. I glanced fervently in all directions, looking for a place to escape.

"Ye see, *lass*...I don't believe you none." He reached out suddenly and took hold of my arm in his massive hand. I opened my mouth to scream, but nothing came out. I swallowed and forced myself to try again.

"Help! Sam! Somebody...please, help me!" I yelled as loudly as I could, as I thrust myself away from him. Leaving no more pretenses between us, I struggled like a wild animal in a trap. But he had a solid grip on my arms, and I felt his nails dig into my flesh, as I thrashed wildly to get away from him.

"Ye best be shutting that mouth of yours, *lass*... ye won't like what I have to do to ya if ye don't." His face was in mine now; his breath stank of rotten teeth and stale beer. I turned away, as he shoved a big, dirty hand over my mouth.

He shoved himself up against me, pinning my back to a tree. My heart was thumping so frantically, it threatened to jump from my chest.

I was able to thrust my leg up into his crotch, as I shuffled around desperately. Using all my strength, I pushed against him. For a brief moment, he bent forward as he grimaced, before coming back full force using his legs to force mine apart. My muscles gave in, spreading my legs outward. I spit in his face, a ditch effort to distract him, so I could make a run for it.

"Ye wee baarrrmy bitch," he yelled. He went to spit in my face but changed his mind, and instead, struck me with his hand, leaving his print on my cheek radiating from the sting. I struggled but felt myself quivering and losing energy, all my vitality sapped from my limbs during my panic. Defeated, I closed my eyes and hoped to get it over soon. The vision of his birthmark blazed in my mind like the brand of a prisoner.

Do what you want—but please let me live, I thought. I resolved to my fate, when all of a sudden, I heard a voice. My heart jumped. The silence was deafening now, as I struggled to listen. *Was it my imagination*? No! There it was. Someone heard me!

"What is going on here?" A man's voice bellowed. I thrashed my head around, as a new surge of energy coursed through me.

"Help me! Someone, please help me!"

The man, reluctantly let go of my arms, never losing eye contact with me and stepped slowly back—the rage still gleaming in his eyes.

Despite the immense size difference, Lord Troy shoved him out of the way and leaned in to help me. They looked at each other briefly, analyzing one other. When unexpectedly, the man spun around and shot off into the forest, running as fast as he could in the opposite direction.

"Are you hurt?" he asked, bending to help me to my feet.

I hadn't realized it, but I was trembling. My knees wobbled beneath me, and I shivered so violently that I had to sit down. He held on to me as I hobbled towards a stump. I couldn't pull my eyes away from my hands as they quivered. Dirt, grime, and blood covered my fingers.

"Did *he*..." He looked down at me. The question reverberated in my mind, sending a chill up my spine. I swallowed the hard lump that settled in my throat and shook my head.

"No."

He looked me over again, rubbing a hand on his neck as he surveyed the area the suspect disappeared too.

"I must go after him."

I shook my head vigorously. *Don't leave me here alone. What if I can't find my way out? What if he comes back for me?*

The thought made me shudder. The weather was stifling, and yet, I felt cold — a chill ran up my spine.

"No!" I summoned all my strength to shout. "Please, please, don't go...please," I begged him.

Don't leave me out here by myself.

I grabbed hold of him with whatever strength I had left. He turned to face me, eyes wide with a pained expression of confusion within them.

"He'll get away..." he said, looking back toward the thicket.

"*Please...*" I heard myself whimper.

He'll come back. He'll find me...and he'll kill me, I thought. He swallowed, and his Adam's apple bobbed up and down in his throat.

"If nothing else, we must get you to safety," he said, as his shoulders slumped with defeat.

I stood up and took a hesitant step, feeling a searing pain shoot up into my calf. I motioned to a stump a few feet away, before hobbling there.

"I think my ankle is hurt."

The pain radiated up my leg, pulsing and throbbing. I felt the constriction around the joint as a sure indication of swelling. *Should I take my shoe off to look at it? Did injury to one's foot, or ankle, trump modesty?* I wondered as I stared at the foot in question.

I peeked up at Lord Troy, the question etched on my face. His brows furrowed as he looked down at me, his hand still nervously rubbing his neck.

"I can call on my doctor as soon as I get you back to my estate. Can you walk? I'll hold you on one side, but you'll have to permit me to do so."

He bent down, looking me in the eye. His eyes were cornflower blue in the light. We'd never been close enough for me to see, and unquestionably, never *this* close.

"Permit me to carry you back?"

"Pardon?"

"Permit me to carry you back to my home...to get you medical attention."

And I shall be painted a dirty puzzle, a fallen angel, I thought, with a look of dubiousness.

He stepped back, letting me sit alone on the stump, and as if he were building a case, continued.

"I can't think of any better way..."

I studied the forest, and a new jolt of fear made the fine hairs on my neck stand up. *What if I don't accept his proposal and we did not make it out before nightfall?*

"Yes." I nodded, swallowing hard.
"Yes?"
"Yes..."

"Stand for just a moment, and I'll lift you," he said, motioning for me to stand.

"Wait!" I blurted, looking down at my dress. It occurred to us simultaneously, that carrying me through the obstacles of the forest in my full skirt would be daunting—impossible, really.

"I'm *wearing*...I have on a crinoline..."

We both stood there in silence for a few minutes, neither of us insistent on bringing up the deduction we'd both made—remove the crinoline and leave *or* stay put and wait for help, *whenever* that may come.

What other options do I have? I thought, drumming my fingers. Surely he's seen more than a lady's ankle, *and plenty of it*, from other women—women he's undoubtedly lain with. My mouth became dry at the thought. But *this*, this was different.

"This *is* a matter of emergency," Lord Troy deduced, looking at me thoughtfully. Perhaps, he was right. I stepped on my ankle again, pressing down gently, testing my limits. The pain radiated like a spark of fire up my leg. I sighed, resigning to the idea with every footstep; *I would have to lose the excess weight to make it easier for him to carry me.* I jerked my chin in the direction of a large Alder.

"Bring me to a tree...I'll need it to steady me."

He held me up, stabilizing me as I stood. I was as wobbly as a skittles pin, but that was to be expected.

"Please turn around..." I could feel myself shake, as the remainder of the adrenaline coursed through my body.

"Oh...yes," he replied, as he grinned sheepishly, before spinning around.

I stood on my good leg, as I braced myself against the tree. I untied the outer skirt, and it fell swiftly to the ground—landing like a floral puddle at my feet. I stared down at it for quite some time, before grumbling to myself. There was no way I'd be able to hop over it.

I leaned my head against the tree and took a deep breath. The sounds of the river came back into focus. I lamented the irony of the soothing sound, as it trickled innocently along during my trauma. I swallowed and gaining courage, I looked over my shoulder.

"I'm going to need a little help."

He turned his head around to look, eyes wide.

"It's out of necessity..." I said — more of a reminder for myself, than for him.

He came over to me, and we both went about our business without speaking, trying our best to avoid eye contact. I could hear his breathing, a measured, but fast pace. It was a queer feeling being intimately close with someone you hardly knew. I took the time to study him unabashed—the filtered light touching the curl of his hair, and highlighting it with the subtle undertones of umber.

I grimaced as his fingers skillfully unlaced the petticoat and then the crinoline, a searing warmth spread across my cheeks at his proficiency. He stripped them off, leaving them pooled on the forest floor, as I held myself up against the trunk of the tree, remarking at his efficiency. I bit down on my lip, tasting the metallic tang of blood on my tongue.

When he finished, he gathered up my petticoat, skirt, and crinoline and laid it carefully across a branch and turned around to wait for me.

I fumbled, but managed to slide a petticoat over my chemise, tying it tighter than normal around my waist—my mother's words of chastity playing in my head.

I was left standing in the middle of the forest in nothing but a corset cover, a white cotton chemise, and a petticoat. I clenched my arms against my chest as I felt the rush of heat flood my cheeks.

"I will send my staff to come and retrieve your clothing once we return. Are you ready?" he asked, holding his hand out to me. I clenched my teeth and begrudgingly, extended my hand to him. He turned, so we faced one another, and bent to lift me. I wrapped my arms around his shoulders and held fast.

"Am I hurting you?" I asked, feeling intensely large and bulky at the moment. He shook his head as he cradled me, treading over tree branches and the various obstacles of the forest floor. He stepped gingerly, in his attempt to avoid jostling me and my injured ankle.

We evaded eye contact, it was too intimate. And instead, I spent the majority of my time, looking out at the surroundings as I saw them bouncing up and down. The labyrinth of forest spread before my eyes, roots, branches, shrubs, and trunks became a blur of greens and browns.

I began to enjoy the strength in his arms as he held me, the gentle sway of his body as he moved. After a while, I could hear his breathing becoming more and more labored. His chest pressed against me, forcing me away with each inhale and closer with each exhale.

"I don't believe I've thanked you for your interference. So, If I may...Thank you, Lord Troy," I remarked.

"Will you please call me Edmund?" He looked down for a moment, imploring me to meet his gaze.

"Mmm?" I tilted my head, so our eyes met.

"You addressed me as Lord Troy...will you call me *Edmund*, instead?"

"If you so wish...*Edmund*."

He made a noise in his throat, half-huff, and half-laughter, as a thin-lipped grin spread across his face.

I closed my eyes and listened to his heart as my head bobbed on his chest.

"Have you had a chance to read *The Count of Monte Cristo*?" he asked, in between breaths. His voice vibrated through his chest, and I felt it, more than heard it.

"I have started..."

"*And*?" He looked down his long narrow nose, until he met my face.

"It is a tragedy that Edmond could not trust Fernand," I stated, looking off into the distance. "To face such a fate, by the hands of someone you trust, so *inexplicably*..."

Edmund locked eyes with me.

"Greed makes even the finest people do things they are not proud of..."

I opened my mouth to respond, but nodded instead, having no desire to dispute.

He stopped for a moment, and we rested against the trunk of a huge sycamore. He took a few deep breaths and put his head down; his hands pressed against his thighs.

"Are you aware of the legend of Prince Jon?" he asked, as he stood back up. I shook my head.

"According to legend," he leaned toward me, as if to tell me a secret, "Prince Jon built a fortress as a gift to a woman with whom he had fallen madly in love. That fortress is out here—somewhere—in this forest."

He turned to look at me; his eyes were shockingly blue from a streak of light that fell from overhead. Taking my silence as encouragement, he continued.

"The woman who he fell in love with, was a Princess named Margery. Margery was from another land—a far off land—a land that takes several days and nights to travel to." His eyes grew wide as he pressed his fingertips together. "When Prince Jon went to her land to propose, offering her the gift of the fortress, he found that his *brother* Prince Francis had *already* proposed to her. Prince Jon and Prince Francis had a long history of animosity, spending most of their childhood in a battle against one another. Always jealous of his brother, Prince Francis went through any means necessary, to thwart his brother's power. *Well*...Prince Jon was able to meet with Princess Margery secretly, and the two ran off together. He took her to the fortress that he built for her, and confessed his love for her...*the problem was*..."

"She was already spoken for?"

"Yes." He nodded energetically and continued.

"Well, there was only *one way* to get out of the proposal."

"Death?"

"*Exactly*..." he said, leaning his face in closer to mine.

"*So*...Prince Francis challenged his brother, Prince Jon for the hand of the Princess. They agreed to meet at the fortress in a fortnight, and prepare to battle one another for her hand."

"What happened?" I asked, leaning in, pressing my chin into my palm.

"Well, during this time, Prince Jon and Princess Margery roamed the villages and surrounding areas, and it was obvious to all who saw, that they were *madly in love* and this *infuriated* Prince Francis." He paused for effect. "A week before they were supposed to battle, Prince Francis tracked them down, and murdered Prince Jon and kidnapped Princess Margery."

My mouth dropped as I looked over at him. A smirk came across his face at my response.

"He forced Princess Margery to marry him ...*but* —unbeknownst to him— Prince Jon and Princess Margery had a *secret* marriage and had consummated that marriage, leaving Princess Margery with child!"

"No!" I replied; my eyes widened.

"The Princess gave birth to the child—a boy— who would later become a *King*!"

"Did Prince Francis ever discover that the boy was not his son? How was she certain that it was Prince Jon's child?" I asked.

"Doesn't a woman *always* know?" He raised an eyebrow at me.

I shrugged, and he started to laugh.

"*Never mind*...shall we continue?" He nodded toward the woods as an indication that we were ready to leave, and reached out, lifting me up into his arms again. I pressed myself to his chest; relishing in the strength of his muscles, as they flexed to hold me. One of my arms locked around his neck, brushing against a dark curl. I tried to glance at his hair inconspicuously; I loved the way it bobbed up and down as he moved. My hands twitched with the desire to run my fingers through it.

"Where *is* this fortress?" I asked, surveying the woodland and finding it to look indistinguishable.

"I haven't found it. But one day, *I shall.*" A smirk appeared on his face; drawing his chin upward into a fine line.

"Will you show me, I mean, when you find it?" I asked, feeling emboldened by curiosity.

"It would be—*my pleasure,*" he said with a grin.

~

We walked for a long while without speaking, listening to the solitude of nature as birds fluttered in and out of branches, and the wind rustled through the leaves.

We reached an area of thicker brush where Edmund lost his footing, toppling down a narrow embankment. He held me firmly to his chest, my ear pressed against his heart. I felt him hit the ground with a loud thud. He bolted upright and shook his head as he dusted himself off. Red welts grew like vines on his arms, where he hit branches on his way down.

"Are you alright?" he implored, searching me over.

I nodded, brushing a twig and a few stray leaves from my skirt. I had a hair-widths' scratch on my elbow, and likely a bruised bum, but didn't mention it.

When I looked up again, my cousin Ezra was standing in front of us, his gaze fixated on us. He had caught a few fish and their silver bodies dangled from a line, their eyes wide and petrified, as if they could still see the terror of their fate.

"Ezra?" I managed to utter.

"Catrina?" he cocked his head to one side and looked at Edmund. I clutched an arm protectively across my chest.

"Are you *alright*, cousin?" he asked, bending down to help me up. I nodded, watching as a renegade tear rolled down my arm. He reached out for me, and I held to him as he lifted me up.

"There was an accident," tears started to well in the corners of my eyes at the recollection of the earlier events. My voice was shaking now, and I found it hard to swallow.

"And your..." he rubbed a knuckle across his mouth, his brows arched as he attempted to phrase his statement. He swallowed and motioned to me, using his hands to form my figure in the air.

"It was necessary for us to remove the excess clothing...so I could carry her."

Ezra cocked his head to the side, assessing. He was eagerly attempting to make sense of the circumstances. He rubbed the bridge of his nose, lifting his glasses in the process.

"It is because of Lord Troy's bravery...that I am safe," I said, giving Edmund a tentative look, before meeting Ezra's gaze.

Edmund stood up, brushing his trousers off, ignoring Ezra's continual gaze.

"Shall we be on our way? We need to get you medical attention." Edmund turned to address me, reaching a hand out to me. He held on to me, the security and solidarity of his body against me felt reassuring.

The lines drawn on Ezra's forehead started to soften as he studied my ankle. It was marbled now, a combination of purple and red, and thick with swelling.

"Ezra, can you head back to my estate and have my staff call for Dr. Bernhoft? By the by, before you leave...have you seen anyone around...in the forest?"

Ezra shook his head but stopped in mid-thought, rubbing his knuckles across his lip.

"There was...*a man.*"

Edmund leaned in, his eyes wide.

"A big man—with a queer mark on his face—on his forehead, if I recall..."

A tingle ran up my spine, and I felt the hair on the back of my neck rise.

"That's him!" I blurted.

"Shall I go off and look for him?" Ezra quickly added. But Edmund shook his head.

"It's unlikely we'd be able to catch him. He's probably made it to the Rose and Crown by now," Edmund deduced, looking off into the direction the man escaped too. There was a moment of silence as we all contemplated the situation.

"Besides, we need to get Catrina back to safety...and get her medical treatment," he added.

Ezra gave him a firm nod before meeting my eyes.

"I will be as fast as I am able."

I gave him a thin-lipped smile, attempting to hide the pain.

He looked over at me with his eyebrows pursed, then turned and headed back through the forest, running off into the direction of the estate, the line of his fish bobbing up and down behind him, shimmering silver whenever the sunlight hit them.

"I suppose this *does* look queer," I said, looking down at my chemise and petticoat.

Edmund didn't respond, his eyes were still fixed on Ezra, as he disappeared into the maze of green.

I took a hesitant step, realizing then, that the pain was growing more intense, paralyzing my leg. I moaned and grabbed hold of the trunk, leaning my weight against my good ankle. Walking would be an impossible feat at this point.

"Come...let's get you back to my doctor," he said, walking over to me and bending slightly to lift me again.

Chapter Sixteen

I sailed out under a beautiful, amethyst sky on my boat; it was a sailboat, a small one, no bigger than a fishing boat. There was a warm, salty breeze that blew across my face, twirling my hair in all directions. The sun had set and nestled into a blanket of thin clouds in the horizon, leaving only the radiantly, purple sky above, and the faint twinkle of some distant stars.

I waved goodbye to the shore. My mama, papa, and brothers were waving back, their faces strangely distorted, but recognizable.

Suddenly, a strong gust of wind came, and I was pushed out to the depths of the ocean—drawn away from the calm, cerulean sea into an ominous, black abyss. I stared back at them, helplessly, as their faces disappeared in a series of reckless waves.

The ocean—like a ravenous beast—swallowed my boat with a single gulp. I could see myself in a whirlpool, spinning inward. The water was gushing in around me, as I funneled into the bottomless chasm. I was gasping for air, pulling and clawing my way against the waves.

Then a face appeared—a face with a marbled, purple blotch. The man grabbed hold of my ankles and pulled. He tugged at me, digging his dirty nails deeper and deeper into my skin, as I held onto the edge of the earth. *Then it was all dark.*

I woke with a violent jerk, the sweat pouring from my forehead. I could hear the muffled sounds of voices moving in and out. *Where was I?*

My head rolled from side to side, as I attempted to reconcile my surroundings. I didn't recognize the mahogany desk, or the portrait of two gentleman fox hunting, nor was I familiar with the ostentatious wardrobe—with its profusion of curlicues and accents.

The throbbing in my ankle brought my memory back almost instantaneously, and I immediately cried out for someone, *anyone.*

"Lord Tro...Edmund!"

A little old lady came scuttling into the room, she had so much rouge on that I wondered if her seeing had gone. She was a squat woman with a thick tuft of honey-colored hair piled on her head, the shape and size of a beehive.

"Miss? You a'right? Can I getcha anythin'? Names' Bee...like the hunna bee..."

I took a deep breath.

"Anything for the pain..." I muttered.

"Whisky?" she asked, her brows knitted.

"Something stronger!"

"a'right...I have jus' the thing..." she said, as she hummed and scurried out of the room like a squirrel on a quest for a nut. I recognized the song as *Too Ra Loo Ra Loo Ral*, an Irish Lullaby my grandma used to sing to me as a child. She returned swiftly with a bottle.

"Open your mouth, dear!"

I opened my mouth. She took a dropper and counted each brown drop as they landed on my tongue. I recoiled at the bitterness.

"Sleep now, dear. You need plenty o' rest," she said, as she screwed the dropper back onto the top and pulled the covers up to my chest—tucking them snugly under my arms.

"Do my aunt and uncle know where I am?" I asked, looking up at her.

The little old lady smiled— a patchwork quilt of teeth exposed.

"Ahh yes, dear...your cousin Edgar?"

"Ezra" I corrected, feeling instantly impolite about doing so. Her mouth contorted and she sighed apologetically.

"Yes, Ezra has let them know. Rest now, dear. Remember a good laugh and a nice long sleep are two o' the best cures..."

I certainly don't feel like laughing, but I nodded anyways.

She turned and waddled to the door, part-singing and part-humming: *"Too Ra Loo Ra Loo Ral...hmmm hmmm hmmm"* the whole way. She shut the door behind her with a soft click, and everything was silent again.

~

I wasn't sure how long I slept, but when I awoke it was dark again, and the nagging pain had subsided. After a few minutes, I decided to attempt sitting. I gingerly shoved the blanket aside and lifted myself up on my elbows and slid to the back of the bed.

It was a grand room, massive for a bedroom. I squinted to make out the small print on the wallpaper, tiny yellow rose buds on blue pinstripes, almost the same sunny color as the thick drapes drawn away from the windows. There was a similar warm glow of yellow from the gas lights. Beside me, someone stirred. I was surprised to find Edmund fast asleep in a chair near the bed.

I leaned over to see his face. His long, dark lashes laid softly against his cheek. His breathing was shallow and alert. A few dark strands curled stubbornly on his head, and I couldn't help but draw parallels to cherubs. I wondered, ruefully, if he had chubby cheeks and pudgy arms as a child.

He stirred again—perhaps he had the innate sense that I was watching him. He raised his arms in the air, as he stretched His eyelids were still closed lightly. He had a book on his lap, and upon closer observation, it appeared to be *Don Juan*. One eye popped open, and then the other, as he took a deep breath—setting the book on a table beside him.

"How are you?" he asked, stretching.

"Well...as well as can be expected I suppose...I have your maid to thank for the medicine she's given me..."

He nodded — a slight grin on his face.

"Yes, Bee is quite...*remarkable*." He took me in for a moment, before clearing his throat and looking away. "You can stay for as long as you need to recuperate."

"That is very kind." I remarked, looking around for my belongings. It occurred to me, that I had no idea where my diary was. I felt a sudden jolt of panic.

"My diary? Is it...here?"

He nodded, before getting up and walking over to the desk, pulling it out from a drawer. *Has he read it? Dear Lord, please say he hasn't read it.* I frowned.

"It was well taken care of while you were resting," he proclaimed, as he handed it to me. I felt my shoulders drop, a sense of relief flooding over me.

"I found it among your things and tucked it safely in my jacket pocket before we left the forest. When we returned, I ensured its security by placing it in the drawer," he said, pointing to the stout, mahogany desk near the wardrobe.

Beads of sweat rolled down my chest in a stream—absorbing into my cotton chemise. It stuck fast to my skin, sticky and moist, exposing the pink of my nipples. I snatched the blanket and pulled it awkwardly up to my chest.

"My apologies...I've instructed the staff to keep the windows open...what with the miasma and such...but it appears that they did not." Edmund opened the window, allowing a breeze to billow in.

I shook my head.

"It's quite alright," I lied.

I was grateful for the draft that blew in. The strong, but sweet, scent of honeysuckle was thick in the air. The window framed the black night, which stood like a stark backdrop to the luminescent glow of the room—where everything had a golden aura. A symphony of nocturnal insects carried in on the breeze, each singing some sort of love song. I peeled back the layer of blanket modestly, allowing the fresh air in and allowing my skin to breathe. Noticing my distress, Edmund leaned forward.

"You look...*uncomfortable*. Can I call for some new clothes for you?"

I shook my head.

"Please, I'd prefer that you don't wake any of your staff on account of me..."

"But we very well can't have you sleeping in sodden clothes," he said, his eyes roaming over me as he rubbed his neck.

He walked toward the door without further explanation, and I found myself watching as he left, the door closing with the same soft click as before.

Was I here? Was I really here? The idea was both absurd and oddly exhilarating. I put a hand on my chest; the firm thud against my palm was a reminder of my vitality at the moment.

And then...Sam came to mind. *Where was he? Was he ever coming back from Bath?* I felt a senseless anger form within me, transforming me as it slithered inside. A mix of guilt, and jealousy, and overwhelming sadness, consumed me whenever I thought of him. I knew it was irrational, but that didn't matter. Emotions are hardly ever sensible!

I was lost in thought, when I heard the click of the door. Edmund walked in, a pail of water swinging slowly by his side, steam rising from it, as he made his way to my side. He sat down, without saying a word, and dipped the rag into the pail, ringing it out methodically.

"If you will permit me?" He held the rag out, his brow raised in question. I nodded, and he pressed the rag to my skin, running it gradually down the length of my arm. I closed my eyes, relishing how the little hairs sprung up.

"I was shipwrecked once," he began, as he moved in a little closer. I opened my eyes to meet his. "It seems as if I am telling you an outrageous tale, but I give you my sacred honor that it is true," he said in a low, quiet voice.

He dipped the rag again and squeezed it out. The water poured from the cloth into the bucket, flinging drops of water in all directions.

"The ship's mast cracked and fell in a brutal storm, it battered the ship, taking a large bit of it with it..."

"What happened?" I asked, sitting upright, eyes wide with curiosity.

"There was yelling, and shouting, and chaos. I was on the back of the boat holding on tight as if the next wave would take me over, but by some sort of mercy, it did not. I said my last prayers. I'm not an overly religious man, but it seemed to make sense to me at the time..."

I nodded and bit my lip.

"It wasn't until I had seen him that I remembered Sam was there with me..."

I put my hand to my heart at the mention of his name. I could feel my breath catch, as if I was standing on the edge of a cliff.

"How did Sam survive?" I murmured.

"Well, he was struggling. He'd fallen overboard. The waves were the biggest waves I've ever seen." His eyes grew wide at the memory. "I vowed I'd save him, didn't know at the moment how, but promised myself I would. No matter my fate..."

I watched as he moved, focused and intent. There was sorrow in his eyes at the recollection, and his pupils gleamed in the light. He dipped the rag again and rung it out as dull gray water dripped into the bucket.

"I saw my opportunity as a piece of the ship floated out to sea. I jumped in and swam as hard and as fast as I could to Sam..." he said as he swallowed, his Adam's apple dropping and rising again.

He was so close now that I could make out the color of his irises, the same color as the sea I loved and missed. A sudden tightening in between my thighs spread outward like a brush fire. A vision of Agatha and Sam appeared like apparitions in my mind—but I shoved them willingly away—watching as they dissolved before me.

"Sam was struggling to catch his breath, he'd lost his energy fighting the waves, and I held him up to me...tight to my chest." He held his arms up, mimicking. "I swam as fast and as hard as I could to that piece of boat, and I held on to it with all my might..."

He ran the rag tenderly down my fingertips, removing the dirt and grime. I clenched my thighs together, feeling the impulses growing stronger and stronger — the fire spreading.

"We were tossed about—the ocean is no place for man alone—and when we came too, exhausted, wet, and cold...we had, by some miracle, landed on the shoreline." He was deep in thought, his head down as he worked. His lashes hit his cheeks when he blinked, long and black.

"Where did you land?" I asked, adjusting myself and leaning forward.

"Greece...Apano Meria."

There was a moment of silence between us. He carefully turned my arm over, deliberately running the rag down to my palm, his eyes following his fingers.

"How did you get home?"

"Well, I didn't. Not for some time. Sam and I spent a long time there," he drifted off. "We drank a great deal of fine wine—malmsey—dined with plenty of fine ladies..." he looked up at me again, and I gave him a wry smile—both of us knew what *that* meant. "Traveled...it was a gorgeous place."

He looked off as if imagining it in his mind.

"I would hike to the top of the caldera. There was an ancient fort there. I'd sit and watch all the ships come in and out of the sea from port Ammoudi. And that is where I fell in love with the sea." He rubbed the back of his neck, as he spoke.

I gazed at his lips, mesmerized by the way they moved. I rubbed my fingers gradually across my mouth, imagining the feel of his lips on mine.

"I can imagine," I said a little wistfully.

"Ah, yes...so you can." He nodded, as he sat back for a moment in his chair, rag still in hand. "Sometimes, if I close my eyes, I can still hear the waves rushing across the shore." He gave me a sideways grin, brushing each fingernail purposely, yet delicately. I could feel my pulse thrum through my neck. The blood was swirling and surging in my veins, hot and thick.

He set my arm on the blanket and motioned with his chin to the other arm. He dipped the rag in the water, and I watched as steam drifted from it in little wisps.

"Why come back...it sounds like a lovely place?"

He stopped and looked up for a minute.

"I wonder that myself sometimes..."

There was a moment of quiet before he set the rag down, placing it back into the bucket, before taking both of my hands in his. I wet my lips with my tongue.

"We have not known one another for long..." he said, holding my gaze." But I feel something *so*..." he drifted off, "I feel a sense of *comfort* whenever you are near..."

I swallowed, feeling my throat tighten.

"I feel the same," I remarked—surprising myself with the truth of the statement.

"I have met my share of ladies, and they are all *dull*...I haven't a single bit of interest in what the color of the season is, or if you can play the pianoforte unlike any other—you, however—there is something so inherently *exotic* about you..."

I laughed, but he gave me a blank stare.

"I'm sorry," I replied, as his face tensed. "I have never heard anyone describe me as ...*exotic*."

"You are *fascinating*...I have not met a woman yet who knows as much about literature and poetry...*as you*. It is no small feat!" he said, his features softening and returning to normal.

I bit my lip, feeling a flush of heat rise from my chest, gradually pervading my cheeks.

He pressed the rag to my neck, urging me to lean my head back—exposing the length of it to him. The water rolled down between my collarbone and into the crevice of my breasts.

He paused, holding the rag above me, allowing the cool drops to bled through my chemise, revealing the rosy pink of my breasts. My nipples stiffened as they brushed against the sheer fabric. Our eyes met and held one another, the blue of his iris swallowed up by the black of his pupil.

He was closer now, so close that I could hear his breathing become heavier with anticipation. I could smell sandalwood and oakmoss on his skin. The proximity of his hands alit something new and curious inside of me, and the world swam in my head— a jumble of chaos, excitement, and bewilderment.

I took his hand in my own and pressed the rag firmly to my neck. I drew it down across my collarbone, savoring the rivulets that tingled across my skin. I exhaled sharply, feeling more than seeing, his lips as they curled into a smile. His breath hitched.

Suddenly, the door creaked, and we frantically grabbed for the blanket. I pressed it to my chest, and Edmund sat back in his chair, the rag still in hand.

"Oh." Bee, who had come in, stopped in her tracks at the door — seemingly analyzing the situation, I now sincerely prayed that her vision was failing her and was thankful for the darkness. Edmund cleared his throat.

"I have taken care of bathing our guest, Bee."

Bee smiled skeptically but was much too wise to say anything.

"Do ya need anythin'...any more medicine?"

I felt my throat constricting by the moment, but I eked out a response.

"Fine...very fine, I have slept a great deal because of it. Thank you."

There was a punctuated silence that felt awkward, and all of us sat staring at one another until Bee spoke up again.

"You need somethin' to drink...I can fetch some water for ya?"

We shook our heads, perhaps too robustly, as she eyed us both. She sighed and turned around, waddling with her ample bottom toward the door as she hummed. Her hands crossed over her chest as she spoke something quietly in Gaelic. I hadn't realized it until she'd said "Amen" that she was reciting a prayer. She shut the door behind her with a soft click, and padded down the hall. Edmund sat back and rubbed his neck, his eyes to the ground.

"I should probably get some sleep," I said.

"Indeed, you should."

He took my hand, and bent down, kissing my knuckles gently. The thrill of his lips on my skin sent goosebumps up my arms. He turned and left, closing the door quietly behind him. I listened to his soft footsteps as he sauntered down the hall.

Chapter Seventeen

"So, I see you had a guest last night?" Imelda chided, as she sauntered through the door. Edmund promptly regretted leaving it unlocked.

"Mmhmm," he muttered without looking up.

Imelda regularly interrupted Edmund's writing sessions, but today he had less patience to deal with it. He didn't look up from his desk — a stack of notices was laid out in front of him.

A nearly extinguished cigar sat in a tray near his elbow, the end was ashy gray, but a minute trail of smoke wafted from it. A glass with a swallow of brandy sat beside the cigar tray, diluted to a pale yellow.

He turned to see Imelda standing at the doorway, dressed seductively for mid-afternoon in an indigo dress with black lace trimming. Her jet black hair, frequently worn loose, was tucked up, exposing a swan-like neck and small elfin ears.

He found it hard to deny that the physical part of his body found her attractive. He felt himself swell uncomfortably in a combination of frustration and excitement that left him confused. He tugged inconspicuously at his trousers, as he cleared his throat.

"I can't say that that's any of your business...who visits me...or who doesn't," he retorted, with a sharp tongue before looking back at his work.

"Perhaps not..." she said, as she did a circle around the room, allowing Edmund's eyes to follow her. She relished the look on his face as she moved, following her dress as it swept across the floor with a swish.

He turned from her reluctantly and plucked a notice randomly from the pile that was splayed in front of him. He sighed and unfolded it, reading only the words: "Final Notice" across the top in large, black block letters before shoving it into a candle, watching as the orange flame licked it. His mouth twitched and then formed into a tight-lipped grin, as the fire greedily consumed it, leaving nothing but a few blackened flakes behind.

"Another notice?" Imelda inquired, her voice wavering on alarm. But Edmund ignored her and attempted to stand up to leave. She quickly, and strategically, straddled him where he stood, forcing papers and pens to make way for her.

"Imelda..." he pushed his chest out squarely against her.

She was pressed tightly against him and his desk, raising an eyebrow in acknowledgment of the feature that, undoubtedly, appreciated her presence. He couldn't deny that he felt a deep, singeing desire for her.

She took his chin with one of her fingers and drew it upward so that their eyes met, her's— an entrancing shade of jade in the light—seared through him, as if she could plunge into his soul. It unnerved him, and he quickly averted his gaze.

"I can give you so much more than *she* can..." Imelda leaned her chest into him, interrupting his thoughts. He huffed, pushing himself against his chair and away from her. He regretted their familiarity, and her ability to manipulate him because of it.

"Imelda...*this*...we *can't* do this..." he said, swallowing the hard lump that developed in his throat. He knew without a doubt, that even as he said it, he was fighting a losing battle. The more she touched him— the more her smooth skin brushed against his—the more he knew, he couldn't resist her.

From his viewpoint he had the advantage of height, as Imelda nibbled the tip of her finger, tracing it into the hollow of her neck and down between her breasts.

She tugged at his shirt friskily, undoing the buttons one by one. He didn't struggle, only shook his head feebly in resistance as he watched her work. His logical thoughts were swiftly tucked away into the recesses of his mind, as his excitement rushed in.

When she stripped him of his shirt, she ran her fingers over his chest—leaving a faint trace of goosebumps in her path. She tugged impatiently at his trousers, wanting to free him from the constraints.

Filled with lust, he decided to act on it and pushed her down onto the desk. He fought this for so long, and for so long, he'd been valiant.

He could smell the pungent scent of her perfume, lemon and bergamot on her neck as he ran his nose along her chin. Their mouths searched frantically for each other, finally finding refuge and relief when they met. He pushed himself back for a moment, pressing his hands on her shoulders.

"Lay down." his voice was gruff and impatient.

It was difficult to undo a skirt and corset, and his restlessness grew by the second. He lifted her onto his desk, pushing the skirt up to her hips, exposing her thighs to him. Using the surface to brace himself, he pushed her legs apart with his thighs and slid inside her. A sense of immediate relief overcame him, and with each thrust, he felt a rush of guilt, aggression, and anger leave his body.

She bent over and bit his lip, holding it gently with her teeth as he moved inside of her. This excited him, and he became more aggressive as he pushed against her harder and harder.

She felt her hips and back press into the mahogany top, as she slid forcefully against it. She gripped tightly to him with her legs, pulling him possessively to her— willing him to control her. She attempted to meet his gaze, but he swiftly averted his attention elsewhere, before closing them.

He couldn't meet her eyes. He felt a simultaneous pang of guilt and regret simmer below the surface, but stifled it, surrendering instead, to his primal instincts.

After he finished, he laid his head tenderly on top of her chest. The scent of their sweat and sex, combined with lemon oil and oakmoss, made a potent eau de toilette.

"I've missed this..." Imelda's voice was soft and sounded different with his ear up to her chest. It had been months since they had been together. What started as a casual agreement to share their beds to stave off loneliness, evolved into something that neither of them were prepared for. It became a ritual of sorts— their passionate rendezvous'—dwindling only when he met Agatha and Catrina.

"I promised..." Edmund began to say, attempting to catch his breath. "I promised myself I wouldn't do it again..."

She reached down to run her fingers through his hair, the unruly, dark curls slick now with sweat. It was then that reality—like a blunt hammer—hit him. A wave of nausea rolled through him, as he pushed himself up and away from her.

He stood up, adjusting himself and hurriedly attempting to dress, as she reached out and grabbed him

"I love you..." she murmured.

He felt a shiver run up his spine.

"I love you—I want to be with you..." her voice quivered, tears welled in the corners of her eyes.

He looked down fleetingly at her hand, wrapped around his arm.

"You know that *can't* be..." he met her eyes for a fleeting instant.

"We can...we can run away. We can find a place to live. We don't need to live here. I'm certain there is somewhere we can be together...no one needs to know." her eyes plead with him. He could see the look of panic and desperation swirling around in her, like a whirlpool. She let him go, pressing her arms firmly across her chest.

"We can go to Scotland—didn't Papa have a place in Scotland? Somewhere in the mountains?"

He felt the word "Papa" jab him unexpectedly, like a sword through the gut. He swallowed hard, ignoring the echoes of shame that chanted in his head, the chorus of a thousand monks that gathered around in his psyche to torment him at his incestuous tryst.

"She's not full blood!" His mind screamed. But it did little to ease the guilt that threatened to submerge him.

He knew, as well as any, that it didn't matter to society whether she was a full-blooded sibling or not. What awaited him, were the chants of angry villagers with pitchforks at the ready, to force him from the estate he'd so rightfully inherited.

They wouldn't care that they only shared the same father. Her mother was the beautiful and elusive, Isidora Flores-Hernandez—the Spanish love of his father's life, the siren that he had to blame for his *own* mother's eventual demise. And yet, he carried no bitterness towards their love child. He'd only grown to become increasingly fond of her—*too* fond of her.

He pulled his arm away from her grasp and walked silently to the door.

"She won't take you...you know that? *No one would*...not with a leg like that!" Imelda's voice choked back tears as she shouted. He paused and turned to face her, meeting her gaze directly.

"Oh, *she* will...I can promise you that..."

She stared after him as he walked away, and without another word, he left her there on his desk exposed to the world.

Chapter Eighteen

I awoke to a fine breakfast of eggs, bacon, scones, jam, treacle, honey, and of course, tea and coffee. The alluring scent of bacon and coffee—like the upper notes of sumptuously delicious, edible cologne—would wake me. It traveled along, like a trickle of smoke, down the corridors from the kitchen and underneath the crack in the door. I ate until my belly was swollen.

Whitman, Edmund's orange tabby, would come to visit me each morning. Following the aroma of the bacon into my room, he would perch on the edge of my bed, waiting for me to break off a piece for him. If he were feeling brave, he would take a few tentative licks before he'd lose interest, and saunter to the window where he'd lay and sun himself.

This morning was different; however, I was halfway through breakfast when I was greeted by my Aunt Beatrice, Agatha, and Ezra. They came to visit me, bringing a few of my belongings with them.

Dr. Bernhoft said that I would likely be able to return to my aunt and uncle's home reasonably soon, as I hadn't broken my ankle as suspected, but had only sprained it. The bruising began to fade, leaving behind a yellowish-green tinge.

I could walk for short distances without it bothering me—which was a cause of irritation and dismay for Agatha—as she desperately wished for me to return home and be nowhere *near* Edmund's manor.

She made it no secret that she didn't approve of my lodging with Lord Troy, regardless of the motivations or lack thereof. Her benevolence toward me was a sign of her growing insecurity at the possibilities that ran amok in her head.

"Why ever can't she come back? She appears to be doing just fine!" she yelled at Dr. Bernhoft.

Dr. Bernhoft glanced over at Agatha, aversely holding back a sneer. He and Edmund shared a look, and he cleared his throat.

"It is my duty to make sure that Catrina heals properly. I cannot send her on her way without the knowledge that she is fully healed, Miss."

He was a stout man with a balding head. The wreath of black hair surrounding the shiny globe of his head was gradually turning gray. It was no doubt due to age, but likely hastened from the anxiety of patients and probing narcissists like Agatha.

He spoke with an aristocratic, nasally tone that grated on my ears. It wasn't enough that he was a doctor; he was *the* doctor to the famous and wealthiest clients in London—something he had no problem sharing with anyone in earshot.

Making matters worse, Agatha made it a mission of hers to come harass me. When lunch was over, and Aunt Beatrice and Ezra were taking a tour of the grounds with Edmund, she came up and beleaguered me.

"What's this?" She gave a slight nod of her chin toward the vase. "What do you have there?"

I bit my lip.

"Flowers...my host has been so kind as to bring me some," I said pointedly. Our eyes met in a game of cat and mouse. She wanted me to run, and I wouldn't.

She scoffed, idly twirling a piece of her hair around her finger, appearing as nonchalant as possible. Her veneer was transparent, however, and she played the part so inadequately, I almost felt a twinge of sadness for her. She was falling apart at the edges. Tears welled up in the corner of her eyes, and I knew one more comment might tip her over the edge, so I drew my tongue in—my own resolve starting to crumble.

"Ezra saw *you*...you know?" she provoked.

"I'm not sure I know what—" I began, but she promptly interrupted, throwing her hands dramatically up in the air.

"He *saw* you!" she cried, as a big tear threatened to leak from her eye.

"What is it that you want with him—with Edmund?"

I shook my head, hoping I'd appear as sincere as I felt.

"I hadn't planned this...you *must* know that," I shot back.

Feeling an immediate sense of sorrow for her, I leaned forward and attempted to take her hands in mine, but she jerked them away with a scowl.

"Heaven and Earth! How dare you!" she snorted.

She shook her head. The tears started streaming down her face, and she angrily wiped them away.

"Agatha...I, I am only here because I am not well enough to return home. Please believe that I want no part of...*whatever* it is you believe is occurring." I pleaded.

A tiny voice in my head defied me and yelled out "Deceiver," but I pushed her aside and continued speaking.

"It is the generosity of Edm...Lord Troy that has allowed me to rest and heal. That is all."

She narrowed her eyes at me again but kept quiet, a promise to continue listening. I spoke up, just barely above a whisper.

"It was awful…if I told you, you wouldn't believe me…"

She took a deep breath in and crossed her arms against her chest.

"But, once I am healed, all will be right again," I said, feeling a strange mix of relief and simultaneous sadness at the thought.

I rubbed the blanket between my fingers, hoping the repetition would calm my nerves.

"Yes, it will…" she stressed, as she stood up and started to walk toward the door, turning to meet my glance before leaving.

"Besides," she said, "this is better for all of us… Lord Troy and I—we make sense…"

Chapter Nineteen

Unlike his sister and mother, Ezra didn't care much for the nightlife or the mass hysteria of people that flooded the theatre. Begrudgingly, he joined his family to watch a show, relieved that it was over and he could finally head home now.

He was surprised to find that it had turned dark while they were in the theatre. The thing that he always found remarkable, was that there was hardly much of a difference at all between night and day in the city. There were lights on all the time. Call him a country boy, but he much preferred the serenity of the natural darkness as it cascaded down across an open field.

Everything about the city was uninviting to him, but nothing more than the abhorrent stench that clung to the air — foggy, dense and putrid. Dung and horse urine stung his nose, no matter which neighborhood he frequented—less so in the elite West London neighborhoods of Piccadilly, Park Lane or Grosvenor Square, obviously, but still apparent. It permeated everything like an unwelcome guest that lingered.

He heard it was much worse in the less desirable parts of town, referred to by his friends as the "darkest London." The stench of smoke, soot and human waste in Whitechapel or Spitalfields, were so intense that you could scarcely breathe. He hadn't been brave enough to venture anywhere near those places, which had become a sort of challenge among some of his brothers at university. One of them came back from a night of "slumming" claiming that he'd been practically beaten to death by an angry costermonger.

He couldn't be sure if the distraction of a night out on the town were more for his sister *or his mother*. He was grateful to see that his sister and mother were discussing something *other* than Lord Troy's intentions, however. He'd heard quite enough about *that* lately.

He knew how much it meant to his family, that Agatha continue to pursue her quest of finding an eligible and wealthy suitor, and even agreed to assist in the matter, by encouraging Thomas Atwell to "appear" at random events where Agatha would be present. His mother encouraged the reunion with Thomas, after discussing the rather precarious, and advantageous, circumstance his cousin Catrina found herself in—being in such close proximity to the Lord.

He wasn't an unsatisfactory prospect...at least not on paper. He came from an affluent and respected family. His father was a lawyer, and his mother was a well-known socialite in the area. And while they didn't live in Piccadilly (much to Agatha's chagrin), they did live in Belgrave, in a fashionable townhome.

Thomas had coincidentally—or not so much—Ezra thought, shown up at the theatre in a row just ahead of them, much to the pleasure of his mother. They all walked out discussing the show—laughter abounding.

People shuffled out onto the sidewalks, creating a mass of humanity as they cheered, whooped and hollered, leaving Ezra in desperate need of escape.

He was itching to get back to have a cigarette and could taste the smoke on his tongue as he closed his eyes, the irritation immediately evaporating away with the sounds and lights of the night along with it.

"Ezra. Is that you, chap?"

Ezra turned and searched the crowd. Through a cluster of top hats, a man he'd recognized from university was bobbing up and down with his arm in the air. He looked a bit foolish, but Ezra pretended not to mind.

"Is that a friend of yours?" his father leaned over to him and nodded in the direction of the man. Ezra begrudgingly shook his head, and a broad grin spread across his father's face.

"Ahh the good ol' days of university," he said, patting his son on the shoulder. "If I could only go back."

Ezra didn't want to spend any more time in the city, but the appeal of getting a beer at the pub with his chum had drawn him in—with the added potential of getting a view of some unholy women.

"I believe that's Leonard…" he said, nodding in return to the man, who was now making his way towards Ezra.

"Will you be coming home with us or shall I let your mother know to expect you later?" his father pulled out a pocket watch to check the time, squinting at the tiny numbers on the face as he put it up to his eye. He didn't want to admit it, but age was starting to rob him of his sight little by little.

"There are plenty of omnibuses to take me home."

"Have a good night, son." his father said as he nodded and tucked his pocket watch away.

His mother and sister were so consumed in their discussion with Thomas that they didn't notice Ezra had disappeared.

He shuffled through the mob, feeling more and more claustrophobic at the minute. Leonard, who had been bobbing up and down unnecessarily as he weaved his way through the crowd, had finally reached him.

"How have you been, chap?" Leonard asked excitedly. A gangly fellow with a mop of black hair and an overbite, he was hardly anything to look at. Ezra realized too late, that with Leonard around, his chances of finding a nice woman to chat with were disintegrating.

"I say! Shall we have a drink? It's been ages. Tell me, what have you done lately?" He grinned again. Ezra sighed and nodded, leading the way to a pub, as he filled Leonard in with the particulars. He cursed to himself silently, as he watched the fellow walk with a peculiar gait behind him.

After they reached the corner, Ezra was grateful to see the crowd dissipate. The sounds of hoof beats and whinnying, raucous laughter, and lively conversations started to fade off, and Ezra was appreciative of the small patches of semi-quiet that now existed.

They approached a pub called the Grenadier and Leonard piped up from behind him.

"Well, I say! The Duke of Wellington frequented this pub in his day."

Ezra ignored him, looking up from his feet to see a group of gentleman crowding around the door.

Standing underneath the lantern lights, he saw the very distinct profile of Lord Troy. *What are the odds?* He thought.

Owing to Lord Troy's good looks and immense popularity, he was shrouded by a group of gentlemen, and Ezra couldn't help but wonder what it would be like to be within such an elite inner circle.

What would the ladies think of him, then? He wondered. A vision of himself being fawned over by gorgeous women clouded his thoughts, and he wasn't going to let the chance slip away from him. He must let everyone around him know that he and Lord Troy are acquainted.

Increasing his pace, he found himself making headway when all the sudden, he turned to see Leonard stumbling. Guilt overcame him, and he turned around.

"I say! It seems I can't quite keep up with your running!" he laughed. *Even his laugh was ridiculous,* Ezra thought. He tried his best not to sneer. *You are a child of God, Ezra. Remember, love thy neighbor?*

Helping Leonard back on his feet as quickly as he could, he turned back, hoping that Lord Troy hadn't disappeared. Thankfully, he appeared to be in the same spot.

Ezra hastened his steps again. This time, making sure he was alongside Leonard in case he should require assistance. Ezra wasn't known for his strength, his height perhaps, but not his brawn— much to his disappointment.

The faces of the men were shrouded in shadow from a distance, but the closer he got, the more confident he was, that Lord Troy was among them.

"A fine night, gentleman," Ezra said, tipping his hat to them.

Lord Troy turned towards Ezra, and his eyes grew wide. The group of gentlemen coldly tipped their hats at him and returned to their conversation. They formed a tighter circle to announce that they had no desire for Ezra's company.

"And to what do we owe the pleasure?" Lord Troy asked dispassionately.

"We were out at the theatre and found ourselves thirsty for some spirits," Leonard responded. He gave the group a smile that slowly faded as he watched them eyeing him like a specimen.

But there was something peculiar about the man opposite Lord Troy. He didn't make eye contact with Leonard, or Ezra. He studied the man for a moment before he noticed Lord Troy glaring at him.

"Ah, indeed. Well, I hear they serve an incredible sloe gin." Lord Troy retorted, oddly curt.

Leonard leaned into Ezra and whispered, "I don't believe that's a man's drink." But Ezra shook it off, meeting Lord Troy's glance once again, his blonde brow raised with a question.

"My apologies gentleman, but we must be leaving." Lord Troy tipped his hat to Ezra and Leonard, not making eye contact with either. He jutted his chin towards the man opposite him, and they all turned, following Lord Troy like a row of hatchlings follows its mother. He and Leonard watched as they disappeared down the road, into a haze of smog and darkness.

"I say! That was rather *peculiar*," Leonard said aloud. Ezra nodded.

"*Peculiar,* indeed," he said, rubbing a knuckle across his lips.

Chapter Twenty

I could see Byron from my window chasing a squirrel. The squirrel, like a brown flash of fur, raced in a circle around a tree trunk before scaling it and out of Byron's grasp. Byron resorted to barking incessantly, until he eventually gave up, sighing and laying down at the base of the tree in hopes the squirrel would come down again.

I was itching to get out and get some fresh air. The room was stuffy, even with the window cracked, and I was growing weary. There were only so many things one can do when confined to bed. I finished reading *The Count of Monte Cristo*, wrote in my diary, counted the tiny flowers on the wallpaper (there were two hundred and thirty-three within my view), sketched a few images of the estate lawn from my vantage point and attempted to scrapbook a few items to give to Agatha when I returned.

The worst part about being in bed, and being alone, were the thoughts that crept in. I attempted to keep myself as busy as possible to avoid thinking of anything that would upset me. But sometimes, when it was late and I was alone, the thoughts would come swarming in—as if I opened the door to them, and they'd been waiting there all afternoon.

I thought of Agatha...and her claim to Edmund. *Was she right?* But even more confusing, *why did that matter to me?* Edmund was strange and stoic at times. He was also moody, arrogant and standoffish. But the more I lost myself in a daydream, the more I realized he was fascinating, mysterious and alluring. The more I grew to know him, the more I was drawn to him, and the more complicated my emotions and feelings became for Sam.

I didn't want to admit it to myself, but I felt an unusual attraction to Sam before he left. And now, those feelings and emotions were rolling around inside of me battling with my growing feelings for Edmund.

When Bee came in with a cup of hot tea, I reached out to her.

"Bee."

She looked down at me, a look of concern in her eyes.

"Is ever'thin' ok, dear?"

I shook my head up and down.

"Yes, oh I'm sorry. Yes, everything is fine…but I'd really like the opportunity to get some fresh air today. Is Edmund around?"

"I'm sorry, dear, but Edmund is away…" she said, as she set the cup down on the nightstand. The scent of black currant drifted over the bed.

"Away?" I asked, pushing myself against the headboard and sitting up straighter.

"He's gone away to Brighton…on urgent bus'ness…he said it couldna wait…"

I nodded at her, but questions stirred in my mind. *Who does business in Brighton?* I thought. Surely, no one I'd ever known of.

The fancy playground to the wealthy, Brighton was a typical holiday spot and an unlikely place to conduct business. Their idea of business was entirely different than my own. I imagined my father laughing at the concept, and a smile spread across my face. Bee continued watching me, amused by my facial expressions.

"He has a good friend in Brighton…'tis a shame he couldna have brought ya," she said, as she began to bend over to collect the chamber pot.

I made an apologetic face as she pulled it out from underneath the bed. Urinating in the dark while attempting to squat on one leg was nearly impossible. She studied the floor around the pot and wiped it with a rag, undaunted by it. I was hopeful that the lavender Edmund brought in from the garden yesterday, would overpower the strong scent of urine.

I stared out the window again, resolved to spend another day in bed. I took a deep breath. Bee piped up.

"Ya know, I believe Sam is 'round." She studied my face to see if this would be an acceptable option. My eyes lit up.

"He's back?" I cried.

She grinned and tilted her head, puzzling things together in her mind before nodding.

"He came back las' night from Bath."

I peeked out the window to see if I could see him, but there was only the great expanse of rolling green turf.

"If you believe it will not trouble him?" I asked, leaning forward, prepared to leap out of bed.

"I'm sure he wouldn't mind a bit if ya join 'im...he spends his days writin' in the garden..." she said, with the flick of a wrist. "I'll call for him."

She shuffled out the door with the chamber pot, leaving me to my thoughts once again.

~

"I come out here every day," Sam said, raising a hand to the sky—showing off the white, puffy clouds and big, golden sun. I had to squint, but I didn't mind. The fresh air hitting my face revived me in a way no amount of rest could. It was here in nature, and with Sam that I felt the most alive.

I hadn't realized how much I missed the way he grinned, and those two deep dimples that appeared, carving into his cheeks any time he laughed. It was as if all sounds faded away from the earth when I watched him smile.

I wanted to stop and turn to him, plead with him to tell me why he left, why he wasn't at Edmund's summer ball, and why he wasn't there to protect me when I needed him most. But I swallowed my questions down, one by one, as I watched him hold onto my arm as we walked.

"Typically, I spend my time writing in the rose garden." He waved his hand in its general direction, "or near the fountain." He beckoned me with his hand towards the fountain that stood near the estate, all pathways leading back to it.

"You are familiar with both... and of course, at our place near the river." He looked at me and grinned, and the world faded away into a watercolor painting behind him.

"I've got different plans for us today," he said, eyeing the book I held at my side.

"Oh, do you?" I asked, fluttering my eyelashes demurely at him. He laughed and pointed a finger out toward the lawn.

"Aye...I do!"

"And what might that be?" I held onto his arm, pressing my weight into my good ankle and using his elbow for stability as we walked.

"Rowing..."

"Rowing? Like sport rowing? Like against teams?" I asked, looking up at him.

He laughed a deep belly laugh, holding his stomach. I felt slightly foolish but grinned at him as he pulled himself back together.

It was good to hear his laughter again, so buoyant and vibrant.

"No, just the two of us...on a rowboat," he asserted, grabbing hold of my arm to offer more stability.

We took our time meandering down the pathways—which led in all different directions across the lush, green grass of the property. This particular walkway wound around a low lying depression lined with neatly trimmed trees.

Once we rounded the corner, a lake came into view. It was considerable in size, forming a giant, tranquil basin in the yard.

A family of ducks gathered around it, waddling, quacking and squabbling amongst each other, before disturbing its placid surface as they walked in. On one side, the grass sloped down to a muddy, narrow embankment where a rowboat sat dredged in the sand.

Sam pointed to the group of ducks who were walking along the bank.

"That's a mother duck and her family...and there's the father. Do you see Papa duck? He thinks he's a king. Now, look at that. There's a lady duck that caught his eye."

I giggled.

He pointed to a duck walking in front of Mama duck and Papa duck waving her tail feathers in their faces.

"She's his mistress..."

"That's very...*observant* of you!" I teased, hiding a cheeky grin.

"I've spent lots of time out here...it gets lonely sometimes..." he countered.

Sam had a particular sort of charm about him that made him undeniably irresistible to be around.

I watched as Mama duck waddled her way over to the mistress duck and had words with her. She used her bill to nibble at the mistress duck, who fought back using her bill to do the same.

Mistress duck turned to walk away, but Mama duck hadn't quite finished with her and lifted her wings up at her, flying a short distance before quaking at her in rapid succession. Papa duck watched, unaware of his status, as the ducklings went about their business digging for worms in the dirt.

"What do you suppose will happen?" I asked.

"I suppose..." he said, "that Papa duck must make a decision...or else he loses them both."

As he said this, he pointed to a different group of ducks a few yards away.

"I'll be bound that there are plenty of dapper ducks in there that would make excellent husbands for Mama duck and mistress duck. Why are they fighting over this one male?"

I chuckled.

"Perhaps he is the wisest duck in the area." I shot him a glance.

"Perhaps..." he said, "or perhaps he has the best sense of humor."

I laughed, and he peeked over at me with a smirk as we continued walking.

A Sam and Edmund duck, I thought to myself as I watched the proud Papa duck waddle to the water and slowly walk in. I thought of Edmund and wondered where he was at the moment. *Had Edmund met up with his friend in Brighton yet? What if his friend was a lady?*

I cringed, feeling my shoulders tense and then shoved the thought away.

"Have you ever been on a rowboat?" Sam asked, interrupting my thoughts.

He held onto my back, as I lifted my leg and stepped into the boat.

"I can't say I have...no, not in a row boat...I've been on plenty of larger boats..."

"Can you swim?" he asked, picking up the oars from the shoreline and setting them down into the bottom of the boat.

I nodded.

"Although it would be quite a challenge in my current state," I jested, and we both laughed.

"Well, you're in for quite a treat," he said, as he thrust against the boat. It took him three good tries before the boat budged and eventually broke the water.

It was tranquil—its surface only blemished by a series of half rings, growing increasingly larger, and dispersing as the boat moved slowly through the water.

I was mesmerized by the serenity of the moment. Sam's arms moved fluidly as he rowed us through the water. The oars bobbed up and down into the silken surface, making a soft 'plunk' sound with each series.

I counted the ducks who lined the shore, giving them each a name. I settled on naming Mama duck, Mildred, and Papa duck, Frederick.

"You seem to have a good deal on your mind…" Sam observed, as the oars made another 'plunk' into the water.

I bit my lip, stifling a nervous giggle.

"It's nothing, really…"

He raised two rugged brows dubiously in my direction.

"I was just giving the duck's names…" I replied, feeling the heat rise to my cheeks. Sam started to laugh nearly dropping one of the oars in.

"What?" I shot back, "you gave them a whole story!"

"It's not that at all…"

I eyed him speculatively.

"They *have* names…"

"You?" I pointed at him, "named them?"

He nodded, laughing again at the irony.

"I did…"

"*And?*"

"Mama duck is Abbie…she looks like an Abbie, doesn't she?"

I tried to locate Mama duck and wondered which one she was. There were eight ducks gathered around the shore, and all looked nearly identical.

"Abigail…" I said with a smirk.

"Very well then…Abbie for short."

"Papa duck," he remarked, pointing to a male strutting his stuff alongside the harem, "is George."

"He does make an excellent George," I agreed.

"Yes, he quite does..." he said, as he scanned the shoreline again and pointed to the mistress duck.

"The mistress, I've called Doris..."

I scrunched my lips up and shook my head.

"No?" he asked, his head tilted in thought.

"No, doesn't seem quite right for her. Not fitting."

"Ok then, what would you name her?" he challenged.

I thought for a moment, putting a finger to my lips.

"Flora."

"Flora?" he exclaimed, mulling the thought over in his head and looking back to the shore.

"I suppose so..." he said, without conviction.

"Do you know a mistress named Flora?" he asked, tilting his head in my direction.

"Goodness me! No!" I laughed. He chuckled and began to row the boat again.

"Well then, now that *that's* settled..." he said, giving me a sideways grin.

~

We rowed for some time until he stopped, pulling the oars in and laying them gently down beside us. We were now in the middle of the lake. I took in the shoreline, surrounded by a hodgepodge border of trees that reflected off the surface—like glittering emeralds. The only ripples came from the soft sway of the boat, as it rocked softly from our shifting weight.

"This," he said, raising his arms in evidence, "is the very best place to write."

He pulled his diary out, catching a glimpse of me, as I took my book out to read.

"Or read," he added with a grin. "You appear to be quite the reader…"

I nodded.

"Writer, as well," I corrected.

He grinned.

"Working on your project, I see," I attempted to peak at his diary, but he slyly pressed it to his chest before I could get a good glimpse, as his lip curled into a half-smile.

"Do you read Dickins?" he blurted, attempting to change the subject.

I nodded.

"Byron? Shelley? Wordsworth? Who else?"

I looked up from my book.

"All sorts. Plato, Shakespeare, Dumas, Voltaire, Socrates."

I saw his eyes light up, and he leaned in closer to me.

"Ahh, a woman of philosophy?"

"Of many forms of literature," I corrected him.

"How did you come to know so much about literature?" he asked, folding his diary shut.

I felt a clutch of homesickness at the thought.

"Well, it wasn't from having the resources at home..." I said, looking up sheepishly at him.

He sat back, giving me his full attention.

"My papa was a man of the sea and made his living from the sea."

I could almost taste the salty air wafting over me from the immediate recollection. Images of sanderling birds came to mind, running up and down the shoreline, their little feet racing to the water's edge before the next wave would appear.

"It was only by sheer luck that I had come across the virtues of reading. I wasn't taught by a governess or nurse or anything of the sorts, all though I'm sure you could likely gather that..." I fumbled nervously with the lace on my dress.

He listened intently. Eyes focused on me. It was faintly unnerving, but I continued.

"At a young age, I became a caregiver for an elderly woman in town, Mrs. Cullwick. She and her husband had retired to the seaside."

An image of the old woman popped into mind, her delicate, opaque skin and cloudy eyes. Her hair was a mix of silver and white that sat on her shoulders. She claimed to be eighty-two and had told a good many stories about the war between France and England when she was an adolescent. She spoke of how her father had been a soldier and lost his foot to battle, how her mother tended to him, and how she lost an older brother to the war.

"She was born into wealth and married wealthy."

"What was his profession?" he asked, leaning forward with his elbows on his knees.

"He was a literary professor at Oxford...a very fine one I might add."

His eyebrows raised as he rubbed his chin.

"Her husband would bring books home for her to read. She had a voracious appetite when it came to reading...She said she saw herself in me, and that we both had something *remarkable* about us. Something that she claimed was almost...*magical*...and now that I say it, it seems *foolish*."

"No, no! She's quite right! You *are* remarkable." he argued.

I felt the heat return to my cheeks as I avoided his gaze.

"No, she was just a polite, little old lady...who loved reading and wanted to share it with whomever she could...I am just grateful that I was the someone she'd decided to share it with."

A smile came across my lips at the memory.

"And your favorite? Book, I mean?" he leaned into the center of the boat.

I bit my lip, wondering if I should divulge the truth. Sam wasn't averse to heckling me.

"You'll laugh," I said.

"*Oliver Twist?*"

I shook my head, feeling my cheeks redden.

"*Candide?*"

I continued shaking my head.

"*David Copperfield?* Come now, what is it? I'll tell you my favorite, and you must promise not to laugh, and then you shall tell me yours!"

"Alright then," I said, sighing deeply.

"*Frankenstein,*" he blurted.

"*Frankenstein!*" My eyes widened. "Sincerely?"

"Of course! What's not to like about *Frankenstein*? I suppose you were expecting something *more*...?" he trailed off.

The truth was I *was* expecting something more, something more *exquisite, cultured, philosophical.* Isn't that the sort of thing that fine gentleman, educated in ostentatious universities, read and enjoyed—the more pretentious, the better?

"I suppose I expected something more along the lines of *The Iliad and the Odyssey*, in all honesty. Isn't that what all gentlemen in universities spew about at any random point in time, as a mark of their wealth...or something else written in Latin or Greek?"

Sam's jaw dropped, and he put a hand to his heart in mock awe.

"You seem to have quite the high opinion of us men of University..."

I snickered.

"Alright now...*your* favorite?" he gave me a nod with his chin.

I held the book up that I was reading, allowing him to read the title.

"Ah, and *that* makes perfect sense," he said sarcastically.

"I beg your pardon!" I gasped.

"I shall say that most women prefer to read the unrealistic versions of their expected future lifestyles. There are no such things as *Fitzwilliam Darcy's* in the world. At least not where I come from, nor anywhere else I've ever known..."

"I sincerely disagree..." I protested.

"Do you? And where have you met a *Darcy*?" he asked, hands out to his sides.

I scrunched my lips sideways, thinking hard.

"Well, he certainly exists... His character *must* have come from somewhere, and most likely, from one of Jane's personal experiences!" I protested.

"Ha! Poppycock!" he scoffed in return.

My lips scrunched tight.

"How else would you define Edmund?" I asked pointedly.

Whatever smirk threatened to appear on his lips bounced back to stoicism.

"Is *that* what you think...of Edmund?"

I nodded fervently.

"I haven't any course to think otherwise..."

Sam pressed his lips together into a hard line and tilted his head quickly to the side.

"I suppose I cannot persuade you otherwise?"

"No," I stated. *What did Sam know about romance?*

"Hmm and how is a *Darcy* supposed to act?"

"He does all the things a gentleman is expected to do—honor his lady, protect her, treat her kindly and gently, attend to her feelings...and be there for her," I said, biting my lip at the last comment, cringing that I let it slip out.

"I suppose then, Edmund is a *Darcy* because I wasn't at the ball, is *that* what you're implying?" he clenched his jaw.

"I mean to do no such thing!" I shot back angrily.

"I cannot deny that it feels as such..." he said, narrowing his eyes at me.

He unleashed a well of feelings that boiled up inside and overflowed.

"Well then, *where were you*? Why *weren't* you there, if you claim to be such a *Darcy*, yourself?"

I hadn't planned to let it out. I hadn't meant to bombard him. But it sat on my tongue, like a jagged spring, ready to bounce from my lips as soon as I willed it.

He set his diary down on the seat beside him and looked up. I felt an odd quiver in the base of my stomach when our eyes met, his—wide and dark.

"I fully intended to be at the annual summer ball...I planned to be with you, to find you." He leaned in, his unruly brows softening. "Didn't you receive my letter?"

"Letter?" I questioned, "I didn't receive a letter."

"My sister called me away to Bath," he said, letting out a deep sigh. "Her husband passed away suddenly from consumption." he looked up to find me, fixated on him as he spoke. "And by some miracle of God, neither she nor the children have any symptoms of the disease..."

"Oh, Sam!" I said, my throat constricting as tears welled in the corner of my eyes. "I'm so very sorry."

How could I have been so foolish? How could I have been so...selfish?

I instinctively reached for him. The intensity of grief had made him a hollow man, and he succumbed to my touch as we embraced. We lingered in each other's arms for a moment, before he pushed himself gently, and gradually away. I felt the intense desire to reach out to him again, to hold him, but resisted.

"Forgive me?" he asked, leaning over and tenderly touching my forearm.

The boat rocked a little from side to side as he came closer to me.

"*Forgive you*?" I remarked.

"Had I been there—*that day*—you wouldn't..." he closed his eyes and took in a deep breath, "*nothing* would have happened to you..."

"Yes, but," I interjected, but he paused and put a hand up to silence me.

"I blame myself," he whispered, his mouth contorted with anguish.

He placed a hand on my cheek, the firm but soft fingers delicately touching my skin as he moved closer. I felt my heart flutter in my chest, promising to burst through at any moment—the faint thud resonating in my ears, as his touch set off fireworks within me.

I closed my eyes, feeling him move closer to me. My breath hitched in my throat, as his lips brushed softly over my own. My mind struggled to make sense of things, bouncing back and forth between Sam and Edmund at rapid speed, before succumbing to him.

In a flash, I felt him shift, and the whole world was upside down. I shot up faster than lightning and started kicking rapidly from the water. My eyes were open, but all I could see was darkness.

Somehow, the boat had tipped, and I found myself flailing. Reaching up with my fingers, I could feel the heavy, wet fabric and immediately started to thrash my arms to clear it. I realized at that moment that my skirt was covering my head. Time stood momentously still; as I clawed my way through the tangle of material, wondering if I'd ever surface again.

I felt a hand poke through the darkness as I struggled. Sam perched precariously off the side of the boat and reached down for me. I gasped, taking in a massive gulp of air as I breached the surface. He tugged at me, bracing himself against the walls of the boat, and pulled me in. He wasn't at all delicate, and I hit my elbow on the seat.

I held my hand to my chest, consciously willing my heart to slow down. My ankle was throbbing from exertion, and my elbow ached from a fresh bruise. My dress, heavy with the weight of water, hung on me like a bundle of chains draped around my chest. I must have looked shocking, a bedraggled heap of material and hair.

Sam was staring at me, a hand over his mouth, his eyes creased with humor.

"Are you...*laughing*?" I asked, astonished.

"No, Miss." he shook his head, and drops of water flew from his hair, scattering to the floorboards.

"You *are*...ugh." My eyes popped open wide, and I was so flustered I didn't know what to do with my hands.

"You are...*unbelievable*. If I could swim in this dress, I'd be off this boat!" I screeched.

My jaw dropped, and out of insanity or madness or rebellion, I started to giggle myself. The chuckle gradually turned into an all-out belly laugh.

"A fine day for a swim, Miss Bennett." He looked over at me sheepishly, as he laughed.

"Well...I can't imagine that Edmund and I would have spent the day like this," I replied.

Sam's eyes met mine and swiftly darted away. I felt my cheeks radiate with heat. A newfound reticence had developed between us within the last few minutes.

"I imagine not..." he said, rubbing his chin, and avoiding my eyes.

"Remind me to never go on a boat with you again..." I teased, as we headed back for shore.

His shirt, soaked through, pressed against his chest and with each stroke of the oar, revealed his muscular upper body. I had the sudden urge to be wrapped up in his arms, to feel the strength of his chest as it pressed against my back. A vision of him pulling me close to him from behind flashed in my mind. I shook my head, pushing the daydream out, feeling the queer sensation that he could read my thoughts.

It wasn't until we were back on shore that we realized that his diary and my copy of *Pride and Prejudice* had sunk to the bottom of the lake.

Chapter Twenty-One

It was pitch black. I was on my boat again, under the amethyst sky. It was evening, as it had been before. The waves rocked peacefully against the bow of the boat, lapping it like a giant tongue.

Then the sky grew darker. A plume of huge, gray clouds, bulbous and riotous, took shape overhead. The waves grew by the second, becoming immense and foreboding, as they lashed about.

The surfs threw the boat up and down, ravaging it from every side before I was flung off. Abruptly, the ocean started to circle around and around, forming a massive whirlpool. I was dangling with my feet into the dark abyss. The sides were swirling into a hellish hole that was growing by the second — the sea became a hungry and volatile foe. I held tight as if my fingers could grip the waves.

I felt pain, pain in my legs. And then I turned around to see the hands gripping my ankles, dirty fingernails gouging into my thighs.

The face. I couldn't erase the face from my memory. I swallowed hard, feeling the lump in my throat. A vision of the man, his deep maroon mark and bushy, black eyebrows, swirled around my head in the Stygian darkness.

I blotted my forehead with my arm, feeling the tack of the sweat stick to me. I had been screaming aloud. I looked around in a panic, trying to determine where I was when Bee rushed in. She drew a washcloth from a bucket beside the bed, wringing it out and placing it delicately on my forehead.

"Dear, dear!" she cooed. "It's a'right...you're safe...you're safe...I'm 'ere..."

I felt my eyelids grow heavy, as Bee helped me lay down again. And then, it was dark.

Chapter Twenty-Two

It was a short trip to Brighton, and Edmund found himself conflicted about leaving. He wished he had come for leisure instead of business. He wished he could have brought Catrina to the seaside.

From what he could make out from his carriage window, the sea was ablaze, sparkling like a thousand blood orange diamonds, he wanted to soak in the last bits of the sunlight, as it sparkled across the waves. He was irksome, however, as he jostled about in his seat, the instability owed to the rough and rocky terrain of the seaside village roads.

It was the inspiration he'd always come back too. Nature had never failed to impress him with its beauty, and thus it became his only devoted lover.

He dreamed about when he had freedom, traveling with Sam to all sorts of fascinating destinations, and bedding all kinds of exotic women. His daydreams often brought him back to the places he'd been and found intriguing, the fine sand of the southern Italian shoreline, the natural beauty of the Pyrenees Mountains, and the indulgences in wine and food in Greece.

Looking out behind him at the ocean, he envisioned himself sitting on the beach with a diary at hand, listening to the waves roll in. Catrina would be there too. She'd be beside him, a book on her lap. When the sun would set, he would draw her away from the beach and find a secret cave where they would make love, waking up in the morning wrapped around one another, in a tangle of legs, sand, and salty ocean air.

The fantasy often unveiled a feeling of complexity that made him uncomfortable. He indulged in his whims and daydreams... and yet, they dredged up something within him that left him...confused.

He wasn't entirely sure what the feelings were, but they clenched him in the soft pit of his stomach. *Was it guilt or regret?* He wondered as he tapped a finger on his pant leg, staring out the window blindly. *Perhaps, devotion?* No, that was *much* too strong. He assumed it was a passing ghost of a feeling, and yet, here it was *again.*

Whenever he thought of Catrina, the sensation came over him. He felt his heart race and his breathing grow shallow. He felt his body tingle, and his fingers yearn.

The fact was, he didn't want to admit it, but he had thought of her on his way here. He'd thought of her today at breakfast. He'd thought of her as he stared out at the ocean. She was ever-present now in his thoughts nearly as often as his writing!

He cleared his throat and set to ignoring the visions, knowing they'd only frustrate him. He had wanted to take out his diary and distract himself with writing prose, but the light would soon be failing him. The thought of being left to his own thoughts, was slightly alarming. He ran his fingers through his hair, which bounced back with rebellion—even his hair was defying him! He thought.

It was moments of weakness that allowed thoughts of Catrina to paralyze him, an image of her nipples as they peaked through her chemise, soft and pink like a juicy, ripe peach or the way her mouth moved, shiny and smooth, seducing him as she licked her lips. He envisioned ripping the chemise off in shreds, exposing her virginal body to him, like an ancient artifact he'd unearthed.

Then it occurred to him, at the moment, that he'd felt these feelings before, *many* times before.

Lust. *That was it.* It was lust!

He sighed, feeling a sense of relief wash over him at the revelation. Once he'd had a chance to bed her, these feelings would disappear, and he'd be free again. He laid his head back and let himself drift off to sleep, content in the control he finally had over his emotions. *She will beguile my thoughts no more.* When I return home, I shall put my plan in action, he thought.

Chapter Twenty-Three

I was tormented at night, by my nightmares of the ocean...but the days were scarcely better. All day long, I fought a battle between Edmund and Sam in my mind.

An image of Edmund, as he drew the rag across my collarbone, letting the water drip slowly to my chemise, forced its way into my mind. I envisioned myself twisting his dark curls around my fingers, as I ran my hands tenderly through his hair or the way he held me firmly against him in the forest, feeling the rhythmic beat of his heart against my ear, as he carried me to safety.

Then a vision of Sam appeared, his head leaned back, lost in laughter. I replayed the memory, relishing in the giddiness I felt whenever I heard him laugh, or the moment when his lips, brushed against mine. I drew my fingertip across my mouth, remembering the short burst of excitement I'd felt at our encounter.

I took my journal from the drawer in the nightstand and wrote one word: *Chaotic*. And shut the book.

I was interrupted from my thoughts when Bee knocked at the door and came in. I was confident that Bee's mother had a sort of premonition about naming her daughter Bee, as I watched her buzz about from place to place. She was a constant source of energy despite her ailing age. She buzzed in with my breakfast before buzzing out again, leaving the door open for Sam on her way out. She gave him a dainty curtsy and scurried toward the door.

He looked dapper compared to his standard dress and had trimmed his mustache and beard. Neither of us could make eye contact with one another. He sauntered toward the bed, rubbing his chin warily.

"How is your…ankle?" he asked pointing at my leg with his chin.

"Fine," I replied rubbing my fingers across the applique rosebuds on my blanket.

"No permanent damage was done from our impromptu swim?"

I looked up from mindlessly fondling the material, to see him give me a genuine smile.

"No." I grinned. "The doctor says I may head back home once Edmund has returned from Brighton."

There was an awkward pause between us. A pregnant elephant could have wandered in, and we'd have pretended she didn't exist.

"I have something for you...*may I?*" he motioned to the wooden chair next to the bed, and I nodded.

He pulled a package from his hand, wrapped in brown paper and tied with a bright purple ribbon, setting it delicately in my hands. I stared it at for a moment, unsure how to proceed.

"I can scarcely wait—I haven't the patience for waiting," he beamed, "go on...tear it!"

I laughed, and as if I were a child at Christmas, I tore into it.

Inside was a book with a brown cover with the title *Pride and Prejudice* in beautiful, gilded letters.

"*Pride and Prejudice!*" I cried.

"It's the first edition," he remarked.

On the cover page, Elizabeth Bennet and Lady Catherine stood together in a pose possessive of the central theme. Lady Catherine, ornamented in extravagance, holds her hand over Elizabeth's arm. Elizabeth, holding a parasol in a simple dress, stands as if awaiting instruction.

"I can't believe this is for me!" I shrieked. I put the pages to my nose and inhaled.

Sam chuckled.

"Whatever are you doing?"

"Smelling the book, of course...don't you ever smell the pages?"

"I can't say that I do...no," he said, eyeing me skeptically. I swatted coquettishly at him.

"Here..." I said, holding the book open to his nose.

He leaned over, and the scent of his cologne wafted through the air, drifting from the pulse on his neck and swirling into an exhilarating perfume of aged paper and citrus. I closed my eyes to take in the scent, hoping I was discreet enough to avoid suspicion.

"I don't smell a thing..." he admitted.

"You don't?"

He shook his head.

"Perhaps only avid readers can smell the scent of a book!" I teased. He gave me a sideways grin and shrugged.

"Perhaps..."

I picked the book up again, cradling it like it was my firstborn.

"Well...it's the least you could do..." I said coquettishly, "now that my old copy has become a favorite in the pond."

He rubbed his chin before fading into a grin.

"They are likely writing reviews on *Pride and Prejudice* in my diary, as well down there," he quipped.

We both broke out into laughter.

"I hope you didn't lose much," I added.

"Thankfully it was a newer one—hadn't but a few pages of prose—and none I'd consider exceptional," he said, looking thoughtfully away, and then back at me.

"That was so splendid of you...to get the book for me," I grinned, as I bit my lip.

"There's more..." he said, leaning over and looking at the wrapping paper strewn on the blanket.

I looked down and noticed something white peaking from beneath. He tied a ribbon around a ream of paper and placed it underneath the book, wrapping the two together. "That's for you...and if you ever need more, I have plenty."

"For me to pen my masterpiece, of course," I remarked excitedly.

"It is for you to do as you wish," he replied, looking down as a grin spread across his face.

Impulse overcame me, and I reached out to grab his hand, but he shied away, the memory of yesterday still fresh in our mind. We didn't dare look at one another either. Our eyes darted back and forth, and I settled for staring at my hands or the window. A cloud of indecisiveness hung in the air, and both of us sat idly, uncertain how to move forward.

"I suppose I should leave you to pick up where you left off..." he commented, after we'd sat in silence for a minute or two.

I raised an eyebrow at him.

"Oh, the book..." I replied, staring down at the book in my lap.

It felt good on my thighs, heavy and firm. It wasn't a thick book, but it was dense and robust.

"That was very kind of you, Sam," I said, feeling my cheeks grow pink.

"It was my pleasure, *honestly*," he avowed.

He took the cue and bowed his head at me as he made his way across the room, just in time to greet Edmund as he came in. Edmund, taken aback with Sam's presence in the room, stepped back and looked over at me.

"Back from Brighton, I see," Sam remarked.

"Mmm, indeed. Hello, Sam...Catrina. Glad to see that you are both doing well." He eyed Sam and then me.

"I've just stepped in to replace something of Catrina's that has met an unfortunate fate..." Sam added, looking back at me.

Edmund looked over at the bundle in my lap and nodded.

"It was my fault. We had taken the rowboat out for a short voyage and, by our misfortune, we tipped. Her book had fallen in the water, and we were unable to rescue it before it sank to the bottom."

"I hope your ankle is doing well after the incident..." Edmund retorted, before shooting Sam a look of disapproval.

"Yes, my ankle is healing well…I can't walk for long distances yet, but all in due time…"

Dr. Bernhoft says I can go home now, please don't make me leave, a voice in my head added. I avoided Sam's gaze. I could feel his eyes staring at me, looking through me. He knew the truth that I could leave at any moment if I wished. But he kept mum.

"Very well then…" Edmund replied, jutting his chin subtly at Sam.

They stood awkwardly for a moment before Sam turned to leave. He gave Edmund and me, a small bow before heading out. I could hear his footsteps treading slowly down the hall.

Edmund made his way to my bedside and sat beside me. I could see the depth of blue in his eyes, just as I could see the glint of gold in Sam's. They were such profoundly different men: Sam— a creature of forests, water, earth and humor and Edmund—a being of art, sophistication, and fire.

His eyes drew to the vase beside my bed. He had Bee keep a steady profusion of freshly cut flowers in the vase, and the ones there now, were limp, sullen white daisies whose heads had curled inward and browned around the edges of the petals.

"I must first do something about that," he said, before walking toward the door, stepping out momentarily and returning with a single white rose.

"Are you aware of the language of flowers?" he asked, before sitting back down beside me.

I shook my head.

"Flowers have meanings."

I examined the bud, rubbing the petals and enjoying the velvety sensation between my fingers.

"I haven't studied the meanings of them much...thankfully, I have a friend who is a horticulturist," he added.

"And..." I looked up at him, "what does a singular white rose mean?"

He cocked his head to one side.

"Perhaps that is a mystery for you to examine," he crooned.

I scrunched my lips together and looked back at the rose, the thorns had been cut off, leaving the smooth green stem and waxy leaves. I put the bud to my nose and inhaled deeply. The sweet and intoxicating aroma filled my nostrils.

"I am glad to be back from Brighton...but I am afraid, I come as the bearer of distressing news." Edmund stared down at his hands folding them. He turned to look over his shoulder, ensuring the room belonged only to us. His eyes darted nervously from me to the doorway and back.

"I have something I must tell you..."

I sat up, pulling myself closer to the bed frame and closer to him.

"What is it?" I whispered.

"You see…" he began, "it's about Sam…"

My pulse began to rise.

"I did not go to Brighton for pleasure," he stated.

"Yes, I know. Bee told me that you have business there."

I blinked rapidly.

"Yes, I suppose I *do* have business there. But not the type of business you would expect…I go to deliver a package." He narrowed his eyes.

"A package?" I leaned back, folding my hands together.

"Yes, I'm afraid so."

"I don't understand," I frowned.

Edmund leaned forward, arms on his knees, hands clasped.

"Sam and I went to Brighton for a holiday a few years ago. We celebrated much like anyone celebrates when they are on holiday." A smile readily came to his lips at the memory.

I nodded, unsure where the story was headed…or how it involved Sam.

"While we were there, Sam met Marianna. She was an artist and he a poet. She was a beautiful woman, whose father owned an Inn in town," he continued.

"They spent days together on the beach—and nights." He glanced at me, hoping I inferred the subtly of his statement, "I hardly saw them the entire holiday…"

A small flame started in the pit of my stomach, but I shoved it down.

"She found herself with child…shortly before we left." His jaw tensed at the observation.

"A child?" My voice sounded foreign to me as I said the word. "Sam's child?"

I felt my palms bead with sweat.

Edmund nodded slowly, his dark waves bounced whenever he moved, one wayward curl, brushed the center of his forehead, projecting him in a more juvenile light.

"But *why*…why didn't he go to Brighton? Doesn't he *care* to see the child? To see his mistress?" I cried.

The words tasted bitter on my tongue. Sam…*my* Sam has a child…*and* a lover! I swallowed the marble-sized lump that had formed in my throat, as the tears welled in the corner of my eyes.

Edmund rubbed his neck nervously.

"The problem is…his mistress is married to another man," he added casually.

I felt my jaw drop. I was too ashamed to cry in front of Edmund, but a renegade tear slipped from my eye and plopped on my hand, as I swiftly attempted to brush it away.

"When they were discovered, he was chased out by the entire village. Sam agreed to pay for the child to attend private school, but Marianna's husband said he could never step foot in the village again..."

"And so...that's why *you* go?" I concluded regretfully.

"Yes..."

I looked at *Pride and Prejudice* on my lap with a twinge of disgust, setting it down beside me on the table, unable and unwilling, to hold it any longer.

"I would not have divulged this to you, but *I fear for you.* I would hate for the same fate to befall you..."

I looked over at him incredulously.

"I beg your pardon," I retorted.

He took my hands in his and held them softly. I noted the differences immediately between his hands and Sam's. Sam's were much larger, brawnier, Edmund's were smaller and softer.

"Please forgive me, I felt it necessary for you to know the character of someone whom you spend so much time with...I care for you," he said softly as he stood up. "I should leave you now, to get more rest."

He bent down and kissed my hand gently, before leaving the room. I sat there for a long time, staring blankly at the door.

Chapter Twenty-Four

Ezra leaned back inhaling the thick steam swirling up from his bathtub. It was a cooler night for summer, and with the window cracked, he could feel the draft of wind inhale and exhale like a large set of lungs. The potent scent of his soap, lemon and bergamot, wafted up with the steam. It had been a long day of apprenticeship with his father, and he felt the welcoming call of the warm water.

He was only interrupted twice, and for these instances, he hadn't minded it. Niamh had come to add more hot water and had also come to give him a towel. He found the maid Niamh to be particularly attractive despite the Irish accent she had. She was thinner than the others, and younger too with an hourglass shape she hid under her maids dress and apron. He liked to imagine what she looked like underneath it from time to time but pushed the thought away tonight to focus on more important things.

Baffling him the most, was the encounter he had with Lord Troy. *Was Lord Troy embarrassed by him*? Ezra so seldom mingled with others that he questioned his own ability to socialize. He much preferred the sanctuary of the forest to human interaction. There, he could be at peace with himself, without owing anyone an explanation for his behavior.

He rolled the thoughts over in his mind, wondering if it hadn't been Leonard that killed his chances of enjoying the night out with Lord Troy.

Even more peculiarly, *who was the man in the group he'd recognized?* Somewhere in the recesses of his mind, he had seen the man. He was burly and stood taller than most men with a thick scruff of black facial hair. Over one eye, he had a purple splotch that, upon closer inspection, appeared to be a birthmark.

He sighed and leaned back in the tub, placing a rag over his eyes. The smooth, hard finish was a welcoming place of rest from the day. He felt the heat soak into his skin, leaving his fingers and toes pruney. He wiggled them under the water exploring the slight wake they made, when *all the sudden*, it hit him.

He sat up, sloshing water over the sides of the tub and splashing it onto the tiles below. He *knew* where he'd seen that man before.

"Bloody Hell!" he said aloud.

That's him! That's the man he saw in the woods, the day he encountered Lord Troy and Catrina.

"Jesus Bloody Hell!" he cursed, feeling instantaneously guilty for his swearing, he signed a "Hail Mary" over his chest.

As he stood up to dry off, the realization hit him. Lord Troy *knew* the man. It was an unsettling revelation that left Ezra reeling. He *must* tell someone, as soon as possible.

Chapter Twenty-Five

Tired of being penned up, I hobbled my way to the garden.

The estate was becoming in the twilight. In the moon's glow, everything took on a new life — the neatly cut rows of lawn transformed into dusky gray, the trees, surrounding the border, loomed like small mountains in the distance, and the warm, yellow light from the windows flickered against the dark. Somewhere, not far from here, a gardenia plant's strong aroma filled the night air with a mocking sense of romance. An accompanying night bird's song made the scene unbearably poetic. *Such irony*, I thought.

I dipped my hand in the fountain, cupping some of the water delicately in my palm. The twinkling lights from the windows were caught in the reflection in my hand—like sparkling golden gems, that disappeared as the water sifted through my fingers. I sat there for a while, gazing thoughtfully at the reflection, when I caught a glimpse of a figure.

Startled, I clutched my heart, nearly toppling over in the process.

"Has anyone ever told you that you should be an actress instead?" Sam eyed me.

I took in a deep breath.

"It's the perfect night for stargazing, don't you think?" he asked, sitting down beside me after giving me a helping hand.

I didn't make eye contact with him. I was struggling with sorting through the troublesome information about him that I'd become privy too.

"May I ask...what *is it* that..." he paused mid-sentence, and I looked over at him waiting for him to finish, but he shook his head. "Perhaps, I should leave you to your thoughts..."

"Is it true?" I interrupted.

His eyes became shadowed in the dark, but the moon had sculpted the outlines of his face leaving it aglow. He had prominent cheekbones and a strong masculine jaw that made him handsome—in a rugged way. I found a spark of arousal spread through me, unsuspectingly. I was so bewildered by it that I shook my head to dismiss the thought.

"Perhaps I do not have any right to ask you this...but after our..."

There was a brief pause where I attempted to collect my thoughts before Sam interrupted.

"Kiss? You can say it, Catrina. Kiss!" He narrowed his eyes at me. A pang of regret filled the air, and I wondered if I had hurt him.

He met my eyes, and I felt the immediate need to blurt it out before I lost my courage.

"Do you have a mistress?"

He leaned back, swallowing hard.

"I beg your pardon?"

"I heard... someone has told me, that you have a mistress."

He shook his head and made a grunt of disgust. I felt the knot in my stomach twisting and growing at a substantial rate.

"Me?" He pointed a finger to his chest. "Is that what you think? That *I* have a mistress?"

I didn't mention the child.

"What do you think? Do *you* think I have a mistress?" he asked, the bitterness tainting his tongue as the words shot out. I couldn't bear to meet his glance.

Did I believe it?

Some part of me did. Some envious being that lived within me had to know — was dying to know, the truth.

"I had to know...I didn't know...I had heard..." I stuttered, fumbling for words, for reasoning, for rationality.

"What difference would it make to you anyway?" he scoffed. "I bid you a good night, Catrina. May you rest easy, you and the Lord. It appears as though you are made for one another..." He bowed curtly, before turning and tramping off into the darkness.

I felt as if someone had punched me in the stomach. I was light-headed. I grabbed hold of the ledge, for something to hold onto, as the world spun around me in dizzying, spectacular agony.

Chapter Twenty-Six

Edmund stared off onto the vast estate lawn, feeling the effects of his alcohol gradually wear off. It was dark, and he enjoyed the sight of the low hanging black clouds draped across the deep blue of the sky.

He heard laughter down the hall and resigned himself to company. Sitting up a little straighter, and attempting to appear a bit more alert than he was. Typically, he'd lose himself to the world of intoxication—drowning out the dullness and madness that he felt—with every swig of his amber gold. But lately, he'd put himself on a probationary period to preserve his self-image with Catrina.

He daydreamt of her often—visions of her long, graceful neck—swan-like as she turned her head and let her dark hair fall around it, her bright, brown eyes—big for her face, but entrancing, the soft, silky skin on her back — that he so desperately wished to touch. He envisioned himself undressing her, and felt the tingle of pleasure run through him.

With every glimpse of her in his mind's eye, he felt weightless. A strange and new feeling he hadn't felt before— this weightless euphoria, like a drug. Like the countless glasses of champagne, he'd partake in after dinner.

He had an addictive personality, he'd known that. Having had trouble with his obsessions with gambling, and now he'd found a new addiction that was serving him well — drawn to her like a moth to a flame.

He found himself struggling to escape the abyss, losing himself in it. It had become harder and harder to come back ashore, and he'd wondered a few times if he would ever let himself sink.

Drawing him back to earth, the voices in the hall grew nearer. The door opened quietly, and it took him by surprise to see Sam standing there. He turned to nod, and gazed back out at the window, relaxing slightly. The crowd Sam had been with, carried on without him down the hall, the echo of their chatter and laughter growing quieter and quieter until it was gone.

"To what do I owe the pleasure, brother?" Edmund took another puff of his cigar, watching the orange blaze burn at the end with the fascination of a child—the mind's way of processing the alcohol still present in his blood.

"*Brother*?" Sam scoffed. "I thought that about us once..." The flickering light danced like phantoms over his face, casting him in a malevolent glow. "What have you told Catrina?"

Edmund took an insouciant puff of his cigar, watching as the smoke rolled out of his mouth. He lingered there for a while, dazed by the gray cloud that he'd created. Whether to further irritate Sam or to come up with an excuse, he didn't know— perhaps, it had been both.

"You and I both know that I have no mistress," Sam started out coolly. He narrowed his eyes at Edmund, who cast a carefree glance towards him before gazing elsewhere.

"I fear that I know so little about you anymore..." Edmund droned as he whirled his chair around to face Sam.

"I fear that I feel the same," Sam shot back, before leaning menacingly over him. "You shall stop feeding her lies about my life...and tell her the *truth* about yours!" His voice boomed.

"I don't recall saying anything about you at all...in fact, if I had, I would have only sung your good graces— as I always do..." he said nonchalantly, as he snuffed the cigar out and leaned forward, looking directly into Sam's eyes.

"I find that incomprehensibly difficult to believe," Sam retorted.

"What do you want with her anyway? She's nothing more than a fisherman's daughter..." Edmund glared at Sam—the dark cascading the features of his face, exposing only the whites of his eyes and teeth.

"I should be asking you the same!" Sam shouted back, as he pounded a fist onto the desk, causing the paper to shake and a pen to roll from its place onto the floor.

"Whether she is a fisherman's daughter...or the Duchess of York, a lord always gets what a lord wants..." Edmund hissed.

Sam huffed, drawing his fists in tightly to his sides. Edmund watched incredulously, tapping his fingers together. He eyed Sam, who stood there lost in between sensibility and anger until he finally relented and turned to leave.

"I bid you good night, My Lord," he said, giving a terse bow before he tromped off to the door.

Chapter Twenty-Seven

Edmund burst into my room after breakfast, wanting to whisk me away to the city. I dressed hurriedly, grabbing a piece of bacon on my way out, and then we were off on our grand adventure.

I couldn't help but notice, that something was distracting him. I attempted to make small talk, but his answers were short. He was drawn to the window, watching as the earth bobbed subtly up and down with each turn of the wheels. I was grateful when the carriage finally came to a stop in front of the Crystal Palace.

I gazed down at my feet, listening to the satisfying crunch of gravel beneath them as we strolled along. There was a steady drone of laughter and conversation abuzz, as couples picnicked and families gathered. The mood was as light and optimistic as the days' weather.

I studied the sketches of the Crystal Palace as a child—wondering what it would be like to see it one day— and now here I was, standing before it. It was awe-inspiring not only for its immensity but also for the sheer amount of glass required to build it. Thousands of panes of glass lined its outer frame— standing like a massive mirror—encapsulating and reflecting the park's glory back to the earth.

I opened my journal, hurriedly adding notes:

—Trip to London with Edmund to Crystal Palace. Most remarkable. Like a mirror to the earth. Beauty in reflection.

Edmund looked on with curiosity.

"Whatever is it that you're doing?"

"Whenever I don't have a chance to write freely, I jot down some quick notes so that I can remember the day, then I go back and write when I have the time."

"Mmm, interesting." He looked on, meeting my gaze, and then his eyes shot off into the distance, lost in thought.

"Perhaps I shall bring my diary along more often...it's quite the *hobby* to get into...*writing*...I suppose it's utterly harmless though...isn't it?"

He'd meant, of course, that it was a harmless hobby for a woman. *Was it a harmless hobby for Jane Austen? Mary Shelley? Elizabeth Barrett Brown?* I felt my fingers twitch and my shoulders tense. Sensing the immediate need to change the conversation, I spoke up.

"Did you know," I asked, looking up from the walking path we had been strolling along, "that my uncle had his hand in designing this place?"

It was his turn to raise a brow. He shot me a dubious expression.

"I give you my sacred honor!" I held a hand up, gently mocking him.

He smirked and took a look back behind us—where it stood like a colossal conservatory—to admire it again.

"That must have been quite the feat!"

~

We stopped at Knightsbridge to browse, after exploring the Crystal Palace, and then headed off to the Burlington Arcade where Edmund purchased a leather-bound journal, pens and a pad of stationery.

He offered to buy me whatever I wanted, but I declined. I only agreed to a meat pie and ginger beer, after he claimed it was one of his guilty pleasures when he visited the city.

"I never leave the city without one of these," he said, as he handed me a meat pie from the merchant, the scent of warm gravy wafted from it in tendrils into the air.

He watched as I took my first bite—eyes wide with anticipation. I bit down into the crispy dough, and the juicy hot meat spurted out, startling me into laughter, as I wiped it from my chin. He gave me a lopsided grin, before leaning in and wiping some from my cheek, brushing his fingers delicately across my face until they cupped my chin.

"There," he said, satisfied.

I took a swallow of the ginger beer to swish down the contents of the pie, relishing the light and bubbly tingle it left on my tongue. He gave me a nod, as I took another sip, enjoying the feel of the hot pie in my stomach and the refreshing ginger beer in my throat.

We found a green space nearby to relax in, and took up residence on a gently sloping hill, far enough from the road that the sound of clattering carriages was a distant thought.

We could hear the "clack" of a mallet, as a group of men and ladies played croquet across the field.

Along the walkway, a group of rowdy boys passed, playing hoop and stick. A brawl broke out between them, ending in a few scrapes and scuffs. When the altercation finished, they picked up the hoop and stick, laughing and frolicking as if nothing had happened.

A woman and her daughter strolled by, pushing lavish baby carriages. The daughter, with a head full of golden curls, stopped to tend to her baby doll. She watched on, as her mother lovingly scooped up her sibling in her arms, rocking the baby slowly back and forth. The baby let out a soft cry, followed by a succumbing whimper, as his mother gracefully lulled him back to sleep.

"Queen's weather," Edmund remarked, as he put a hand into the air.

We'd both finished our pies and ginger beers, and neither of us had moved. The consensus, as gathered from my corset now digging into my sides, was that we'd felt too full to get up, and we're both enjoying the entertainment.

He leaned back onto the slope, pressing his elbows into the earth. Following his lead, I sat back; the grass tickled my palms, the refreshing scent of it drifting up from my fingers.

"Your ankle...is it well?" he asked, meeting my gaze.

I looked down at my ankle instinctively and nodded.

"Very well...thank you."

"And it's healed?"

I nodded.

The bruise had all but disappeared, leaving only a secondary crater shaped yellow spot behind.

I wondered temporarily, how this would alter our growing interests with one another. *What would happen between us when I did eventually go back to Aunt Beatrice and Uncle Harold's...or further away, back home?*

I pushed the thought aside for a moment, taking in the beauty of the sky above us—a cheery, brilliant blue. Thick tufts of puffy, white clouds hung from an invisible string—appearing entirely too heavy to be suspended in the blue without support.

"Let's play a game," I suggested.

"Mmm?" Edmund turned his head to me, the sky a near match to the blue of his irises.

"Let's find objects in the clouds," I said, tilting my head back to gaze above. I felt Edmund's eyes on my neck. Slowly, he tipped his head back, propping himself up by his elbows.

"Very well then..." he agreed, scrunching his lips with concentration as he studied the sky. "There...that one!" He pointed a finger at a large, bulbous cloud.

"What's that?"

"Byron...do you see...even his tongue is sticking out," he said with a chuckle.

I tipped my head, analyzing the shape.

"So it is," I giggled.

I looked out at the sky, the clouds moving lazily across the blue emptiness.

"There." I pointed up at a round cloud with a peculiar wisp of a tail.

"And what might that be?" Edmund rolled over to face me, one elbow still propped in the grass, his eyes hooded with intrigue.

"A lamb shank...of course," I fluttered my eyelashes at him playfully, and we both laughed.

"I suppose Ag..." he began, but stopped short, swallowing a lump in his throat before looking back up at the sky.

"No, I don't suppose Agatha would be excited about finding a cloud shaped like a lamb shank," I gave him a sly grin before looking back up at the sky. He rolled back over also, eyes fixed to the heavens.

"There!" he pointed, "it's the Crystal Palace."

"Goodness me!" I said, looking at an unidentifiable mass of cloud, "that looks nothing like the Crystal Palace!"

He raised his shoulders, a smirk on his face.

"It does to me." he ran his finger along the edges of the cloud.

"I have to say, that is rather...*imaginative*," I cooed.

He gave me a broad grin, as a curl fell across his forehead.

"Edmund."

"Mmm?"

"I must ask you something..."

He looked over at me, head cocked.

"When I asked Sam the other day about...well, you know...about the mistress and—"

"Yes...I know..." he interjected, averting his eyes to the ground, where he had plucked a piece of grass and was now shredding it between his fingers.

"He...got very cross with me..." I added, attempting to meet his eyes again. I bit my lip, feeling my brow furrow.

Edmund sat up from his elbows, dusting his palms off before putting his knees up.

"No one likes to admit their weaknesses, Catrina," he said, glancing at me, before plucking another piece of grass and shredding it. When there was nothing left, he dusted his hands again and sat up straight.

"You must listen..." he looked around, eyes darting from side to side, "you cannot trust Sam. He has a history that you know nothing about."

I felt my forehead and stomach simultaneously tighten.

"Whatever do you mean?"

I pressed my arms against my chest.

"Well, you only know two of his secrets: Marianna and the child, but I assure you, there are more...plenty more." He sighed deeply.

Chapter Twenty-Eight

Ezra's mind ran a million miles a minute. He had run through every possibility, before coming to the conclusion that it was absolutely necessary to tell someone what he knew.

He was a reasonable man, and not anyone who would want to be involved in any kind of drama, least of all any involving potential for his cousin to be wed to a Lord. But he always was a man of the truth, and thus felt it was his duty to give her the information—be damned with the outcome.

He didn't want to alarm his mother and father, and certainly not Agatha. She was already sensitive about the interactions between Edmund and Catrina and bringing this up to her would devastate her.

He set out on his horse Ollie, giving his parents vague answers about his proposed whereabouts. It was a beautiful summer day, and he hadn't had a chance to take Ollie out in quite some time, what with being held up with his father's business negotiations. He was a passenger in everything, he thought.

He patted the shiny black mane of his horse and smiled at the thought of the freedom he'd felt, as he galloped away. He had forgotten how much he loved the feel of the horse's muscular body beneath him and the feeling of the wind as it brushed past him.

"Good boy, Ollie," he murmured.

~

Like a line drawn from the sky, the wilderness relinquished to the meticulous bedding of bright green that was Lord Troy's estate lawn. The tall trees ran parallel, in a contrast of man-made and nature that was startling.

He could see the sky, faded blue and free of obstruction, holding the sun on its descent into the horizon. In the distance, a manor graced itself, perched high on the hilltop like a mama bird on a nest, surrounded by soft rolling hills that made way for gardens and hedgerows.

Despite his initial feeling of freedom, the overwhelming and debilitating thought continued to drone on in his head—*what if he was wrong?*

He held tight to the reins, feeling the grip lessen and slip in between his hands from the sweat. The oily film made it difficult to keep his glasses from sliding down his nose. He pushed them up, for what felt like, the hundredth time and tipped his head back.

His mind kept dragging him back to the moment outside the pub, replaying the sequence where he could identify, with certainty, the man with the red mark on his forehead. He had never seen another man with such a mark. And to have seen two men with the same mark in the same spot would be... unlikely. More than unlikely, he thought—*highly improbable.*

This thought enlivened him, further motivating him on his mission. The tightening that had threatened to consume him lessened its grip in his stomach.

He sighed, taking in the fresh air as he slowed from a gallop to a canter. He was getting close.

~

The door flung open, allowing the afternoon light to spill inward and Ezra was startled to find Sam, who seemed in a hurry himself, on his way out. Sam stopped though, and turned to Ezra, giving him a bow. Ezra nervously rotated his hat between his fingers, attempting to make words from all the thoughts that permeated his mind. The sound of a grandfather clock punctuated the silence with its sharp 'tick tock.'

"Is there something the matter?" Sam asked, as he rose from his bow.

Ezra hesitated for a moment, the round lenses of his glasses making his pale blue eyes look like owls, wide and alarmed. He inhaled deeply, before blurting out.

"We must talk!"

Sam's brows furrowed.

"I do apologize, but what matter is it that we shall speak of?"

Ezra looked around, content with the absence of anyone else in the large foyer. The light streamed in from the afternoon sun and fell harshly across the Persian rugs that ran the length of the hall, tainting their rich burgundy and yellow colors.

"It is a matter of much importance, regarding the Lord...and his acquaintances." Ezra blinked, his bright blue eyes peering from behind his round rims nervously.

Imelda had appeared seemingly from nowhere, startling both Ezra and Sam. She had taken up behind a doorway into the parlor, and rounded the corner at that moment, her green cat-eyes narrowed and alert.

"I believe I may have something that would also be of interest to you..."

She held out a piece of paper, which had been folded and unfolded numerous times by the creases, and Sam reached for it. He read the first line, before looking back at both Imelda and Ezra, eyes wide and mouth agape.

Chapter Twenty-Nine

By the time we left the green, the sun was setting, leaving a warm orange glow in the horizon. The life of the green changed during the twilight hours. The chaotic and playful spirit of the day gave way to a mellow, somnolent force.

The children, who once filled the hills with their games and laughter, had dissipated, drifting off in all directions towards home and the assumed warm dinners that would fill their bellies. In their place, adults funneled in, roaming across the walkways toward town, the spirit of night evident in their actions and speech.

We spent the better half of an hour meandering through fields and pastures, making our way back to Edmund's estate, savoring every last bit of the glorious summer afternoon. It wasn't only the weather or even the magnificent sights of the day that I was savoring. I had a dizzying sense of euphoria that came over me, leaving me light-headed.

Our conversation—which had started out on neutral territory, identifying the most influential authors' of our era— had transformed somewhere between here and the city limits. It blossomed into something more *personal*—delving into the stories of our childhood, our future goals, and our biggest fears.

We meandered our way to the edge of town when Edmund noticed the sky was changing—burning out from the orange blaze of the evening to the cerulean blue of a storm at sea. The thick and white, puffy clouds of the afternoon were slowly transforming—blanketing the darkened sky in an ominous profusion of gray. There was a storm on the way, and it was coming on quick.

"We aren't far, but I fear we won't make it." Edmund motioned to the sky.

All at once—as if his words provoked the sky—the heavens opened up, and big, fat drops of rain fell, hissing as it came down in sheets. It was so thick that it looked like opaque curtains closing off the world in front of us.

Just then, a crack of lightning flashed overhead with a long, low pitched boom of thunder. Startled by the clash, I fell forward and landed on my palms in the mud. It was so dark now; it looked as though night had fallen in a matter of minutes.

Edmund swiftly helped me to my feet, pulling me towards his chest—pressing his body to me. The heat rose from his skin, as the brisk drops of water flooded down on us. Somewhere deep within me, a wildfire was kindled and spread throughout my body.

"Are you hurt?" he had to yell over the hiss of the rain.

I shook my head, feeling the water flick off in all directions from my hair. I took a glance at my palms for abrasions, finding them to be red, but otherwise unscathed.

"Hurry, come closer," he shouted, waving to me in the darkness. All I could make out was his silhouette, as it flailed through the storm.

He grabbed hold of my hand, and we ran together down the road—the mud flinging up behind us with each hasty footstep.

The earth was alive with the overpowering scent of ozone, as another crack of lightning rang out through the sky. It webbed against the darkness, like veins, illuminating us for a fraction of a moment.

I grabbed hold of his hand, racing along beside him, fighting the slick beads of rain that slid between our fingers.

My skirts were so thoroughly soaked they clung to me like iron weights, dragging me down to the ground. I felt the strange and uncontrollable urge to laugh and threw my head back letting the rain hit my face.

We increased our pace, slipping and sliding over the mud until we eventually made it to the estate lawn.

"Follow me," he bellowed, the sound of his voice almost disappearing in the drone of thunder.

I looked ahead, cupping a hand over my eyes to see the blurred vision of a building. It took me a few glances to make out the characteristic atrium shape of a conservatory.

Running the last few steps with renewed vigor, he thrust himself against the door, and we nearly flopped over one another. He hurriedly shut it behind us as he held onto my arm.

"That's better," he snickered, the water rolling down his hair and dripping from his nose.

"We're absolutely sodden," I chuckled, taking in the full weight of my ensemble. I hadn't noticed until I looked up, that he was studying me.

"You are quite handsome when you're wet," he said, with a smirk. His eyebrows were glistening with moisture. I gave a clumsy curtsy, and we both sniggered.

There was a strong aroma of rain, wet earth, and vegetation inside the conservatory. A variety of plants lined the walls—orchids, palms, bromeliads, and exotic ferns, splayed across the ground like a miniature jungle—spreading upward against the glass—soaking up whatever light cascaded in from the outside. In the center, under the dome, a few wrought iron pieces of furniture sat— four chairs, diagonal of one another, and two couches, each with red and white pinstriped cushions and pillows.

Edmund peeled at his shirt—the wet cotton clinging to him like a second skin. Finally free, he dropped it to the floor with a satisfied grin. I was shivering, but it seemed entirely unrelated to the chill of the rain.

He gazed at me, our eyes meeting, answering an unasked question within them. He took my hand in his, and pressed my fingertips gently to his chest, drawing them slowly down toward his navel. The hairs sprang away from my touch, making me flinch. I pulled my hand away instinctively, as if it burnt.

Patiently, and without words, he took my hand in his again, seductively drawing the lines of my palm with his fingertips. He spread my fingers out, before pressing the whole of my palm to his chest again. I sighed, relinquishing my resolve. I closed my eyes and willed myself to let go.

He ran my hand down his chest again, over the soft curl of his hairs until I finally reached his navel. My thighs tightened, and I felt a pulsation that I knew only with desire.

 I leaned back, allowing his hands to remove my corset, dropping it to the side with a heavy thud. My breasts, free from constraint, dropped gently to my chest under my chemise. My nipples puckered at the draft of brisk air, brushing the inside of the wet cotton and exposing their pink flesh. I shivered reflexively as they grew more sensitive to touch.

 He came closer now, pressing his hips to my own, his smooth and taut hip bones protruding awkwardly against my fleshier thighs. His eyes, consumed fully by his pupils, were now wide and black. The rain pounded down on the glass panes in a symphony of white noise, but I could scarcely hear it over his heavy breathing. His nostrils flared, arousing me with anticipation, as he untied my skirts and crinoline. When he finished, I stepped cautiously out of each, wondering if he could see me tremble.

 He took my hands and placed them on his trousers, willing me to undo them. I fumbled nervously, my hands twitching as I loosened them. I watched wide-eyed as they fell to the floor beneath him.

He stepped back, taking me in— a look of deep satisfaction and contentment crossed his face. I felt myself hunch inward at the vulnerability, crossing my arms and folding them over my chest.

"You have nothing to be afraid of," he whispered, a raw huskiness present in his voice as he came closer.

I closed my eyes, taking in the sensation of his hands as they moved over my curves. He ran his fingers along my collarbone, tracing them up to my chin, where they grazed my lips. He bent inward, slowly and tentatively, pressing his lips to mine, quiet at first, and then hungry.

We searched frantically, consumed with the desire to become one with each other, our arms and hands going in all directions before he guided me, pushing me gently toward a couch where he laid me down. I felt his body on mine, the soft, slick skin molding into the more ample portions of my feminine chest. For a brief moment, I could see the encompassing gray of the sky above, the fat drops of rain plopping on the window pane unceremoniously, before rolling down to the earth.

"Are you...*alright*?" he whispered, meeting my eyes. I nodded and bit my lip, willing him to continue.

He pulled my chemise up to my hips, taking his time to do it slowly. I felt myself quiver uncontrollably as he entered me—sending a shiver up my spine that splintered in a thousand directions. It was exhilarating— a simultaneous sense of pleasure and pain that radiated from between my thighs, as the sensation pulled me into myself at every thrust.

I held onto his shoulders, feeling the rhythm of his movements as our bodies met, the residue of rain gliding across our bodies. I bit down gently on his shoulder, tasting his moist skin. He tasted of sweat and male effort.

With each thrust, he grew more determined, his focus steady and intent on his actions. I closed my eyes, drawing him closer to me as I pressed him inward with my thighs, feeling the sleek wetness between my legs. I gasped at the pain, but he didn't notice...or didn't seem deterred by it, for he seemed to grow more restless, his eyes glazed with arousal.

He lunged deeper and harder, as his rhythm grew faster. I held tight to him, forcing myself into him—the thirst and fire that flickered within, being quenched by the very motion of his hips. I bit my lip, holding onto him until he let out a primal groan. He quivered—his whole body shaking as he held me firmly, his chest rising and falling in quick succession.

We laid there for a long time after, listening to the patter of the rain above our heads.

~

When we finally reached the manor, we shoved open the door, and fell into a heap on the floor—the water dripping into dirty puddles on the marble beneath us. Our laughter echoed across the hall, as we attempted to untangle ourselves.

He sat up, pulling me up with him, our foreheads touching. His eyes creased, divulging secrets between us, and brewing a silent storm within me with his touch. He kissed me affectionately, his lips grazing mine and lingering. I felt a tender tug in between my thighs—a reminder of our new intimacy.

Dazed and light-headed, I looked up to find Imelda glaring at us from above, her eyes brimmed with tears. Before Edmund could say a word, she spun around, her hair whipping from side to side as she raced off in the other direction sobbing, her feet tapping wildly across the floor.

Edmund cleared his throat, taking his time to stand up before helping me to my feet. I felt his eyes on me, as I looked down the hall. He reached for my hands, taking them in his.

"I do not care what Imelda thinks of this..." he raised his hands slightly to inform me that he was referring to "us," but I felt a shiver run down my spine.

Imelda reappeared momentarily with Sam and Ezra by her side, and I knew then what was bothering me. Sam's face was contorted with rage...or sorrow. It took everything in me to look at him—his broad, beautiful grin nothing but a memory. I felt my stomach twist into a knot, boiling and churning. I bit my lip, hard.

Imelda, tears streaking her cheeks, turned with a jolt of her head, her chin held high as she walked briskly away and disappeared back down the hall.

"What do we have here?" Sam asked, his voice choked with emotion despite his apparent effort to remain collected.

I rubbed my hands nervously together. Edmund stood up straighter, his shoulders squared as he faced Sam.

"I do beg your pardon, have you forgotten your place? Now if you'll please, Catrina and I must be getting back to our activities for the evening," Edmund shot back, brushing shoulders with Sam, his nostrils flared with anger.

Something came alive in Sam's eyes, at the comment, and he put an arm out, pressing his hands against Edmund forcibly. Edmund leaned back, eyes wide with astonishment.

"Have you forgotten whose manor this is?" he snarled.

"Ezra...will you do the honors?" Sam asked, turning to Ezra and ignoring Edmund.

Ezra, who before now, stood with his eyes downcast in the corner, took a deep breath and stood to face Edmund.

"What is the meaning of this?" Edmund scoffed.

"I know..." Ezra began, feeling emboldened, "that you are acquaintances with the man that attacked Catrina..."

Their eyes meet, Edmund's narrowing before he turned away. I looked at all three men, as they glared at one another.

"That's blasphemy," Edmund scoffed, pushing his shoulder into Sam in an attempt to walk past, but Sam's broad shoulder acted as a blockade, and Edmund was jarred back, looking somewhat stunned and annoyed.

"Ask him...Catrina. Ask him if he knows the man that attacked you in the forest." Sam's gaze shifted from Edmund's face, to mine, stoic and emotionless.

I felt a wave of nausea roll through me. The pit in my stomach began devouring anything in its wake—feeding on the unknown— and threatening to swallow me whole. *No.* I shook my head. *It's not possible, he wouldn't. Ezra is mistaken. Edmund was the only one there to save me. In fact, had it not been for Edmund...*

A shiver ran up my spine.

"Ask him!" Sam shouted, startling me.

I walked up to Edmund and swallowed hard, feeling my jaw tense.

"Is it true?" I asked, no louder than a whisper.

He looked down, his eyes the same intense blue as the open sky.

"You cannot possibly believe that!" he snapped. "And from Sam nonetheless! I know of no such beast."

"That's a lie!" Sam fumed, throwing his hands up, he was moving about now, pacing uncomfortably.

Edmund turned to me, his hand outstretched in my direction. I bit my lip hard, tasting the metallic hint of blood on my tongue. It was a moment, a fraction of a second and yet time stood still. I looked at Sam, with his large brown eyes, pleading, and then at Edmund, his face contorted with rage. Everything was pivoting on me.

I started to reach for Edmund when Ezra interrupted me.

"Catrina..." He shook his head vigorously. My hand froze in space, halfway between my body and Edmund's. He looked me in the eyes. "I know this to be the truth..."

I swallowed hard now, looking back and forth between Ezra, Sam, and Edmund.

"What is it that I have here?" Sam interjected, pulling a folded piece of paper from his pocket. He pretended to read it, skimming over the words, before holding it out to Edmund.

"Whatever it is, it's hardly important or of any relevance to me. Come along now, Catrina," Edmund snapped.

But I stayed put, feeling both the urge to run and the simultaneous urge to remain rooted to the ground, peering now curiously over at Sam and the mystery letter.

"Oh," Sam spun around, walking casually, an air of disdain in his voice "But...*it is*."

He turned then to face me, and I felt the icy fingers of doubt run along my spine.

Edmund looked down his long nose at Sam, who stood just inches away now. "I highly doubt that..."

"Catrina," Sam called to me. "Do you recall when I left to see my sister in Bath?"

I nodded slowly, feeling my chest tense up.

"This letter—the one I hold in my hands, is the letter I sent to Edmund with my regards for missing the ball."

He handed me the letter.

I have been called away to Bath by my sister for an urgent family emergency. I looked up at Sam, attempting to read his blank expression, but to no avail. I read through it, line for line, pausing at the phrase: *Please send my condolences of my absence to Catrina.*

A pang in my heart resonated like a coin falling down an empty well, tumbling and free-falling in the dark until it hit bottom with a loud "clank."

"You *bloody* bastard!" I shouted, narrowing my eyes at Edmund. "How *could* you? How could you lie to me?"

"That's enough of this. I will tolerate no more of these barbarous lies! Every word that comes from Sam's mouth is a falsehood, and I will play no more to this party!" Edmund hissed, backing himself up against a wall. His words shot from his mouth like daggers, and yet, he sank into himself, running his hands against the wall, searching for a place to escape.

"Lies?" Sam retorted "What truths have you told her about your life, Edmund? Edmund's face was red hot, like the burning glow from an ember. His fists and jaw clenched as he held himself back, but he uttered no words.

"Have you told Catrina that you hired—yes, *hired* someone to attack her just so that you could be her savior, her protector, her big, brave lord? Isn't that right, Edmund?" Sam moved in, stalking Edmund, pushing him closer and closer to his confinement.

All of a sudden, Edmund lunged at him, shoving his hands hard into his Sam's shoulders. I watched in horror as they fell on to the floor with a dense, loud thud.

Edmund bit his lip, pushing with all his might, to force Sam off, heaving and rolling over one another. A flurry of fists and elbows and feet followed, Edmund at once punching Sam repeatedly in the face. Sam blocked most of the blows with his forearms, before pinning Edmund down again and giving him a hard blow to the face.

Bright red blood oozed from Sam's eye. He dabbed it with his sleeve, before coming toward Edmund like a freight train. Edmund braced himself, jotting around a statue of a half-clad Roman god near the wall. It was an almost comedic scene of darting back and forth that ensued, with Sam threatening to run up or over the statue, in an attempt to get his hands on Edmund. Finally seeing his shot, Sam lunged, pinning Edmund up against the wall, squeezing his large hands around his neck.

"I will *kill you*...I won't hesitate!" Sam yelled, gripping harder.

"Grhrrhrlllg..." The sound of saliva bubbled and spluttered from Edmund's throat with each exhalation.

It all happened in a matter of moments, and I found myself whirling with confusion as I looked on.

Edmund's eyes—bulging and furious—locked on Sam as he grimaced.

"Glkhghhh Dooo...ittt Bassglltard!" he managed to utter.

I hadn't realized it, but I was screaming. Sam, finally hearing the shriek, turned around to see me standing frozen behind them.

"Stop this!" I screamed.

They both froze, staring at me curiously.

"You are going to kill each other!" I shouted, feeling the adrenaline race through my arms, my fists clenched by my sides.

They both let go, moving slowly away from one another.

"That was the plan!" Sam retorted. His hands shook, and I could see the resentment forming in his eyes at being forced unwillingly away. They were breathing heavily, gasping for air, and their chests were heaving up and down at the effort.

Edmund's shirt was torn; large slashes ran the length of it. He wiped inefficiently at his nose, where dried blood had caked. Edmund rubbed at his neck, thankful he could breathe easily again.

Sam's eyebrow had a gash that he dabbed at bitterly. He looked at his sleeve, at Edmund and then patted his brow, repeating the series.

I stared down at them, as they looked up at me in tatters. Two men, two men so wholly different—the sun and the moon—and *both of whom I loved*.

"This is *enough*!" I cried.

I could feel the hot stream of tears running down my face as I ran to the door. Sam raced after me.

"Catrina, stop Catrina!"

I raced down the hall so hard and fast that my heels throbbed. At that moment, my world spun into chaos.

Chapter Thirty

Edmund was in later than usual. His butler Raymond greeted him at the door as he always did and then he was off. Byron, happy to see his owner, greeted him with his typical exuberance. Edmund rewarded him with a warm embrace and a firm, but loving, pat on the head before heading into the kitchen.

Discouraged with the state of things, he yelled at a kitchen maid. What was her name again, Maria or Mary? He could never remember. It didn't matter, as she hadn't been there long. He also didn't know if he planned to keep her around much longer anyway, considering she didn't know how to fold napkins all too well and had forgotten several essential items at a dinner he had recently. He'd made a mental note to speak with the head kitchen maid Gretchen about his feelings on the matter when he had a free moment, but for now, his stomach growled, and his nerves were frayed.

He scavenged around for something warm, settling on a thick slice of ham and a chunk of cheese before heading to his office instead of waiting for his kitchen staff to make him something.

The last he'd eaten was at a street vendor on Regent gulping down a Ginger beer and a small handful of warm hazelnuts. He'd planned to get something at a more formal eatery, but decided against it, finding the idea of eating alone off-putting and strolled around the park instead.

He was hardly ever alone. He surrounded himself with people; *purposefully* He didn't care much for being alone, as it left him with too much time to think. Of which, he *almost always* went down a path he regretted. But, as the weeks wore on, he found himself more alone than ever.

He frequently awoke, covered in sweat and unable to fall back to sleep. He confided in Byron, hoping the feel of his warmth as he lay in bed with him, would drive away the nightmares. And when that didn't work, he relented, spending the wee hours of the morning writing in his office.

He found himself writing poetry, most of which was about Catrina. He had stacks of pages all with the words: *"My Dearest Catrina,"* and nothing else. He wondered if he were going mad, his mind was perpetually swimming with his growing and uncontrollable obsession with her. He'd never been plagued like this before, and something about it felt so *unnerving*, so *sinister*.

He hadn't seen her in a few weeks since she stormed out, the same argument that tore him and Sam apart and caused a rift between him and Imelda. *Was he so wrong?* People had done much worse...

He felt the blood rising into his head, making it feel hot and heavy. He took the paper and crumpled it up, throwing it across the room where it hit the window with a light thud and fell to the floor. He'd spent many hours doing this, starting to write her a letter and the words failing him. He felt *betrayed* by words, at once a comfort to him...now a burden.

He'd tried to take comfort in women, something he'd always found particularly useful during his times of stress, but something about it now felt...*foreign and lackluster*. His libido didn't suffer, and for that, he found temporary relief. But something else unnerved him, and he'd find himself, even more discouraged the following morning.

Eliza, his fleeting companion of the night, had come to him recently. Their rendezvous had left him satisfied momentarily...until he could think again. Then he was plunged back into the depths of despair, clamoring to reach the top of the twisted gorge in which he'd seen himself.

And the dreams. Nightmares. They came often. Catrina, a siren of the sea, would rise from the waves and bewitch him, leaving him entirely powerless to her will. That part, oddly, had not bothered him. It is when she *left* that he'd felt the tug of her absence. He sat on the sand and begged for her return, as the waves rushed in and out with no care for his desires.

He had other nightmares—one in particular reoccurring one with Imelda and Agatha as angels, each in a flowing gown of sheer and silky white. They called to him, luring him in with the sweetest melody he'd ever heard. And when they opened their mouths to speak, nothing came out but song.

He was dragged from the safety of the earth, finding himself dangling from the clouds. They had him within their grasps, holding him there with their power when their delightful and ethereal glow, transformed into one of evil and condemnation.

Their judgment of him final, they gave each other a simple nod of approval, before he found himself falling to the earth below— his legs and arms flailing and waving in the air, as he attempted in vain to reach out.

He shook the image from his head, as he looked back down at the blank paper beneath his elbows, and took a gulp of his whiskey. He uncorked the bottle and poured himself another glass, feeling immediate relief as the amber liquid hit the bottom.

He stared down at the page, rubbing his head. The words were growing fuzzy. He attributed it to his mounting headache.

On top of the mounting pile of paper with the only words scrawled *"My Dearest Catrina,"* sat the endless amount of fines and late notices he'd been avoiding. He took a few of them randomly and crumpled them, turning it into a sport of sorts, as they hit the window with a light 'thwack' and fell to the floor.

He looked down at his leg again, covered in the blue pinstriped trousers and envisioned his mangled leg beneath, a scowl forming on his lips at the thought. His life was falling apart around him, and he hadn't a clue what to do or where to start to pick up the pieces. He drank and drank until his lips felt numb.

"My Dearest Catrina," he wrote again. This time the words flew from his pen. He gave a subtle nod to the whiskey in his glass as he kept downing them one after another.

When he finished the letter, he put it in an envelope and wrote "*Catrina,*" sloppily across the front before flopping over onto his desk, not waking until daylight appeared like a harsh spotlight across his face.

Chapter Thirty-One

Sam unfolded the letter, as he sat down on the last remaining stone stair of the fortress.

He was by himself, spending much of his free time exploring the wilderness. He felt such freedom in the outdoors. After their fight, he resorted to spending much more of his time in the forest.

He'd heard of Edmund's story—about the fortress in the forest—and came across it by chance one evening. A part of him lit up with excitement at the discovery, and then quickly faded, at the sudden realization that he and Edmund were now at odds with one another. *It shall be a secret all my own*, he thought.

He knew Edmund—knew him too well, in fact, and yet, still couldn't reconcile how Edmund could so easily betray him. The only thing he could deduce was that Edmund felt similarly about Catrina.

The fortress was enveloped in the thick and unforgivable arms of ivy—hidden away from the roving eye. Nature—an affable beast—was devouring it slowly. On the one side, a steep wall speckled with narrow openings was visible—the last remaining piece of its foundation. All of its softened walls sat lopsided, in various states of decay.

He envisioned Catrina here, wondering what she would think or say about such a place. It still stung to think of her, and he attempted his best not too, and yet here, he sat with her letter...waiting to be read.

He looked down at it again, folding and unfolding it, until he finally built up the strength to look down at it.

Dear Sam,

I've written this letter to you a hundred times and still...the words...they feel so wrong. And now as I sit here (for the hundred and first time), I still do not know how to say to you how I feel.

Part of me wonders if you will even open this letter, so if you have, I suppose that I have a chance to explain myself.

I have been foolish...more than foolish. You see, I always thought of myself as very wise, until I found you. I thought I knew how to follow my heart; I thought I knew who I could trust; I thought I knew who Edmund was...it seems as though I know none of these things.

The only thing that I do know is that I miss you. I miss the way your dimples carve into your cheeks when you grin. I miss the way your eyes light up when we talk about something ridiculous. I miss the way you name ducks...and even as I write that I grin, because it's so ridiculous, and yet, I miss it so...

Forgive me, for I do not even know

myself.
  With my love,
  Catrina Bennett

Sam folded the letter and closed his eyes tight, as he whispered to himself— "But *I* know you."

Chapter Thirty-Two

I stared blindly out the window of my guest bedroom at Aunt Beatrice and Uncle Harold's. It had been a few weeks since I returned, and the weather was growing cooler, as it does at the tail end of summer. The strong scent of wildflowers and sunshine was changing swiftly to the aroma of brisk night air and frequent rainstorms. With the changing weather, came the ever-changing ways of life.

With the dissolution of her relationship with Edmund, Agatha spent her time refining her etiquette and spending the remaining time with her new beau, Thomas Atwell.

In the past few weeks, their relationship blossomed. Agatha, reticent initially, now laughed and grinned freely when in Thomas' presence. She had confided in me after their first introduction at the ball that she hadn't found him particularly attractive, but now, you could see the glow on her face whenever their eyes met. She was the happiest I'd ever seen her, glowing from the inside out. I knew, without a doubt, that it would only be a matter of time until he proposed.

Aunt Beatrice's mood seemed to evolve as well, in light of their anticipated future. She was already spouting wedding ideas to Agatha during dinner. Uncle Harold *well,* Uncle Harold was Uncle Harold, and he just grumbled as he continued eating, more than likely lamenting the idea of spending lavishly on a wedding.

Ezra was more than thrilled to have avoided the attention, using whatever free time to his advantage to escape into the woods. He was always out fishing, hunting or trapping with some of his chums.

It hadn't escaped Uncle Harold's notice, however, much to Ezra's chagrin. Uncle Harold continued to argue the virtues of working hard, particularly in one's job as a civil engineer. He hadn't quite resigned to the fact that Ezra had entirely no intentions of following in his footstep, despite his continued insistence that he would.

The day was bright, seemingly mocking my emotions. I spent the better half of the morning writing another letter to Sam, that Ezra was gracious enough to deliver.

Truth be told, Ezra had grown quite fond of Imelda lately and used my letter deliveries as an excuse to visit her. He hadn't admitted it...but with my letters going out, he always had an envelope with her name on it, scrawled in his characteristically, lousy handwriting.

It had been a fortnight since I'd written to Sam. Every day, I yearned to hear the arrival of the post, so resolved that *this day* would be the day that he would write back. And yet, nothing ever came. Every Tuesday passed with a pang of disappointment.

I only had myself to blame. I knew that, and yet, there was nothing more I could do, or say, than ask for his forgiveness—something that occurred to me that he may be unwilling to accept.

Aunt Beatrice noticed my melancholy mood, and found me out in the garden one day, fingers curled up around *Alice in Wonderland*.

I was spending more time watching the bees, as they hovered in and out than reading, studying them as they bustled around the bee bush—landing on the small, fragrant white blooms to collect pollen, before hovering off to their nest in a nearby silver birch.

The world was such a vast place, and here in a tiny garden, a whole society of bees worked in complete oblivion to the immensity of their universe. So soon they would have to hunker down for autumn.

"Catrina," Aunt Beatrice's voice disrupted my thoughts. "My dear…"

I set the book down and met her eyes.

"It appears that summer is drawing to an end, and autumn is near."

I knew before she had a chance to explain that she was asking if I was ready to return home. The truth was, I thought about it. I spent a good many nights, wide awake, wondering what I left, and what I would return too.

"I've received a letter from your mama and papa," she said, handing the letter to me.

I sighed, reading through it, tears springing to my eyes. I had written them back and forth the entire summer, but this letter bore a small hole into my stomach, the longing to see their faces, mama, papa, Miles, Seth, and Morgan, the sound of the sea as the tide came in, the salty sea air and the smell of fish stew burbling on the stove.

"Perhaps it is time…" I said.

~

I was huddled up in my room, reading *Oliver Twist* when a vigorous rap on my door interrupted me.

"Who is it?" I cleared my throat.

"It's Ezra. Can I come in? It's urgent!"

I hurriedly rubbed my face and pushed any wayward strands of hair from my eyes, as I sat up.

"Come in," I called back.

Ezra rushed in suddenly, and from the look on his face, I could tell it was serious. He was halfway out the door, his body turned as if he were ready to dart at a moment's notice.

"It's Imelda!" he sputtered.

My eyebrows shot up.

"You have to come with me...no one can talk her out of it..."

"Out of what?" I asked, leaning forward, ready to get up and run with him.

"She's on the bridge..."

I felt my heart start to thrum wildly.

"What do you mean?"

"Come with me quick..." he motioned to me, and we were out the door.

~

We raced out to the yard where Ezra fetched Ollie. Id' never seen him so determined in all my life, and it dawned on me that his feelings for Imelda may have been stronger than I initially guessed.

The trees and landscape rushed by in a blur of greens and browns, as we sped through the wilderness. The sun beat down between the trees, determined as it was, in the fleeting days of summer. The crisp scent of pine filled the air, as the wind rushed past us, swirling my hair in all directions.

Ezra was galloping at high speeds, and I felt uneasy on Ollie's back. I held tight, pressing myself against his back, keeping in the tears that threatened to escape.

I hadn't quite known how or why they were there. Imelda had never been particularly cordial to me. But the idea, or sense that someone was in danger, had elicited a well of emotions, just under the surface, that sprang free at the notion.

My eyes stung with the thought of her balancing precariously on the edge of the bridge, a vision of her dangling there, hands gripping to the side. What if she wasn't there when we got there? *What if we were too late?* The thought brought fresh panic; my breathing became shallow, as if someone had placed a large rock on my lungs.

Tears streamed down my face, and I rubbed them secretively away. Ezra hadn't seemed to notice...or if he did, he was too kind to say.

~

When we finally reached the bridge, I was able to take a deep breath. She was still there—still alive.

The torrent of water beneath swirled and churned, an ugly mud color that gulped anything close enough to its edges. The scent of river water was in the air, moist earth, humidity, and decay, an appallingly, unpleasant aroma that drifted over the surrounding land.

I hurriedly slid off Ollie, as Ezra fastened him to a nearby tree. I didn't know what to do or say when I reached her, but I was determined to do something. I felt my heart skip, my hands clenched to my side with fear. I walked slowly, but resolutely, not wanting to startle her.

Sam was there, right beside her—the look of fear and panic etched on his face even from a distance. He was attempting to reason with her from the looks of things, but she hadn't budged.

She looked over at us, feeling our presence more than hearing our footsteps, and I could see the depth of the despair in her eyes. The usual brilliance behind her jade-colored eyes had been replaced with dull, lifelessness as she gave me a numb glance and turned back.

I could hear the rush of the river growing stronger as I walked closer. The sound of it roaring and rolling down the bank made the hairs on my neck stand up.

Sam reached hesitantly out to her, his hands almost grazing her fingertips. But she stayed gripped tightly to the side, unwilling to move. Her knuckles tensed, turning white—her fingers losing their circulation with the intensity of her grip.

"Imelda," I said, not recognizing my own voice. I choked up and had to clear my throat— finding the strength I so desperately needed.

"Imelda," I said again, this time forcefully.

She stared blankly at me. I could feel my pulse pressing against my temples, my jaw clenched.

"You need to listen to me. I don't know what has brought you to this place, but whatever it is, we can fix it."

Something in my speech aroused her, just enough for her to sigh in my direction before looking back at the water below.

Her hair fell down her back in silky, raven-colored strands, stick-straight. Typically, it was coiffed, but today, it hung bitterly to her head, as if it too were despondent.

I reached hesitantly out to her, placing my hand near hers.

"There is nothing in this life that cannot be changed or altered for the better good, except death," I said assuredly.

The word "death" seemed to jar her, and at that moment, I saw her tremble. Her lips were quivering as she turned to me.

"We will not leave here without you," I urged, moving my hand closer to hers.

She shook her head slowly and looked back out toward the water, the rush of the river was deafening—a sign of looming danger that appeared to be getting closer.

Ezra laid his hand on Imelda's. I was surprised to see that she didn't flinch.

"This world is a more beautiful place with you in it," he whispered to her, squeezing her hand briefly. She met his gaze, with a look that asked if he meant it, and then took a deep breath.

"You don't understand...I can't," she said suddenly, her eyes wide and alert now—the mesmerizing green color becoming more apparent in the rays of light that peaked through.

Sam leaned in as cautiously as he could.

"What is it that we don't understand? If you tell us, we can help you. We aren't giving up on you," he asserted, leaning into her.

A tear swelled in the corner of Imelda's eye and became so fat, it rolled down her cheek plopping onto the ground.

"I can't fix this! You can't fix this! *No one* can fix this!" she yelled, flinging Ezra's hand away angrily.

Ezra, undeterred, grabbed hold of her hand firmly.

"We will not stop until whatever demon you are facing is defeated," Ezra swallowed, the lump visible in his thin neck.

I grabbed hold of her other hand, meeting her eyes. I could see the energy draining from her, the tenacity to keep fighting us was crumbling with every breath she took.

Whatever history we had with one another dissolved at that moment, as I held her hand and felt the life and warmth in it. I looked down, remarking at the peachy pink of her skin and the way her pulse throbbed through her wrist. I could feel its steady rhythm thumping against my fingertips.

    She broke down, letting tears stream down her face as she sobbed and leaned into me. Surprised, I took hold of her with all my might and held her there, promising myself I wouldn't let go until she was safe. If she were to jump, she would be taking me with her. I felt the smooth wet heat of her cheek on my shoulder and smelled the sweet scent of lavender on her hot skin.

    The rush of the water gradually subsided, becoming less and less of a threat, as I held her. The sounds of everyday life started to reappear—the chatter of birds in the trees above, the horse's whinnying, the faint sound of a train whistle somewhere in the distance...

    When I felt her wanting to let go, I saw Sam and Ezra move in to take hold of her. They guided her gently, but resolutely, over the ledge and back to the safety of the road. I took a deep breath as her feet hit the earth again, feeling the weight rise and evaporate like steam from my chest.

I went over to her again and held her tightly as if the instinct to survive and protect had overtaken me. She stared at me, and I could see the genuine look of appreciation flash in her eyes. We stood there a long time until she spoke, her body was shaking like a leaf. Ezra reached out to her and held her in his arms.

"I have something to show you..." She turned to Ezra and Sam, and we all gathered around.

"*This*!" she swallowed hard, "*this* is why!"

She placed her hands gently on her belly, framing a small, round bump that had gone unnoticed.

A look of shock overcame Sam and Ezra before they composed themselves. Ezra began pacing, his fists clenched together.

She came to me, reaching out for my hands and taking them in hers.

"I don't know how to tell you this..." I stepped back, pulling her hands from mine, feeling a tingle of pure adrenaline rush up my spine. A pang of denial sat like a threat in the back of my mind, crouched and ready to spring at her words.

"It's Edmund's child," she said assertively, placing a hand over her swollen stomach and nodding at me.

I felt my lungs compress as a whoosh of air from the bottom of my chest escaped, as if my ribs had been pressed together with a vice.

"*His?*" I asked, still in shock by the announcement.

She nodded sheepishly and looked away from me.

"Does he know?"

She shook her head.

I could feel my heart pound in my ears, and the nausea rise in my belly. It whirled around inside of me, heavy and foreboding, looking to anchor somewhere.

It shouldn't matter...*but it did.* Somewhere deep inside, I still harbored something resembling jealousy and resentment for him, for her, and for the child, she now carried of his.

Imelda spoke up, her eyes focused on the ground. Every once and awhile she glanced up at us, just enough to meet our eyes. She crossed her arms, protectively over her belly, her head bowed.

"I don't have anywhere to go. I don't have family nearby. The only family I have left is an Uncle who lives somewhere in Spain. I have nowhere to go! We had a place in Scotland, but I have learned recently that it is no more..."

She choked up at the last part, and I saw a tear fill her eye. It rolled gently down her cheek—a silver streak against her flawless, olive complexion.

"Imelda, I need to know. Did he? *Was it?*" Sam stopped pacing and reached hesitantly out for her hand. He bent his head, eyes looking up into hers—searching.

"Oh, Lordy me! No! It wasn't forced. I was such a fool. I wanted to be with him—for him to marry me—for so long, and when he gave me the opportunity..." she drifted off, unwilling to finish the sentence, leaving the silence punctuated with the knowledge of the affair.

Ezra moved into Imelda, wrapping his arms around her. I watched as her shaking calmed to a mild-quiver in his embrace. He towered over her and could comfortably rest his chin on her head if he wished.

We stood there for a moment, all lost in thought until Sam spoke up.

"Ezra, do you have anywhere you can take Imelda that will be safe?"

Ezra's fair brows scrunched as he thought.

"It won't be safe for her to return..." Sam added for emphasis, the obvious having no need to be stated, but for the sound, it made as it filled the awkward silence.

"We can find a place," Ezra asserted, looking down lovingly at Imelda. It was so genuinely affectionate that I felt myself begin to blush...but not without feeling the unwelcome emotion of jealousy creep in. *Would someone ever look at me that way?*

"Very well, then." Sam nodded at Ezra, who took it as his sign to get Imelda to safety.

Sam— being the gentleman that he was—helped Imelda on to Ollie. She held tight to Ezra, as he craned his head back to ask if she would be safe behind him. She nodded, and Ezra squeezed her hand gently in return, an acknowledgment of a bond grown stronger by a near tragedy.

Ezra tipped his hat to us before Sam slapped Ollie on the back. The horse raced off into the forest, his copper coat gleaming in the sun, leaving me watching until I could no longer see their figures darting through the thicket.

Sam was busy readying his horse, fixing her saddle that had slid on his ride here. He tightened it up, straightening it with a jerk before he turned around to face me.

"I suppose this means that I will be delivering you to your aunt and uncle?" he raised an eyebrow in my direction.

His tone was sharp and short, and I felt a small piece of me dissolving in his presence.

He leaned up against Beulah, the brown of his jacket contrasting against the sleek and shiny black of her coat. His arms crossed defensively.

"That would be...I would be very grateful for that," I replied, bowing my head.

What I wouldn't give to be able to see those bright, brown eyes again, and to know that they held my gaze.

He pushed himself up, leaning down to me and offering his arm, as I pushed myself up on the stirrup.

"Aren't you going to put your arms around me so that we can be on our way?" he asked.

I nodded and timidly held on to him, lightly at first and then more firmly. He flinched, pulling his shoulders tight before succumbing to the idea.

We rode along, the steady rhythm of the horse's sleek body rocking us back and forth, like the waves in a boat. I pressed myself against him, breathing him in. *When would I ever smell his scent again?* He smelled of pine and sweat, sunshine, and sandalwood. It was a heady scent, leaving me light-headed.

"Did you get my letter?" I leaned in, feeling emboldened. He was quiet for a moment; I felt his breathing, shallow and soft, in his chest as I held onto him. Then I felt him nod.

"I did."

"And?" I asked impatiently.

"And?" he replied.

"Well, didn't you reply?"

"Should I have replied?"

I hunched my shoulders, feeling the strong desire to clench my fists.

"Isn't that the proper etiquette?"

"*Proper*...I suppose that is the *proper* etiquette!"

"What is that supposed to mean?" I shot back. I pushed myself away from him, holding onto him as little as I could manage.

"I suppose there are plenty of proper ways of doing things...I didn't know that you subscribed to all of them."

"I beg your pardon!" I hissed.

"Please do," he retorted unfazed.

"You will let me down off this horse, right now!" I demanded, inching myself even further away from him.

"I will do no such thing...until you are delivered safely home. Is that not the *proper* way of doing things?"

"Urrrgphmm," I growled, feeling my blood pulse wildly in my temples.

I looked down at the ground and wondered how badly I would be injured if I decided to jump. We were doing no more than a canter; it would hurt more than if Beulah were trotting, but not quite as bad as if she were galloping.

"Shall I make my own exit then?" I added with a flourish of drama.

He made a reluctant noise of anger in his throat.

"I suppose I *could* jump," I leaned to the side, feigning interest in leaping from Beulah's back. He swiftly put an arm out and shoved me back into place.

"I am a man of my word..." he said, "certainly something more to be said about that than Edmund."

"What has this got to do with Edmund?" I asked, feeling immediately foolish for doing so. *Had I opened Pandora's box?*

"Wha...what has this got to do with Edmund?" he replied, turning back to look at me fleetingly. "It's got plenty to do with Edmund. In fact, it's *all about* Edmund."

I hunched over, feeling the desire to leap stronger than ever.

"It's true then?" I blurted, desperate to end the speculation that still swirled around in my head.

"I beg your pardon?"

"That you have a mistress...and a child. Else why would one not return a letter?"

He groaned.

"I will not justify that with an answer...if you know me to be the gentleman that I am, you shouldn't be required to ask me of that," he grunted, pulling a little tighter on Beulah's reigns, eyes dead set ahead of him.

"Well then," I huffed, "I suppose I can make my way back from here. Let me off this instant!"

He pulled on Beulah's reigns, and she stopped abruptly. I jerked back and forward so quickly that I smashed into Sam's back. But my pride was the only thing that hurt, so I hastily slid to the side and dropped off of her back.

"It gets rather dark out here, I would hate to leave you alone," he added vacantly.

I took a look at the sky. From what bits of it came through the sliver of trees, I could see the telltale signs of evening on the way, as the tangerine orange glow gave way to the gentian darkness. I shivered.

He hopped off of his horse, holding onto her reigns as he walked.

"What are you doing?" I asked, crossing my arms.

"Walking along with you," he replied, patting Beulah's large dark head. Her big black eyes stared back at me, daring me to defy her adoring master again. I sighed.

"I told you, I am a man of my word," he retorted, staring blankly ahead.

Chapter Thirty-Three

He promised Sam he'd get Imelda to a safe spot, but the thought of bringing her home wasn't an entirely promising one.

He'd have to claim that the child was his own. To risk one's livelihood and life for a child born out of wedlock that wasn't even your own child, would be preposterous, outrageous, and unquestionably unacceptable.

Most certainly his parents would be disappointed, perhaps even outraged. He liked to think of his parents as socially liberal, and yet, he couldn't imagine that their response to such a thing would be tolerated.

He felt his shoulders stiffen, and his posture tense as he jostled over the rugged landscape. Ollie was a spry, young horse and had little difficulties with the terrain, Ezra however, felt himself clench tighter and tighter to the reins. His neck was stiff, and his stomach was weak. He wondered if Imelda could feel the tension in his shoulders as she held on to him

What would she think? Would she trust him to take her somewhere safe?

Jesus, even he didn't know where that was.

He went to make a "Hail Mary" across his chest at the thought but realized it would be too difficult and dangerous to do as he held onto Ollie's reigns.

You will have to forgive me, he thought, *without the use of the prayer.*

Almost perceiving his fear, Imelda spoke up.

"Take me to Edmund…"

"What?" He turned his head to the side with a jerk. "I will do no such thing…I promised Catrina and Sam that I'd bring you to saf—"

"I have something that I need to do before I go. *Please*, bring me to Edmund. Then we shall leave," she pleaded, holding to him tightly. She laid her head on the back of his shoulder.

He loved the feel of her there, the warmth and embrace of her arms as they wrapped firmly around his waist and the solidness of her head on his back. He couldn't help but imagine how she would look when she woke up in the morning, her hair twisted and disheveled from sleep, his arms laced around her body. He sighed, wondering how he became so entangled with Imelda and her affairs—and how he'd done it so willingly.

He thought for a moment then nodded, pulling the reins so that Ollie stopped. He turned around, trotting past the trailhead that led home, and turned towards the trailhead that led to Edmund's estate.

Chapter Thirty-Four

We didn't speak for a long time. The only sound was the distant rushing of the water from the river, which ran parallel, and the constant clatter of Beulah's hooves, as she walked steadily along beside us.

We wandered through the forest where it eventually gave way to fields. The fields were laden now with tall, yellowing grasses that swayed back and forth—as if a giant billow blew across them. The sky had grown darker— the colors of evening dissolving gradually away at the horizon, leaving behind the violet color of night. The air had become brisk with the disappearance of the sun, and I felt myself hunch inward to conserve my heat. The sounds of nocturnal insects were starting to appear, first a chirp and then another, breaking out into a chorus across the meadow.

"Well, I suppose we should make camp," Sam turned in my direction, making a statement more than posing a question.

"Make camp?" I muttered.

"Beulah isn't fond of the woods at night. She gets spooked, and we have quite the walk from here," he explained, tying her reins up to a nearby tree—a massive oak, the only tree in the field.

She whinnied, almost in agreement, as he patted her head gently. Her eyelids closed in response to his touch, exposing her swooping lashes. For a moment, her foreboding dark eyes weren't focused on me.

We were in an oasis, of sorts, surrounded on each side by forest and field. The night sky—painted like a giant dome of deep blue— seemed at both immeasurably large and strangely small, above our heads. Stars—spread like confetti—flecked the sky with white. The oak, our shelter from rain and wind, stood sentry over us. Her branches, black as pitch, twisted and turned, reaching up toward the heavens. And while I had never spent the night outside, I could think of no better place to do it, than here.

"I suppose I should make us a fire," Sam commented, rubbing his hands together.

We only spoke from necessity, both of us still holding tight to the tension that boiled just beneath the surface—threatening to expose itself at any moment.

He commissioned me to find field stones to surround the makeshift fire pit. It wasn't an easy job in the dark, but I managed to find enough to make a small circle. I searched the surrounding area for a few sticks for kindling, and when I returned, there was a fire in the fire pit.

I was grateful for the heat, standing as near to it as I could, enjoying the warmth that permeated the chilly air around us. I was also thankful for the light, which highlighted the details of Sam's face, exposing to me the dark hollows of his eyes as they glowed in the honey-colored light. His cheekbones were high and smooth, giving way to shallow hollows and two long deep dimples. A scruff of beard covered his chin—nearly two shades darker than his hair on his head. He looked different somehow in these past few weeks.

I studied him, taking in every detail of the topography of his face, focusing much of my time on the shape of his lips—soft and broad, yet masculine. I rubbed my hands subconsciously over my mouth, wondering how his lips would feel on my own. And then the crushing uncertainty came over me, *would I ever feel his kiss on my lips again?*

Resolved to focus on something else, I sat down in a hollow near the base of the tree and pulled my diary from my bag. There was just enough light from the fire that I could write.

I tapped the pen methodically to my chin, unable to clear my thoughts when Sam came and sat beside me.

"Edmund met Marianna when we were on holiday," he spoke softly, just above the crackle of the fire.

I looked up from the glow of the flames to meet his eyes—the dark shrouding them with mystery.

"When we were to leave, she found that she was with child...and she proclaimed that it was, indeed, Edmund's child."

There was a moment of silence—a pause to soak in the new information. Sam picked up a stick and jabbed at the fire, stirring the red hot embers in the bottom so they sparked and hissed. I hugged my arms around my chest, feeling a shiver in the cool night air.

"Edmund panicked, asked me to flee with him in the night...I convinced him to do the right thing after some time, and he begrudgingly agreed. He worked out some sort of financial arrangement to pay for the child, declaring that he wanted to be in no part of the child's life." He gazed aimlessly in the distance, lost in memory.

I swallowed, feeling a large lump dissolve in the base of my throat—a sense of relief and guilt welled inside of me, conflicting with one another.

"And that is why he goes to Brighton...on business," I concluded.

He didn't look over, but nodded slowly.

There was a long, poignant silence where we both sat, huddled near the fire—attempting to make sense of the world. I wanted so badly to reach out to him, to feel his skin on my skin, to touch his hand...but I refrained.

"Anyte," he said, finally breaking the silence.

"Hmmm?" I asked, taken aback.

"Anyte...*you* are Anyte of Tegea," he added, watching my face with curiosity.

"Who is Anyte?"

"Anyte is a poet. One of Greek's finest. She wrote about women and children and animals. Her work is *so* impressive that she has been compared to the likes of Homer."

"But I don't write about women and children. Nor animals," I replied, pressing my diary shut and laying it on my lap.

"Perhaps not, but your love of nature is what unites you," he surmised, picking up a piece of grass and shredding it. He had an odd habit of doing that with vegetation.

"She never wrote of love," he added.

"Why do you think that I never write of love?" I rebuffed, pushing myself up straighter against the trunk of the tree.

"To write of love, you must know what love is," he glanced at me, before plucking another piece of yellow grass from the earth.

I huffed, setting my diary down on the ground next to me.

"Is that what you think? That I do not know what love is or that I am not capable of love?" I felt my pulse heighten, and my voice rising with each word.

"No, I simply know that you do not know love when you see it."

"And how is that?"

"It is simple," he said, standing up and brushing off his trousers. "You chose him."

"You're wrong. *He* chose me. *He* wanted me!" I stood up now, facing him, feeling my hands clench into fists against my sides. "Why does it matter?"

He was so close; I could see his nostrils flare. I could hear his breathing and feel his breath as it left his lips. For a brief moment, I was transported back to the boat, sitting in front of him, waiting to feel his lips on my own.

"I must...there is a truth of which you don't know, and I cannot bear to live any longer like this, but I fear that it is too late..." he spoke softly, brushing a strand of my wayward hair away from my cheek and tucking it behind my ear. He glanced wistfully at it, as his fingers grazed the length of my cheek back to my chin. A tingle ran up my spine at his touch, and my whole body yearned for more. I felt my stomach tighten, as I leaned forward, urging him to continue.

"I don't understand," I uttered. I felt my breath catch in my throat. My world started to spin, and I suddenly felt a strong desire to lay down. He took my hands in his, and I felt my heart begin to race, threatening to leap from my chest.

He leaned in slowly, tipping my chin delicately up as he pressed his lips gently to mine. An intoxicating euphoria gushed through me, like a dam let free.

"Do you know the truth now?" he asked, the depth of his eyes exposing a new layer of him—raw vulnerability.

I nodded, feeling my thighs shiver. I tried to steady myself but felt the strange sensation of weightlessness. He moved in closer, his lips brushing against my own as he whispered.

"I know what happened between you and him. Am I too late? Do you love him?"

I shook my head, feeling the heat from his breath.

"You said it yourself," I whispered back, "I did not know love."

Chapter Thirty-Five

Edmund holed himself up in his office. The door opened quietly, and it took him by surprise to see Imelda standing there. They hadn't seen much of one another lately, since their brief rendezvous, and he preferred it that way. She was a means to an end, and nothing more. He turned to nod, and then looked back out at the window, relaxing slightly.

He took another puff of his cigar, watching the orange blaze burn at the end.

"Edmund..." her voice wavered, as she stood near the door, peering in. He didn't look back, just motioned with a finger for her to come in. He didn't want to be bothered with her but knew she wouldn't leave without speaking with him.

She came into the room, shutting the door behind her, and the golden light from the hall disappeared.

"I have...news," she spoke softly, and Edmund could scarcely hear her.

"What is it?" he retorted gruffly. She always had a way of interrupting him when he was enjoying himself, he thought. He took a long drag of his cigar, watching as the smoke wafted out of his mouth, attempting to calm himself.

"I have something I need for you...to know," she continued.

"Come on with it then! What is it?" he sneered. He snuffed his cigar out, before turning around to find her shadowed figure just a few short feet in front of him. She looked different, but Edmund could not put a finger on what was different about her. She was disheveled, for one. Her beautiful, glossy black hair hung lifelessly around her shoulders, and her gown was a simple, sunny-colored cotton one. He'd never seen her in anything less glamorous than silk.

She framed her belly—at once revealing the telltale bulge.

"I'm with child," she cleared her throat, "*your* child."

He leaned back, shaking his head in disbelief. He felt his head spinning in a million directions, the room became as dark as coal. He already had a child. He didn't need any additional expenses. His inheritance was running dry, and if he didn't produce a few good well-paying books soon, he'd be living with a title without means.

He swallowed hard, envisioning the walls of the manor falling in on him as a draft of frigid air drifted in through the cracks. He laid huddled on the floor, dramatically gasping for his last bit of breath, his lips a pale shade of blue and his dead eyes set on nothing. He'd be driven out of town if they found out that he was indeed the father of his sister...*half*-sister's child.

"No, no, no, no, no, I don't believe it. I can't, this can't, don't you realize?" He stood up then and paced, pressing his hands against his temples and shaking his head while Imelda stood in the dark. He raised a fist in the air and banged it down hard onto the desk, startling Imelda, who stood stone-still beside him.

"Nonsense. I will claim no paternity for this child!" he shouted, shoving an entire stack of haphazardly placed papers off of his desk, in a fury.

He shook a hand at her, his fingers clenched.

"This child is not mine. He's the child of a whore!"

Growing more irritable by the second, he slammed a hand down on his desk again and shouted.

"Get out!"

She twitched but didn't let it deter her. She came closer to him, and took his hand, guiding it to her belly, laying his palm flat against her. He flung his hand away as if he'd touched fire.

"He is your son," she asserted, meeting his gaze. Her eyes were the same jade ones they'd always been, but this time, there was something in them he didn't recognize, a sort of assuredness that alarmed him.

He shook with rage as he pointed to his door.

"Get out!"

She walked away, gradually and calmly, as he pounded his fists and threw books and papers from his desk, cursing and screaming long after she left.

Chapter Thirty-Six

I rolled over and nuzzled deep into the side of Sam's warm body, I could hear the soft and rhythmic sound of his breathing in my ear with each breath. A small area of pain radiated within my thighs, but I pushed it aside, as I tucked my chin and burrowed myself in next to him. I took a deep breath in, soaking in the scent of his bare skin against my cheek. He smelled of male musk, sweat, and earth.

The early morning sun was peeking over the horizon, its warm, orange glow spreading like fingers across the earth. The birds were wide awake, chittering and chattering amongst one another, singing delightful songs and melodies that made me grin.

Sam leaned over and kissed my ear so gently I almost didn't feel it.

"You're an Elizabeth...not a Jane," he whispered.

I grinned to myself.

"Is that so?"

"Mmmpfhh," he grunted as he pulled me close to him, and I melted into his side—like two pieces of a puzzle.

"Nothing wrong with a Jane, if you're Mr. Bingley," he added.

"So you are implying then, Sir, that *you* are Mr. Darcy?" I turned around to face him; our noses were nearly touching one another. In the early morning light, his eyes were the color of coffee—a speck of gold gleamed in each of them.

"Well, I'm certainly no Mr. Wickham," he smirked, as he leaned in to give me a lingering kiss. When his lips left mine, I felt myself float off somewhere above the trees.

"I thought you didn't believe in Mr. Darcy," I teased, still gazing intently at his lips.

"Ahh, that's because I *am* Mr. Darcy. You see, Mr. Darcy did not think of himself as a *Mr. Darcy*," he retorted, shifting himself.

"Whatever do you mean?" I pushed myself up onto my elbows and looked down at him. We laid in a thick thatch of grass on the meadow floor, his jacket beneath our chests.

He rubbed his chin lightly with his fingers, feeling the rough scruff of his hair there. I reminisced at the touch of it on my chest, as he grazed down my collar bone, and felt myself tremor.

"He sees himself as a gentleman, and simply that. If all gentlemen cannot see themselves for that, then they are Mr. Wickham's," he declared, as he lifted his head and his eyes met mine. "Oh this conversation reminds me that I have something I'd like to show you," he said, rolling over onto his side. He rummaged in his bag, pulling his diary out and setting it flat out in front of me.

"What's this?" I eyed him.

"Open it."

I looked down and tentatively lifted the cover.

"The Lord Poet?"

"My project," he replied, as he gave me a satisfied grin, "I'd like you to help me with it..."

Chapter Thirty-Seven

Aunt Beatrice received the post and idly thumbed through it. She hadn't heard from Ezra in a week and was an absolute wreck because of it. She'd done everything she could to find him, even calling in the police brigade, but nothing turned up. Then, as she feverishly tore through the post, her eyes lit up.

"Harold, Harold! It's him, it's him!" She ran as fast as she could, down the hallway. Uncertain of her husband's whereabouts, she raced right past his office, having to turn around abruptly when she heard him respond.

"I'm here," he added in his usual blunt manner. He had a pipe dangling from his mouth, his smoking jacket on, as he hung his head out of his office doorway.

She ran to him, flitting about, as he combed his desk drawer for an envelope opener. She danced excitedly in her spot while he opened the letter and laid it on his desk.

Dear Mother and Father,
Firstly, do not worry about me. I am well! Better than well, in fact!

I have eloped with a lovely woman, and we have left the area. I have feared to tell you this, as I concede, I will no longer be focusing on my career in civil engineering. Please send Father my regrets.

We shall keep in touch. God Bless and Farewell.

Your son,
Ezra

"Confound him—that fool! That damn fool!" Harold shouted, slamming his fist on his desk before he got up. He paced near the window, while his wife timidly followed behind him, attempting to calm him. He shooed her away with his hands while he ranted, his thick, salt and pepper mustache twitching with irritation.

"Have you ever heard of such a thing? What kind of witchery is this?" he bellowed.

He made such a ruckus that some of the staff came to see what the matter was. Beatrice gently shooed them away before Harold saw. Harold had become so upset that he left in a hurry, walking straight to the back garden to work off some of the steam he'd built up.

Content that he was away, walking off his anger, Beatrice picked up the letter and reread it, running her finger along each line. A small smile spread across her face as she folded it and pressed it to her chest.

"God Bless you son...and your new wife," she whispered.

Chapter Thirty-Eight

Edmund sat down at his office desk and stared blankly out the window. He rubbed his eyes and pressed his fingers above the bridge of his nose to alleviate some of the pressure he felt. He had been drinking himself to sleep most nights to avoid the nightmares that had become so frequent. His sleep had been so disjointed that he wondered how he managed to stay awake most of the day.

A parcel, wrapped in brown paper and tied with a purple ribbon, sat on his desk. That was queer, he thought, picking it up and analyzing it.

"Raymond!" he called out the doorway, leaning back in his chair.

Raymond dutifully arrived a few moments later. He had appeared to grow shorter recently, his back hunched from old age, and yet, he was abnormally tall for a gentleman.

"Yes, My Lord," he replied, attempting to stand up as straight as his aging body would allow.

"Where did this come from? This package?" Edmund turned it around and raised it for Raymond to see.

"It was delivered this morning, My Lord. By post," Raymond confirmed with a nod of his head.

"Mmmm," Edmund murmured as he studied the package, lifting it to feel its weight before setting it on his desk again. The package did not appear to have a wax seal or postage mark of any kind. That was quite queer, he thought. He rubbed the back of his neck as he looked it over again.

He flicked a wrist at his servant, who unconcernedly turned around and disappeared back down the hall.

He took an envelope opener from the drawer and carefully slit one side of the package. Peeling a thin layer of the paper away, he could see, what appeared to be, the cover of a book. He ripped at the paper, this time with less finesse, exposing the entire face of a novel.

"*The Lord Poet*," he read aloud.

Peculiar, he thought. *Where could this have come from? And why had he received it?*

He flipped it open, to the cover page to find a handwritten inscription:

"I have always had more dread of a pen, a bottle of ink, and a sheet of paper, than of a sword or pistol,"

Alexandre Dumas, *The Count of Monte Cristo*

He looked down and almost dropped the book from his hands. His jaw hung agape. His heart felt as though it seized in his chest.

The Account of the Life of Lord Edmund Troy. Written by: Catrina Bennett and Samuel Elliot

He felt violently ill as if someone had kicked him in the stomach. He pushed himself back from the desk and stared it at disbelievingly. He bent over, clutching himself with his arms and then sat up again, rocking back and forth, unsure of what to do. He stood up, nearly knocking his chair over in the process, and bent to pick up the book and inspect it again.

He felt his shoulders tighten and his jaw clench, as he begrudgingly opened the first page and read the words that caused him to topple over his chair.

"*My Dearest Catrina,*"

She had taken the note he had written to her...and used it in a book about him. He read it, feeling his eyes widen and his jaw clench.

Had he actually written this?

His memory suddenly jogged, an image appeared of him waking up in a stupor the following morning. The alcohol made him confess his darkest secrets—his love affair with his half-sister Imelda, his admission of hiring the man to attack Catrina, his jealousy of Sam for his love for her.

He'd professed his love, devotion, and purity to her, and she *did* this? In a fit of rage, he threw the book across the room until it hit a bookshelf and fell to the ground. He flung himself at his desk and shoved all of his paperwork and pens from it in one fell swoop.

"SON OF A BITCH!" he yelled.

He feverishly ripped at the brown wrapping paper, shredding it into such minuscule pieces, that a gust of wind from the window scattered it across the ground like snow.

"Those...blackguards...those sadistic..." his mind search frantically to fill in the void.

Byron, confused by his master's anger, came dutifully by his side, waiting for a pat on the head, but Edmund didn't notice. He just sat there. Head tucked in.

"Edmund," Raymond called from the door, his bald head peeking in hesitantly. "There is someone from the bank at our door, My Lord." He turned around and shut the door quietly behind him,

Edmund's knees shook. Unable to quell the rage that had steadily built up again, he took his pen suddenly and chucked it at the window, where it spilled black ink down the pane. He watched mindlessly as it dribbled down the clear glass and onto the floor.

"Son of a bitch!" he shouted again, before falling to the ground on his knees.

Chapter Thirty-Nine

George Eliot once said: "Gossip is a sort of smoke that comes from the dirty tobacco-pipes of those who diffuse it: it proves nothing but the bad taste of the smoker." But I am much obliged to disagree. *Gossip* is what divulged the truth, fueling the sales of the book Sam and I wrote: *The Lord Poet*, funding our rent and reputation as authors, serving karma when karma needed a direction. *Gossip* was the driving force behind the truth. A truth that Sam and I exposed. The truth about who Lord Edmund Troy *truly* is.

It has been said, that Edmund couldn't go anywhere in public, without the crowds following him. His vanity, it seems, would have been fueled by the attention, if it weren't for the fact that it was, nearly always, to question his ill motivations.

After the widespread success of our book, Edmund simply disappeared. One day, out of curiosity, Sam took a carriage to Edmund's estate, and found that the entire manor had been abandoned. The beautiful, white exterior used to glow with the vigor of its parties—but it now sat vacant, shrouded by the gold, red and brown leaves of its manor's trees.

It's been heard around town that Edmund moved to another country, as his reputation had been so damaged, he ran off to hide from it. Some people say he moved to Italy, others to Greece, some even say that he's gone so far as to sail across the ocean to America!

On account of the popularity and instant success of our novel, *The Lord Poet*, Sam has been able to quit his job as an article writer for Punch, and is able to focus on writing future books. He spends most of his time curled up under the tree in the field where we met…with me by his side.

I've decided to stay. I visited my mama, papa and brothers in Weymouth, telling them all about my time in London, but returned shortly after. I have plans—plans that include reading and writing, dancing and exploring, and possibly even marriage…if Sam ever plans to propose.

The fall came with a gust of autumn wind, blowing away the warm summer nights and leaving us time for reflection. I snuggled into Sam's lap, nature our only witness, as the crisp autumn air brushes across our cheeks, and Sam flips open our book, grinning as he reads the first few words aloud:

"*To my dearest Catrina…*"

Made in the USA
Monee, IL
20 July 2022